THREADS OF RANIC

THREADS OF RANIC

SONS OF CYRUS, BOOK ONE

BY C. E. MARTIN

Tranquility Press 2019

For information:
Tranquility Press
TranquilityPress.com
723 W University Ave #300-234
Georgetown TX 786626

ISBN 978-1-950481-09-5

Dedication

To Beth,
without whom I would never have found the courage to
move forward with this project.

To Jann,
for your love and support, and for every day that you
cheered me on during the writing of this book.

To Greg,
for your botanical know-how.

To my children, Lauren and Arran,
make your presence felt upon the earth but do it with
kindness and know that I will love you always.

To Guy,
my husband who has always encouraged me to follow
whatever path I choose
and has never stifled my creativity.
Thank you, my love.

Contents

In order for fiction to become fact, ancient beliefs long held to be true must be shaken, torn apart, re-assembled and accepted by all. If one person continues denying the evidence before them, then that once-immutable fact may shift again, disassemble, then reassert itself in what is perceived to be its rightful place in the universe.

Prologue

T HE MAN MOVED through the canopy, silent as a puma, high in the rain-soaked treetops. He jumped with little effort between the branches and landed with feline grace as he explored a world normally hidden from mere mortals. Done for the day with diving in the frigid northern Californian waters, he was drawn back to the redwoods and their rich, woodsy scent.

A young woman squelched her way in muddy boots through the woods toward him. He fought to keep the threads within himself...

Chapter 1

in which one is lost
and one is found

I MUST BE seriously deranged. The thought took root and spread its tentacles insidiously throughout her grey matter. Charlotte paced frantically up and down, wearing a groove in the time-worn, wide plank flooring at her boss's second home. They groaned quietly in the way old things often do as her delicate feet worked their way through a sitting room half-marathon.

The problem that had driven her to distraction should have been either curled up in his bed taking a nap, or standing on the deck watching the deer peacefully grazing in the meadow below. He was, however, nowhere to be seen. After her first few sips of a gloriously fragrant cup of coffee, she'd noticed that Atlas had not shown up for his morning kibble fest.

She'd only been house-sitting twenty-four hours, and she'd already managed to lose Cam's precious pooch. Charlotte told herself she wouldn't panic just yet.

The cheerful chirp of an incoming text interrupted her

pacing. Never far from her sight, the cell phone was a welcome intrusion into her panicked musings.

How r things up there in the promised land?

Cam's message flashed on the screen like a neon warning sign. *Oh, lordy.* Was she going to lie or merely "forget" to tell him that his beloved pooch was AWOL?

Everything is great, she replied. Just sitting out on deck admiring the view.

OK. wood out in the shed if it should get cold.

Will do, catch you later.

Relieved, she let out her breath. She'd dodged a bullet as he hadn't asked about Atlas. That gave her a few more hours, or maybe even a whole day if she was lucky. Time enough to get that lovable but hectic dog back into the house.

She threw the remaining dregs of what was now lukewarm coffee down her throat and pulled on the rain boots that were sitting forlornly in their own puddle of old, dried mud just inside the back door.

The northern California weather had turned decidedly wet the day she arrived, and now rain fell in unending torrents. There didn't seem to be any chance of a break in the downpour anytime soon, so she braced herself against the wind, turned up the collar of her jacket, and headed down the steps and out into the storm.

The home stood quite alone on a small hill. Towering redwoods surrounded three sides like sentinels, facing whatever Mother Nature chose to throw at them. At the rear of the house grew a large and lovely garden with thoughtfully planted flower beds and natural pathways that wound in and out of the redwoods. In the spring it would be dotted throughout with daffodils, but now in the dead of winter it was just a lot of mud and a withered layer of last fall's leaves underfoot.

Charlotte made her way down the steps off the back deck and gingerly jogged down a meandering bark pathway and out into the redwood forest that encircled the rear of the property. She kept up a constant calling, hoping Atlas would put in an appearance, but after half an hour was no closer to finding him and she was soaked to the skin, the rain plastering her hair to her head.

As she made her way through the looming redwood tree trunks, something glinted on the ground at the edge of the trail, half hidden under a piece of fallen wood, winking at her in silent invitation. Slowly she picked her way toward it, looking down and not up into the branches overhead as she walked.

Had she been looking up, she would have seen him drop silently from a height of maybe thirty feet. His descent was fast, but instead of landing in a mass of broken bones on the forest floor, he slowed his descent and stopped falling just short of the ground, gently descending the remaining distance just an arm's length from her. Slowly and gracefully he bent to retrieve whatever had been lying in the leaves.

Astonishment clamped Charlotte's throat shut as prickles of adrenaline gave her mind amazing clarity along with a peculiar disconnected feeling, as if she was watching this unfold from a great distance. Even though she was soaked through, beads of sweat gathered on her breastbone and trickled down inside her sweater.

The man stood up and turned back toward her, holding a small, spherical object in his outstretched hands. It flashed brilliantly, first in a luminous aqua the exact color of the ocean before it washes up on a Caribbean beach, and then in a startling pink, hot and vibrant, before it faded to gently pulsing flashes of white. As she stared at him, he closed his long, slender fingers around it, cutting out the light completely.

Slowly the world came back into focus as Charlotte tried to make sense of what just happened. She pushed her wet hair out of her eyes and stared at the man who stood mere inches from her. She rubbed her eyes, trying to see a little clearer through the driving rain.

Every fiber of her being screamed at her to RUN! But the message wasn't getting through to her feet, which remained firmly planted on the wet ground.

He was very tall, possibly four or five inches over six foot; and although he was broad and obviously strong, he had a lithe look to him with incredibly long, supple limbs.

He blinked slowly and deliberately twice and then, with a lightning-fast motion, he threw the object he'd just retrieved high into the sky, where it flashed bright as a star, spun faster than she could follow, and vanished into the clouds above.

At last her feet got the message. In terror, she ran faster than she would have ever thought possible, especially considering the conditions in the forest. She never looked behind her and hoped she could run long enough to get away, hopefully to another house where there might be people around.

After a while she thought it must be okay, he wasn't following her; but then she saw him again, and this time he was way ahead of her, standing on the path right where she was headed.

How did he manage that?

He closed the distance between them in the blink of an eye. Charlotte gaped, swallowed hard, and her world spun on its axis before everything went black as she tumbled to the ground.

Chapter 2

in which the river meets the sea

Charlotte's first thought was that this was a very unhygienic way to wake up. A long, smooth and very wet tongue was repeatedly washing her face with an energetic and somewhat smelly, slimy swipe, from chin to forehead.

"Atlas, stop that," she admonished the dog, who promptly moved away to inspect an interesting smell lurking nearby.

I really have totally lost my mind, was the second thought that invaded her now fully conscious brain, closely followed by, *Oh, my good God, what the hell just happened?* and *Okay, girl, get a grip.*

She fought the fog that still wound its way around her head and tried to get her legs to support her as she pushed her way back up to a standing position.

Atlas returned and leaned against her, his wet fur slick on his body. They were both cold and wet through to the skin. She gave up trying to think it through and pulled on his collar, dragging the hound toward the steps and into the kitchen. His big, wet paws left puddles on the floor as they both stumbled through the house. In the great room she fell on the sofa, her breath coming in heaving gasps as her body reacted to what had occurred.

I could not have just seen that. A man dropping out of a massive tree, for God's sake. Who does that in a rainstorm, or any time for that matter? The events of the past ten minutes spun around in her head, filling every corner of her brain with images and sounds until at last she conjured up an explanation.

I'm a grown woman and there's no way I saw that. I must have fainted because of the donation I gave to the blood bank yesterday. Maybe they took too much. Simple and succinct. Enough to allay her fears and put her firmly back in the driver's seat. After she calmed down she made her way upstairs and took a very long and very hot shower.

This time her cell phone's chirping was a source of relief, a moment of normality during a very unusual morning.

Hey there, forgot to ask earlier how's Atlas? The text from Cam was short and to the point.

Just fine Cam, she typed back. He took a walk and he's a bit wet. I'm going to spend the rest of the day cataloging some of your new sketches.

With her boss's concern over Atlas allayed, it was time to get dressed and get some fresh air as the rain had finally stopped. Time enough to work later. She grabbed the dog's leash and the pair of them took off down the driveway and started the descent down to the Russian River.

She loved the river. It meandered through towns, vineyards, and, in springtime, meadows of mustard interspersed with live oaks. It then continued through towering redwoods with little beaches scattered down its length, where on warm summer days small groups of people sunned themselves on the shoreline.

It only took a short while to get down to the shore. Charlotte picked her way over rocks and pebbles until they reached the water. Atlas tugged on his leash.

"Oh, no, you don't," Charlotte said. "You're staying right here."

The pooch seemed to understand. He trotted back to her. She reached to scratch his head, but he darted away. Instead of slowing down when he reached the full length of the leash, the dog seemed to give an extra burst. The leash pulled out of Charlotte's hand. With an ecstatic bound Atlas was off into the churning water with the single-minded goal of catching a little black duck that was beating a hasty retreat into the greenery on the opposite bank.

"Atlas, please come back," she pleaded to the dog. Instead, Atlas paddled furiously toward the opposite bank, in hot pursuit of the poor duck. With the occasional deafness that seems oddly pervasive in the pet world, he blithely ignored her pleadings. The duck was now long gone and Atlas seemed a bit confused.

He turned to make his way back across to Charlotte, who was pacing the bank making wild promises of treats and cookies and anything else she thought the dog might like, trying to get him to return to her.

He swam about half way across but then got caught in an eddy. The non-stop deluge of the past twenty-four hours had turned the usually calm river into a fast-moving body of water that was rushing inexorably towards its outlet at the nearby Pacific Ocean. The dog was caught in its ferocious pull and although still swimming he was being carried downstream much faster than she could run. Eventually the small beach ran out and Charlotte could go no further.

"Oh, please God, no." She sank down on her knees and cried, unconsciously clutching the necklace of her mother that she wore constantly. The all-too-familiar feeling of stress gripped her stomach, leaving her shaking and nauseated.

Loss was an emotion that she was only too familiar with since losing her parents. A fairly minor earthquake had pancaked their home down on top of them, while she was safe at school. The memory of that awful day and the tilting her life took as the world around her shook, leaving her an orphan, was never far away and it left her longing for love and stability.

Suddenly she remembered her cell phone and yanked it out of her jacket pocket. Of course, out here away from the house with its Wi-Fi, she couldn't pick up any signal. Cell coverage was sketchy at best in the more remote parts of the county and this area was one of the worst for a lack of signal. She didn't even have the one bar needed to send a text.

She had to get help for Atlas and get it fast. Charlotte ran back up the beach and stumbled over the rocks to get back to the road.

The man appeared again. His dark shape emerged from the trees and stood statue-like in the shadows, unmoving and vast. The sight of him brought her to a screeching halt, her heart thumping madly from both the stress of losing the dog and the run back up the beach. This time when she looked at the stranger lurking at the edge of the tree line, it wasn't fear or shock that was her first thought but more of a feeling of awe.

He moved gracefully forward out of the gloom and stepped onto the beach. The rain suddenly ceased, allowing a brief ray of sunlight to slice down through the branches overhead, illuminating him. His entire body seemed to pulse gently with an energy like nothing she'd felt before. The sensation emanated from him, washing over her in waves of heat until her entire body was on fire.

As he walked toward her, his body moved in a graceful, feline way. His mouth tilted up at the edges as he smiled radiantly at her, and try as she might she just couldn't look away. His eyes were a deep forest green with an outer circle of gold and long, thick lashes. The overall effect was stunning in the extreme. Oddly, his dark hair didn't seem damp from the rain as it waved down his neck, ending just at the collar of his perfectly fitted bespoke leather coat.

She got her wits back fairly quickly and spluttered, "Please can you help me? The dog I'm supposed to be looking after, he's in the water..." Her hands gestured wildly toward the rapidly flowing river.

He tracked his gaze downstream with hers. The dog had completely disappeared. He slowly turned back to her, his lovely smile replaced with concern etched between his brows.

"Come," he said, holding out his hand to help her over the last few rocks. She hesitantly took the proffered help and in no time they were back on the road. Parked on the grass was a silver SUV, sturdy and practical. He led her toward it but she balked when he opened the passenger door for her to get in.

"I'm not getting in the car with you," Charlotte said. "I don't have any idea who you are."

"Do you want to find the dog before he's sucked out into the ocean, or not?" he said, turning to her with a look of frustration.

"Of course I do, but...but I don't even know who you are or why you keep showing up around me." Her voice trailed off in a confused muddle.

"Very well," he said as he let go of her hand and walked

around to the driver's side.

At that point she concluded there were two ways this could pan out. The first one left her standing at the side of the road alone and without her car or Atlas, and by the time she got back to the house she'd lose the dog for sure, never to be seen again.

The second was risky but at least she would stand a chance at finding Atlas and every second counted.

"Okay, okay," she countered, clambering in before her nerve left her. The man slammed the SUV into gear, screeching out onto the road that led to the ocean so fast it left her blinking in surprise and gripping the dash to hold herself steady. He drove well, aggressively but sure and precise.

Charlotte was stunned to realize she wasn't scared at all. He never looked at her but kept his gaze locked onto the road ahead, anticipating every twist and turn it sent their way.

"When are we going to stop and look for him?" she asked while sneaking a look at his profile and hoping he wouldn't catch her staring at him. "Do you think the river washed him downstream as far as the ocean?"

"I doubt he's gone that far. The Russian River takes so many turns that we could be well ahead of him already. Try not to worry. We'll find him." His voice had a lovely musical, lilting quality which even Charlotte, with her keen ear for accents, couldn't quite place.

Hmm, I wonder if he's European, maybe Irish or... She wasn't able to continue her musings as the road widened and around the next bend the ocean spread out ahead of them, grey and ominous under the wintery sky. He pulled off the road next to a half-hidden sign that showed the way to a track leading back down to the river.

"Come on," he said, running swiftly through the bushes that lined the path. She had trouble keeping up with him as his legs were longer than hers and even though she seemed to live at her local gym, he was obviously even fitter that she was. She ran as fast as she could, stumbling often on the smooth pebbles that seemed determined to make her lose her footing.

When they made it out onto the riverbank she was relieved at the chance to stop and catch her breath. He stopped and waited for her to catch up to him.

They stood side by side and looked out at the water, searching for any sign of Atlas. There was nothing, no dog alive or half-drowned anywhere in sight.

Then she spotted him. Barely visible at the water's edge, he lay half out of the water, his head twisted round at an awful angle. She knew instantly that they were too late.

It was at that moment of horrible realization that everything went black again as she crumpled onto the sand.

She felt a whisper on her skin, a touch as light as a feather stroking her face. She couldn't quite open her eyes so she gave herself up to the soothing touch with relief. It was a great deal more pleasant than the doggy wake up that had brought her around the last time this happened, just this morning, she realized. *There seems to be a pattern here.*

"Open your eyes." His demand was curt and invasive and startled her into full consciousness. "Now, damn it."

The blackness receded to the back of her brain and light made its way back inside. She looked up into his big green eyes that were just inches from her face.

"Are you feeling better? Can you stand?" He held her gently and eased her up to stand in front of him.

"Thanks," Charlotte managed. "I'm fine." She shrugged off his hold on her arm and looked back down the beach to where Atlas lay still and silent on the rocks.

"I can't believe I couldn't take care of a dog for a single day, without him ending up dead." She stared at the poor drowned creature, unable to tear her eyes away from the horrifying sight. "He doesn't even belong to me. I'm supposed to be looking after him, and that's just a cruel joke. I'm so useless. Cam will be so upset, and I know he'll fire me. So not only have I killed his pet, I'm unemployed. Oh, yes, and homeless to boot, since I just gave up my lease to stay at Cam's place for the foreseeable future. Not to mention the fact that I keep fainting dead away so I must be getting sick or something."

The reality of her situation hit her with a cold and uncompromising kick in the keister. That familiar knot in her stomach once again put in an unwelcome appearance, making her anxious and vulnerable. Nothing in her life ever went right. Just when she felt she was getting back on track, something would happen to wreck it.

"I'm stuck out here now, so is there any chance of you giving me a ride back to town?" she asked him.

"Of course, and the dog as well."

"Atlas, his name was Atlas. And thank you; you're being very kind."

He walked over to where Atlas lay and gently scooped him up. The animal must have weighed well over a hundred pounds with all that long, wet fur, but the man lifted him as if he weighed nothing at all.

Holding Atlas against his chest, he made his way back up the path to the car. She followed a few paces behind and it was then, as she watched him walking with that lithe gait, that the memory of the morning came flooding back again.

Oh, my God! She hadn't imagined it. He really had been there. She stopped cold, her heart thumping, terror replacing grief as her primary feeling.

Sensing the lack of movement behind him, he turned around and gently lowered Atlas to the ground.

"I'm not going to hurt you." The words came out as a whisper and they echoed in the air, hanging there like a softly spoken threat.

She wanted to run, to scream, something, anything, but her feet rooted her to the ground, stuck as solid as if they were implanted in concrete. She couldn't have moved if her life depended on it; and the sad reality was that her life could very well depend on it.

"Did you hear me? I promise you, nothing is further from my mind. I want to help and that is all. Please relax; you're wound up so tight I can see the bands around you." He said that part louder, and slowly his words penetrated her mind. She relaxed a little and nodded.

"Who are you and why have I seen you twice within a couple of hours and how the hell did you get so far up into that tree and what was the light thingy that you flung into the air and..."

He cut off her verbal volley by merely holding his hand out to her. His fingers uncurled, revealing a small sphere two inches in diameter, the palest glistening silver color.

As she gazed at it, the surface seemed to pulse and it quickly changed from silver to aqua and then to the hot, almost neon, pink she'd seen earlier, then finally to white, at which point it shot upward, this time of its own volition, and vanished into the leaden skies above.

Her mind crept inexorably toward a startling conclusion. The realization that he was not human arrived and it was too much. There was a limit to what her feeble human brain could take. This time the blackout was faster, deeper, and lasted a good deal longer.

Chapter 3

in which the moon turns blue

T HE RANIC INTERPLANETARY high court was in an uproar. Never before in the exceedingly long and illustrious history of the Raniculan race had this happened.

Elyian repeated the short statement that had reduced the members of the court to babbling idiots; this time, however, his voice lost its normally gentle, melodic tone and had a cutting edge to it. "I claim the human."

The high justice stood and leaned over the crystal table, making his shimmering mother-of-pearl necklace skim the table's surface, and nodded his head sagely before he began.

"Succinctly put, Elyian, but just because you make that claim does not mean that it will be so! You continue to defy us and the rule of law. We, as the ruling members of this court, cannot allow this to happen. It would mean the end of everything that we hold to be true. This human does not belong here. We never transport species, so why do you feel that you have the right? You may be the ruler, but we have laws in place that you cannot change at will!" The high justice wagged his long fingers at Elyian as he spoke, as if that would make his point clearer.

Elyian, who had been leaning casually against a huge pillar of stone, stood straighter and slammed his fist against the pillar's surface, so hard that it trembled and a large fissure appeared, zig-zagging its way down the length and leaving little crumbs of stone scattered on the floor.

"No, High Justice, it is you that is wrong," he countered. "This is not the end of the debate, but I have other matters to attend to; I must leave and we will continue this at another time, and at my convenience."

At that he bent and pulled hard on the chased hilt of his sword, retrieving it from where it was embedded in the marble floor, the result of his temper getting the better of him earlier in the proceedings.

At the rear of the cavernous room, a stunning male dressed in hunting clothes watched the entire scene play out. His green eyes flashed as he memorized everything he saw and heard. As court recorder, an honorary position allotted him when he abdicated the throne in favor of his son, it was his job to faithfully preserve the day's proceedings for future reference and to oversee the secrecy of the race's existence while visiting Earth.

It pained him to spy on his son but he was obligated to do just that. He rarely saw Elyian act so arrogantly and was intensely curious to discover why a mere human could put his son in such a tailspin. So he began to make plans.

With a quick movement Elyian slid the sword back into the sheath at his waist and strode out of the vast hall. His long legs ate up the distance between the hall of justice and his living quarters at the center of the city.

Once there, he slammed the great slabs of wood that formed his chamber doors shut. He knew he was getting worse. The band of pain that encircled his head tightened with a vice-like grip. In the past he got these headaches only when exhausted, but now they were a part of him, as frequent a visitor as the mood swings.

He sat on the edge of his sleeping platform, swung his leather-clad muscular legs up onto the bed, and willed his mind to close down. Sleep was the only way to get some relief from the pain. So with a deep sigh he gave himself over to peaceful oblivion.

When he awoke much later, it was to the sounds of the household in full party mode. He could hear his brother Jendal berating the servants who, he assumed, were as busy as always, scurrying around the palace carrying enormous pitchers of Yalon, the viscous, dark brown, coppery-tasting liquid which comprised the mainstay of the Ranic diet.

"Hurry up!" Jendal's voice rose above the general hubbub. "You know he'll be awake soon, and your life will be a whole lot easier if he's in a good frame of mind."

The heady fragrance of flowers and spices mingled with the rich scent of the Yalon. The combination was enough to persuade Elyian that sleep was highly overrated when compared to the delights of the palace banqueting table.

He rose quickly and, after standing in the wet room to cleanse and rejuvenate himself, left his chamber and went to join Jendal in the long hall. It was decorated for the festival of Arn with fluttering, lustrous banners that hung from metal ropes spanning the width of the hall.

Arn was a High God and it went without saying that this was a celebration no one dared miss. The court judges were harsh in the extreme if they discovered that a citizen had chosen to do something else on this holiest of days.

Everyone had to be in attendance. Punishment was swift and severe for any who missed it. Banishment was the most likely sentence, and the terra planets were favorite places to send the offenders.

There were four terra planets. Three were in their own solar system, but the fourth was in the sun's solar system. On Ranic that one was known as the blue planet. It was Elyian's favorite. He called it "Earth," as did the species of humans that inhabited the diverse world.

In the long hall, great throngs of people milled about sharing stories, gossiping, comparing notes on clothing and chiding the children for being disruptive.

Under one of the stone arches, a tiny, delicate woman followed Elyian's progress through the crowd, her turquoise eyes never leaving him. She was about to step forward to talk to him when she felt a hand grasp her upper arm.

"I wouldn't," Jendal said gently. "It would undoubtedly go badly for you." He moved her back under the arch, well away from Elyian's view.

Jendal walked away from the woman and quickly sought out Elyian, who by this time had been encircled by a few gorgeous females. They were positively glowing from being in his vicinity. He looked awkward and did not enjoy being the center of their undivided attention. His mood darkened with every passing minute.

"Jendal!" Elyian welcomed his brother. "I do believe the time has come for my brother and I to spend some time in each other's company." He nodded to the women. "Please excuse us."

The two men beat a hasty retreat, much to the amusement of some older residents who watched the entire scene with the patient, time-worn wisdom of the elderly.

"I just learned yesterday of your return, brother. You were away much longer this time and I missed your company. Please, tell me what was said in the high court that had them all wound up earlier. Of course none of them, not even our father, will divulge to me, the lowly younger brother, the machinations of the court. It was interesting to see so many of them steaming mad when they exited the hearing." Jendal was eager to hear the news, but Elyian was reluctant to tell his brother the reason the justices had been all in a lather.

"It was nothing that important, they were just testing my resolve on an issue of state matters and I disagreed with them, as is so often the case. Let's forget it for now and go down to the caves. I left a full flagon of well-fortified Yalon for us to share. I believe it will have fermented nicely in the time I was away!" Elyian threw an arm over his brother's shoulder and the pair left the hall, with Elyian grateful for the timely intervention.

After a short and pleasant walk through the city streets, they reached the stone obelisk that marked the entrance to the meandering labyrinth of catacombs that ran beneath the palace grounds. They were careful not to brush against the walls, which glistened with minerals and silver, as they entered.

Raniculans detested silver. Even the slightest touch of it caused massive welts to appear on the skin for days; and if they ingested it, the metal reacted with their nervous systems and could cause heart failure, normally within a few hours. It was a favorite tool of the criminal to commit murder, as once ingested the Raniculan body chemistry neutralized the silver and it became impossible to detect after death.

Elyian and Jendal chatted as they wound through the catacombs, and before long they stood in the cool, dark interior, where a vast, round table studded with gemstones took pride of place in the Leverium2 chamber. The cold, silvery-blue metal was harder than any substance known on earth and was used for everything from building materials to jewelry.

Gemstones such as rubies and diamonds were commonplace on Ranic. In places they lay on the ground profusely and so were not prized.

That honor was given to something not found on Ranic. Their single ocean contained no salt, ergo no abalone, with its gorgeous mother-of-pearl interior, lived in its balmy waters. Above all else, Raniculans prized the mother-of-pearl they found while diving on Earth.

Considered the most beautiful thing on the planet, it was carved into fantastic tiny sculptures, inserted into rings of Leverium2, and used as the currency of the Raniculans. It was traded, bought, sold, and stolen, and wealth was measured in the weight of the carved mother-of-pearl buttons one possessed and wore as currency. Threaded onto an unbreakable twisted cord of Leverium2, these buttons hung on the necks of the wealthy and were sewn onto clothing.

For thousands of years, the Ranic race had travelled across the universe to cull abalone and its prize from the chilly waters of Northern California, sending hunters out to gather the shells wherever they were found. There were only two rules. Never be seen; and never drink human blood while traveling, but only Yalon. Any hunters whose alien identities had been compromised or who had consumed blood were routinely refused entry back into Ranic and had to live out the rest of their natural lifespan of a thousand years on Earth.

Elyian and Jendal made their way into one of the massive caverns, stooping under an overhang that then opened up into a narrow room off the cavern. At the center stood a large storage jar of unfermented Yalon. To one side were a dozen or so tall pottery jars, sealed, marked READY FOR CONSUMPTION, and stacked carefully so they wouldn't topple over.

The men sat down and with matching sighs of contentment drank together, sharing the contents of one of the jars. It wasn't until they had finished the third one that Jendal heaved himself up to his feet and dragged a decidedly drunk Elyian from the cave to return to the party.

They should make their presence felt in the gathering. Elyian had fences to mend, and although he wasn't inclined to do that, he knew the members of the high court were powerful and influential. It would not serve him well to alienate them when he needed their support.

Many centuries ago when they'd learned of Elyian's first human interaction, they made a single deviation in the rule of deportation due to his rank, and allowed him to stay on Ranic. The high court judges did not think well of this latest event.

Elyian swayed slightly, attempting to fight the effects of the alcohol. *Damn,* he thought, *I should've had more sense than to go and get drunk.* He needed his wits about him, and at the moment his wits were more than a little addled.

He spent the rest of the evening stroking the egos of the arrogant court members, until eventually the last stragglers left and Elyian and Jendal retired to their respective rooms.

Elyian reached beneath his sleeping platform to pull out a box. It was an unremarkable container, considering how critical the contents. Lying in a nest of aqua silk was a shiny ball a mere two inches in diameter. It pulsed with a life all its own.

He picked it up and stroked the surface gently. At his touch the ball shifted color and the pulsing quickened in his palm. It had been with him for as long as he could remember, but until his last visit to Earth there had been nothing different about it. The ball of Leverium2 had been inert. Up to that point, it was the same as any other ball found at any common merchant in the city.

Until the day he saw her, the woman on Earth with hair like fire. Then it had wrenched itself out of his hand to lay on the ground near her. It had come alive, and he had come alive along with it.

Elyian returned the ball to its resting place and, with a lightening of his heart, pulled back the curtain that shrouded the window. A matching pair of blue moons hung in the purple sky, casting a dancing light on his windowsill.

Have I found her at last? Is she the one that can make my life worth living?

Chapter 4

in which fantasy becomes reality

CHARLOTTE GROANED, TURNED over, and tried to fluff the pillow under her head. It felt wrong. Too flat. And it smelled weird.

Note to self, buy new pillow, she thought before she was fully awake. Then the smell made her come around. It was peppery, metallic and somehow familiar but unsettling. Blood.

Oh my God, I can smell blood everywhere! Her eyes flew open, convinced she'd find herself covered in the stuff.

The reality was different but equally disturbing. The first thing she took in was the fact that although it felt like nighttime, light peeked around the covering on the window. Not yellow sunlight, but a strange color. An odd purple shade.

The next thing she realized was that she was not in Cam's guest bedroom. She didn't recognize this room, with its stone floor and beautifully eclectic array of furnishings, at all.

Every available flat surface featured a few stunning objects, displayed with obvious pride and the skill of an accomplished interior designer. It looked as though every century of porcelain and fine glassware was represented.

Interspersed with the obviously high-end antiques were oddly shaped chairs and cabinets that didn't appear to belong to any familiar era. Some had strange symbols etched onto the surfaces and were upholstered in fabrics that constantly shifted color.

As she contemplated this, a tiny creature with greenish fur, inky black bulbous eyes, and huge ears, scuttled across the windowsill and disappeared over the edge. Charlotte screamed and clutched the thick quilt around her. She screamed so loudly her throat tightened up and began to cut off her air supply.

At the start of a second scream the door flew open and a huge body flung itself through the doorway and stopped dead at the end of her bed.

Elyian was frantic. He'd heard her scream once and was out of his room and into hers before the second one had left her throat.

She stopped. Everything stopped. Her heart, breathing, screaming, everything came to a complete stop. She looked at the man standing there with panic written all over his face.

He was beautiful. The pale, lilac light that escaped the curtain bathed him in its glow. His skin was luminescent and pale, his hair a rumpled mess of long black waves, his head further enhanced by a long, straight nose framed by high, chiseled cheekbones and those shockingly green eyes with long, black lashes. Heavily muscled arms were at the moment clutching a long and lethal-looking dagger.

She screamed again.

"Will you please stop the screaming? You'll awaken everyone in the building and it's still very early," Elyian pleaded with her. "I know this is scary and confusing but please do calm down, so I can talk you through this."

He sat down at the edge of her bed and lowered the dagger. "Sorry about the weapon. I thought you were in imminent danger, with all the noise you were making."

Charlotte made a few spluttering sounds and swallowed hard. Then she rubbed her eyes, tried blinking and sat up in the bed, hoping she was asleep and that none of this was real. Although she had to admit, the man squashing her feet with his heavy body wasn't bad for a dream guy.

"It's you again," she said, managing to get a coherent sentence past her lips. "Why can I smell blood?"

Elyian reached over her and picked up a small glass

from the top of a cupboard next to her. "I think you smell the glass of Yalon I left here for you. Here, have a drink. You must be thirsty; have some, please."

She was thirsty, so she took the cup and downed some of the contents without looking first. Severe retching overtook her instantly.

"Oh, that's awful. It tastes like—yuck, I don't know what, but it's disgusting. Please, can I have some water?"

He smiled and his array of white perfect teeth glowed in the light. "Of course. I'll be right back."

She sat unmoving, her breath coming quickly as she tried to calm herself. Everything about this was beyond strange. She had no idea where she was; the last thing she remembered was being down on the beach at the river with this man.

It was just moments later that Elyian reentered carrying a large glass of water. She drank it down, even though it, too, had a strange taste; the water was so much better than the foul liquid she'd first sipped that she didn't care. Charlotte looked bravely up at him.

"I think it's time you answered some questions. Such as, who the hell are you, exactly?"

Elyian paused, and then with a smile that would melt an iceberg he spoke. His voice was careful and measured as he tried to ease her into the reality in which she now found herself.

"My name is Elyian Trainor from the third house of Ranic, but please just call me Elyian. My father is Amun and I have a brother, Jendal, as well as some uncles. All good men, except one uncle, the hideous Havvol Vax. You are at my home and you are safe. Neither I, nor anyone else who lives within these walls, will cause you any harm. You have my word on that. I brought you here because you were unwell and I knew that you would recover quickly if you were here with me."

"I would have recovered anywhere!" she interrupted him.

"No, you probably would have died if I had left you at the river. Every time you lose consciousness you're out for a longer period of time. This time your pulse was very weak and your core temperature was plummeting. I made a snap decision to bring you here. Not something I normally do, I must admit."

"So where is this place?" Charlotte was beginning to

think she wasn't going to like his answer. She suspected her world was about to be turned upside down yet again. Her mouth went dry and as she sipped the water he continued.

"This place is called Ranic. That's the name of both the city in which I live and the planet on which it is located."

She spluttered on the last sip of water before he resumed.

"I know this is all going to be hard for you to understand, but maybe this will help." He strode over to the window and motioned for her to join him. As he slowly drew back the covering, she jolted backwards with absolute incredulity.

They were standing high up in a round, stone tower, and spread out before her was a landscape unlike any she'd ever seen before. Two huge moons of pale blue hung heavy and low in a purple sky.

The town below, spread under the glow of the moons, was meandering and huge. There were stone buildings and pyramid structures mixed in with pathways and rivers that intersected the town like a spider's web. Great pointed towers of gleaming metal rose high into the air. The streets were wide and seemed spotlessly clean.

Although there were trees, none of them looked remotely familiar to her. She could see bushes on which hung some strange, reddish-brown, bulbous shapes. They were sitting in pots just outside most of the doorways. Maybe an edible plant of some kind? She wasn't sure.

As she was trying to take it all in, a dark shadow moved over the ground from one end of a nearby street toward the tower in which they stood looking out at the view. It grew in size until the object that created it was fully in sight. A large wagon, drawn by a pair of creatures she initially wanted to believe were horses.

As they came closer she was sure that they were most defiantly not equine. They had the bodies of something that looked reptilian with heads that were almost human. Slits of orange eyes stared out from white pearly skin and drool dripped in long, sticky strands from sharp fangs that extended way beyond the jaw line. Their long talons clicked on the stone pathways as they pulled the wagon slowly down the street, passing under the window where Charlotte was now barely standing on a wobbly pair of legs.

She turned slowly away from the window and looked searchingly at Elyian, who was eyeing her with more than a little trepidation.

"Are you all right?" he asked her very gently, as if afraid that speaking too loudly would shatter her as easily as a drop on concrete would a piece of the finest crystal.

"No. I'm so far removed from all right it would be hilarious if it wasn't so terrifying." She'd come to the odd conclusion that she was ensconced, much like a damsel in distress, high up in a tower on a planet far, far away. She was living out the plot of a movie, for God's sake.

The one thing holding her in check and stopping her from entering a full-blown meltdown could now be found striding around the room. His long, muscular legs moved him in concentric circles around the perimeter of the tower. His face always turned in her direction, swiveling on an enormous neck, never looking ahead. He quite literally could not take his eyes off of her.

She couldn't help but be drawn to him. He pulled her in like a magnet. He was everything she'd ever fantasized about. Dark-haired and handsome and those eyes of his flashed with shades of the darkest green, emerald and gold. Charlotte had dreamed of meeting someone like him, had wanted to feel strong arms holding her in their powerful but protective grip, had melted at the thought of lips like that crushing her own beneath them. He was the embodiment of her fantasies. But was he holding her captive?

Elyian suddenly stopped pacing and closed the distance between them so swiftly that she gasped when he stopped in front of her.

Never before in his very, very long life had Elyian been speechless. Now, with the heady scent of this woman filling his senses, his power over her native tongue fled, leaving him almost mute. His upper jaw ached and he longed to release his fangs from their trap. But he knew it was too soon for that little secret to come out of the closet.

"I don't know your name, either," he finally stammered out. That surprised Charlotte; she'd assumed her stalker knew everything about her, but apparently that wasn't the case.

"I'm called Charlotte," she answered him. When her name left her mouth, the air around her face moved his direction. He breathed in the expelled air and his world spun on its axis. Her breath coursed through his veins and heated every fiber in his body. He had to have this woman.

"Elyian," she tested his name and it sounded right.

Perfect. She had so many questions for him, but right now they could wait. For the time being, nothing was going to change where she found herself. Deep down in the very center of her being, she knew she was safe. This man she'd just met was the most important thing that had ever happened to her.

Charlotte wanted him on a purely animalistic level. It was illogical and bizarre, but her longing was so strong that there was no hesitation in her next move. Without any forethought she reached out and gently touched his face. Tracing the line of his generous mouth with her fingertip, she felt shock waves hit her and wrap her in their heat. Her core trembled and the life she had known before shattered into crystalline shards.

They came together like magnets, drawn by a force out of their control, and as he pulled her down to the bed they were both blissfully unaware of the storm that gathered outside the seclusion of his quarters.

Much later they lay curled around each other, wrapped in a tangle of coverings of the softest fabric she'd ever had next to her skin.

"There are plenty of clothes in that closet," Elyian pointed to a doorway on the opposite side of the room. "I don't know if you'll find anything you like, but don't worry; we can always have some made for you."

Charlotte smiled and stroked his well-defined chest, admiring the sweep of his muscles and his taut, lean stomach. "Thank you; it would be lovely to have something clean to wear."

She dragged herself away from him and made her way to the closet, peering inside. She didn't know who the clothes belonged to, but whoever it was had wonderful taste. Row after row of gorgeous gowns, silky tunics of russet, silver and green, and a rainbow of delicate leather slippers were neatly arranged. Boxes filled with delicious satiny undergarments vied for space with masses of more casual clothing such as leather leggings and soft, warm, woolen tops.

She delightedly pulled on a soft tunic of the palest sage green and silver-grey leather pants that clung to every curve of her long legs. Then she wrapped a wide leather belt around her tiny waist and cinched it tightly.

Elyian's breath caught in his throat as she emerged from her clothing cocoon. She was beyond beautiful, her copper hair glowing in the moonlight and her body undulating across the room clad in those sexy leather pants.

At the curve of her breast hung a large gold ankh that she never removed. It was pitted and scratched with age, and it held a single piece of mother-of-pearl in the center loop, which was glowing against her pale and perfect skin. Seeing that pendant, he had realized with a shock just how special she was.

Charlotte had eyes that in the right light would almost match Elyian's. With pale skin and an upturned nose, she was tall with delicate bones and a tiny waist but curves in all the right places, and legs that were long and toned. As she moved toward him she reminded him of an elongated elfin creature. All she needed were little pointy ears, but those she lacked.

He spoke at last. "Good, you're dressed. Let's eat." Elyian took her hand and opened the door. They stepped out of the room, and into chaos.

Chapter 5

in which history is rewritten

Ranic in the century of the shining moons
Earth year 1592

ONE HUNDRED YEARS after Christopher Columbus reached the New World, Elyian made his first trip across the universe. He was young for a Raniculan, a mere child that still had more than a thousand years of life left to him.

This was his first mission to cull mother-of-pearl from the oceans of planet Earth. His father hadn't wanted him to go and claimed he was being foolhardy and risking the future of Ranic by placing his life in danger. But it had gone well so far.

He was accompanied by a few other highly skilled and lethal hunters whom his father sent to be both his companions and guards to protect him. After a few nights of diving, Elyian managed to bring in a hefty harvest of the much-prized shells.

While diving in the ocean, Raniculans' body chemistry changed, slowing their metabolism and allowing them to stay submerged for extended periods. Thus they were able to remain undetected as they went about the business of collecting abalone.

Stealth and secrecy were of paramount importance. Under no condition were they allowed to be spotted by the local population of humans. All diving was done after nightfall, with only the glowing, handheld orbs to guide them down to the shellfish beds.

On their last night on Earth, all of them were hunting in a single cove. The net bag Elyian left on the shore bulged with shells and he was delighted to see how many he'd found. He dove down to retrieve the last abalone in his section; but before surfacing he decided to explore a little further, beyond the sweep of rocks that sheltered the cove. After a while he surfaced and came up dripping onto the beach.

The light of the moon illuminated a lone figure, walking quickly and furtively along the edge of the water ahead of him, stumbling occasionally in the dark on the slippery, seaweed-covered rocks. She wore animal skins of some kind.

A large male stood waiting for her at the base of the cliff, under an overhang that hid the entrance to a cave. The man raised his arm, beckoning to her, and she made her way up the beach to him. Once there she took his hand; then the darkness swallowed them up.

Elyian, who had a youthful mind, sharp and curious, wanted to know where they had gone, so he followed slowly and at a discrete distance.

"Elyian! Stop!" His fellow hunters had seen his body stiffen in reaction to the girl and tried to prevent a potential meeting between her and their leader's son, which would undoubtedly end badly. They raced across the sand to catch up to him. One hunter grabbed him by the arm and tried some gentle persuasion.

"That's not a good plan, Elyian, sire. We need to stay as far away as we can from these primitive people. They're not nearly ready to understand who we are and where we have come from. They are without knowledge of any world outside this planet, let alone understanding our universe. And you know we can't follow you for protection. The court will have our lives if we're seen by any circumstance not accidental."

Elyian frowned and shook his arm free of the hold the hunter had on him. He replied with the arrogance of youth and the decided lack of good sense that often accompanies a youthful, hormone-driven mind.

"They are so interesting to me. I don't care if you want

to leave; that's your decision. But I want to learn all I can about this planet, and this is part of the process. Anyway, I'll be careful. So stay here if you wish, or leave, it is of no great matter to me."

With that he suddenly bounded forward and ran at full tilt to the cave's entrance, leaving his companions behind. Or so he thought.

He was silent, every movement made with the knowledge that he must make no sound at all. He stood without so much as the single smallest twitch of a muscle at the entrance to the cave. As his eyes adjusted to the darkness, he took in the scene before him.

She was naked, and her skin glistened with the damp of the cool night. The male was wrapped around her, and the heady, musky scent of mating lay heavy in the salty air. Elyian hardened instantly, and before he could stop himself a long, deep growl emanated from him as his fangs descended.

The couple spun around in shock, taking in the sight of the terrifying figure stalking toward them with enormous white teeth protruding down from the curve of his lips.

"Get him! We have to take him away—he's not about to go willingly," one hunter said to another when they saw that Elyian had been spotted by the couple. With a single, united movement they bound Elyian's mind to their own and vanished into the chill of the night, taking Elyian with them.

So it happened that on a lonely beach on the west coast of a vast continent that had yet to see the invention of anything more complex than an arrow, two native people who had stolen away for a brief interlude with each other, had instead the first human interaction ever with a Vampire. Every now and then, a Raniculan slipped up and a human saw them for what they truly were. Each encounter added yet another story to the legend of a monster in the night.

It took another hundred years before Elyian was allowed back on Earth after that, his first major interplanetary infraction. Once permitted to return, he travelled there often and grew to love the planet with great blue oceans and snow-capped mountains. He enjoyed exploring every country and watched, intrigued, as man changed the face of the land with roads, bridges, and cities.

The Ranic high court gradually relaxed their rules, and Elyian spent time on Earth in human houses, wearing their clothing and eating their food—though human food passed through his system without his body absorbing any fats or nutrients. This was just as well, as he developed a passion for fried chicken when he spent a decade living in the deep south; and his craving for chocolate was a source of constant frustration when he was back on chocolate-deprived Ranic.

Elyian never again revealed his true nature to humans, always exercising self-control to keep his fangs well hidden. He'd learned his lesson after that first infraction of Raniculan law and had no desire to be Ranic-bound again.

He always missed the taste of Yalon when he was on Earth, as it was a vital and much-loved part of the Raniculan diet. Human blood was a good substitute; it had the same rusty tang and viscosity. Elyian tried to never take blood directly from a human's vein, but preferred blood banks as his primary source of food during extended stays.

As the centuries passed, with inevitable slip-ups by various hunters and an increasing numbers of Raniculan criminals sentenced to life on Earth, sightings of them became more frequent. But human beings are a cynical lot, and most of the Vampire killings were passed off as gang incidents, with the accompanying paperwork cataloging the exsanguination of victims becoming lost under ever-increasing mounds of bureaucratic red tape.

This was due to the dedicated work of a few Raniculan men and woman who lived on Earth permanently and dedicated their lives to the cause of keeping the race secret from everyone on the planet. It was their job to do anything necessary to make sure the human race never knew there were alien beings making shopping trips to the planet. They spent their days losing and altering files; and as the computer age got up and running, they introduced the PC gremlin, a microscopic creature from Ranic that was amazingly efficient at messing stuff up.

Every now and again a case would slip through their fingers. Rumors of Vampires would run rampant through the village or town where the attack occurred. What they always failed to mention was that almost every incident was precipitated by a violent crime, and the victim of the Vampire attack would have been the prime suspect had he or she lived to see justice served.

The Raniculan hunters were very careful and did everything in their power to hide their innate power and bloodthirsty tendencies from humankind.

Elyian blatantly ignored this law. As the current ruler, he did as he pleased. For centuries, Elyian watched human history play itself out from the sidelines, often from a favorite vantage point in Paris. He would sit on the roof of the gothic Cathedral of Notre Dame, next to one of the many gargoyles, and watch the procession of humanity below. He was bemused by the violence endemic on Earth and saddened by the wasteful loss of life that accompanied every change of power. The toll was massive and seemingly never ending.

During the twentieth century, he watched in worried fascination as the planet's population exploded from one to over six billion souls. It was then that Raniculans became concerned that their precious source of mother-of-pearl was being threatened. It turned out that humans liked abalone as well as Raniculans! They, too, went diving for them and ate large quantities of the shellfish; but thankfully, humans didn't seem to treasure the shells and often tossed them into piles behind seaside restaurants. Then, if they didn't feel like getting wet, the Raniculan hunters were able to go dumpster diving instead of deep sea diving.

Every hundred years or so, some female caused a major slip in Elyian's self-control. The last one was back in 1898, when he bedded a fine young woman who matched him in passion.

She had perished when her father tried to shoot Elyian for sleeping with his daughter and inadvertently put a bullet through her heart instead, killing her instantly. Elyian was so saddened by this that he cried off human women for good.

Until he met Charlotte.

It was in the spring of 2019 that Elyian spotted Charlotte near the house where she was staying. He'd been out at the ocean all night diving for abalone and had just returned when he heard her clear voice calling out as she stood on the back steps of the house next door to his own temporary home.

Curious, he far-stepped deep into the woods, losing himself in the shadows as she approached. He climbed up the nearest redwood tree and perched himself on a branch, looking down.

As the light caught her face, he was mesmerized. He stared in awe at the girl making her way valiantly through the driving rain. She was nearly six feet tall, an extraordinary height for a human female, with long, lean legs and at the height of her beauty with a chiseled face and just a hint of a cleft in her chin.

But it was her hair that first caused his blood to pound in his veins. The color of russet leaves with flashes of burnt orange and red, it held an entire firestorm of color within its mass of long waves, glossy and shimmering in the light even though it was getting soaked in the heavy rain.

At that moment the small, heavy ball of Leverium2 squeezed out of the pouch hanging at his waist on a leather thong. With a will all its own, it dropped silently to the ground, where just a moment later she spotted it in the damp, leafy undergrowth.

Elyian was stunned when the ball changed color. It had never done that on Earth, and he was well aware of its meaning. With his senses in overdrive, he descended to the forest floor and stood stock still, doing a marvelous imitation of a marble statue. Only his fangs moved. Unbidden, they exploded down and throbbed with the need to sink into her throat.

He watched her approach and then gently lifted his teller orb from the cradle of leaves in which it had landed. The orb had given him the knowledge that she would have a huge influence on his life. Exactly how this would happen was still a mystery to him—a mystery he was only too keen to unravel.

Chapter 6

in which reality bites

ELYIAN AND CHARLOTTE forgot about getting anything to eat as soon as they left his chambers and beheld the activity unfolding in the corridor ahead.

Several young men were manhandling a squirming, screeching woman, pushing her against her will down the corridor away from where Charlotte and Elyian stood. She yelled at them to leave her alone but they blatantly ignored her.

Charlotte started forward to go and help somehow. She hadn't taken more than one step before Elyian held her fast and stopped her progress.

"What? No! Let go, Elyian, I need to help that woman, or you do. Don't just stand there!"

He turned her away from the scene and with a determined move held her face in both hands and kissed her soundly. She shoved him away, amazed at his disregard for the fate of the petite woman. Charlotte still heard her protests, though by now she'd been removed from the scene by the men.

Elyian looked suitably abashed and winced slightly when he realized how upset Charlotte was.

"I am so sorry, Charlotte." He almost growled the words at her. "I had to make sure she didn't see you...yet."

"This is just the latest in an endless stream of weird things happening. My mind is so bemused I can't take it all in. Can you take me to get something to eat? All of a sudden I'm absolutely starving." She looked up at him and he took her hand and led her off in the direction of the kitchens.

As they walked through room after gorgeous room, she tried to absorb the sights that unfurled before her. Raniculans had a definite addiction to anything silver in color, and the gleam of polished surfaces were everywhere. The rooms were stately but comfortable, with enormous full walls of glass that gave uninterrupted and sweeping views of the city below.

When they passed a small group of what looked like servants cleaning a curved staircase, Charlotte was puzzled when they all dropped their heads in a submissive gesture to Elyian.

"Why are they doing that?" she asked.

"There's something I've neglected to tell you, Charlotte. Let's sit here by the window and I'll explain." He showed her to a soft and comfortable nook that housed a massive, grey, velvet-like sofa. She sat and waited for his explanation. He was about to begin when a servant arrived seemingly unbidden. He handed Elyian a glass and bowed as he left.

"Thank you, Arun," Elyian said, then turned to face Charlotte.

"Here on Ranic we have two dominant races. Mine is the ruling race and we are, as I have told you, the Raniculans. The other race is the Frey, and they tend to end up as servants in the households of the Raniculans. Not always; I know many Frey who own their own businesses and have brilliant, inventive minds. There are even some who are quite independently wealthy. However, many Frey don't have the mental capacity to live without help in housing and work from the Raniculans. We call those Frey *Greylings*. Their brains are compromised at birth in almost every case. It is our greatest wish that this tragedy could be rectified. Nobody knows why this happens, but we spend much time and effort trying to find some way to put this right. It is my goal to see that happen, and if it doesn't I'll be the one to blame. Because as they say so succinctly on Earth, 'The buck stops here.' Although I frequently wish it wasn't the case, I am the ruler here. That's why the Frey you just saw bowed to me."

Charlotte laughed, a great loud laugh that reverberated around the massive room. She laughed until tears fell unbidden from her eyes; and as the first salty rivulets tracked their way down her cheeks, her laughing turned to sobbing until she was retching from lack of oxygen. Elyian held her gently and waited for the storm to pass.

"You're their king! Really? I can't do this anymore. I need to go home. Oh, God, please, just take me home. I need to feel human again. This is just too much." Her stomach was clenched in knots and her eyes were red rimmed from the crying.

Elyian felt awful. He knew she was traumatized by everything. He'd been such a jerk. He even took her to his bed, knowing she hadn't had any time to adjust to him absconding with her.

"I know you need to go home, Charlotte," he said, so softly she could hardly hear him. "But I don't know how I can let you go."

She stopped breathing, and as she looked into those wonderful green eyes, she knew her life had just gotten a whole lot more complicated.

"I have to go back, Elyian. I don't belong here any more than you belong on Earth. Please just take me back home," she begged.

He stood up, and with an inclination of his head gestured toward an open door at the other end of the room. He looked devastated but was obviously trying to keep his emotions under control as he replied. "I'll take you back after we eat."

As they sat at a long, highly polished wooden table, Charlotte took her first bite of unearthly food. Elyian had asked the cook to prepare a meal close to what she might find on earth; but since the cook had never stepped foot off Ranic, his idea of a hearty casserole was not quite the same as she was used to seeing. It had a very odd color, a murky greenish hue that gave it the unsettling look of rancid meat.

She was so hungry that she closed her eyes and took a small, tentative bite. Not bad. It had good flavor, and as long as she didn't look at the meal, she reckoned she'd be able to finish it.

Elyian sat across from her with a face like stone. Unreadable, but his eyes were flashing and she could feel vibrations emanating from him in great waves.

"Aren't you going to eat?"

"Yes, of course," he said, as a young Frey entered, bowed deeply to Elyian, and placed a chalice in front of his king.

Charlotte looked into the large, ornate cup. It held a gruesome-looking liquid, brown and thick, with a rusty smell. "Yech, that looks just awful." Elyian laughed at her and the tension in the kitchen eased.

He raised the cup to his lips and drank in great gulps until the entire thing was drained.

"When I first went to Earth, I tried your food and found it sadly lacking, but I must admit it has grown on me. I adore chocolate and I could eat fried chicken all day long." He laughed again, remembering his first forays into the gastronomic delights of the United States during the mid-twentieth century.

"What you call TV dinners are just dreadful. I question why they are still in existence after all this time. We don't have to eat human food at all. We really shouldn't eat it, as most of it is bad for our systems, but some of it we quite enjoy and so I do indulge in that one vice. Here on Ranic we drink mainly Yalon. Fermented or not, it contains all the nutrients we need. Any other food we eat is simply a supplement to that. When on earth for any extended time, we need a substitute, and the closest thing to Yalon is blood."

She paled at his last statement. Her mind wandered.

She stood suddenly, knocking over her chair. Her voice shook as she said, "On earth we have stories about creatures that prowl the land looking for victims whose blood they can drink. They're called Vampires. Of course they aren't real or anything and I know you exist, and you don't have fangs and you haven't tried to rip out my throat or anything..." her voice trailed off.

Elyian watched her carefully, trying to judge her mood, which changed like the wind over the Ranic upper plateau. Making up his mind to be honest with her, he far-stepped.

She cried out in alarm at his sudden disappearance across the table, and re-appearance next to her. "What... how...I'm not going to like this." She kept her voice carefully moderated.

"It's time," Elyian growled. His lips peeled back as his fangs descended, white and gleaming and very, very sharp. He backed a few steps away from her so she wouldn't feel threatened.

It didn't work.

Charlotte reeled when she saw the huge teeth. Everything she thought she knew about him came crashing down in that instant.

She whirled around and fled. She had no idea where she was going, and the palace was huge with long corridors leading in a multitude of directions. She just knew she had to be alone. She needed to think.

She ran until she couldn't run any farther. She'd reached a dead end. The corridor stopped at a bricked-up wall, so she leaned her back against it and sank down on her haunches. Another of those little furry beasts went scuttling across the floor, but this time it merited barely a glance from Charlotte. The sight of Elyian's fangs was a lot scarier than that tiny furry thing which was now sidling up to her, making an odd sound between a squeak and a purr.

She absently reached down to pet it. The creature jumped a good three feet in the air and bit her upper arm, hanging on like a persistent tick. She yelled at the stabbing pain and pulled at the creature until it let go. The red, angry mark left on her arm hurt like hell. As she looked at it, the inflammation spread rapidly outward, creeping up her arm toward her neck.

Elyian's disembodied voice came out of thin air. "Charlotte, I wish you hadn't pulled it off; it may have just bitten you and not injected venom if you had let it be. I have to go and get something to help you. Just sit here quietly and I'll be right back."

He far-stepped away and a few minutes later reappeared at her side holding a piece of cloth from which dripped a clear blue liquid. "Let me help," he said. He wrapped her arm carefully in the cloth, knotting it together to hold it in place. She tried to pull away from him but he held her fast.

He slid his hand to the nape of her neck and held her head gently in the palm of his hand. "Charlotte, please listen to me. I was never going to hurt you. I was showing you what I really am. I don't want there to be secrets between us." His sincerity showed in every line of his face.

She wanted to believe him. At the moment, though, the pain throbbing in her arm was so distracting she couldn't think about him.

Elyian started to panic. It was a new emotion for him. He had a short temper but was never scared. The knowledge of what could have happened to Charlotte from this bite scared the shit out of him.

"We don't have time to talk about this right now." Elyian spoke urgently and even he could hear the quiver in his voice. "I need to get you up to the infirmary. We don't have a lot of time; the venom from this creature works fast." He scooped her up in his arms as if she weighed mere ounces and far-stepped the short distance to the royal infirmary.

The physician was having a bad day. His assistant was away on an errand that had taken three times longer than it should have, and he'd dropped a large flask of liquid all over the floor. He was in the process of mopping it up when he saw a pair of massive combat boots right in front of his nose.

His gaze lifted skyward, up the long, strong legs and on to the girl being held in the arms of a very worried-looking hunter. When he noticed the Leverium2 and mother-of-pearl talisman engraved with the royal seal swinging from Elyian's neck, the physician blanched visibly, instantly realizing the identity of the imposing man looming over him.

"Sire," he stammered while getting to his feet. "Please, how may I help?" Elyian peered at the man as if he was completely stupid.

"Obviously, you can help me by taking care of the female draped in my arms!" Elyian's panic had taken him over the edge. He was terrified he would lose Charlotte.

She drifted in and out of consciousness as intense pain moved up her arms and into her torso. Searing heat licked at her heart and exploded into her head. Within minutes she was floating in a blissful sea of black.

Chapter 7

in which the chicken came before the egg

Her DREAMS WERE Technicolor vivid: purple skies and double blue moons, weird green creatures and men with white fangs. Everything was wrong, yet it all felt right.

Slowly, reality began to creep back, and when Charlotte woke up, she was—again—not where she thought she would be. She awoke in her bed at Cam's house, tucked securely beneath a cozy comforter with the smell of eggs, bacon and fried chicken drifting up the stairs to her room.

As she moved in bed her PJ's felt different, a lot tighter than they should have been. Quite uncomfortable. Peeling back the sheet, she yelped at the sight of her skin-tight leather-clad thighs.

She didn't own leather pants.

Before she had the chance to process both pieces of information, there was a loud bang and crash from somewhere downstairs, followed by choice cursing in a booming male voice. Then she heard him moving around the kitchen, with drawers opening and closing and flatware rattling.

I guess the burglar's hungry, she thought wryly.

Charlotte felt Elyian's presence in every fiber of her being. She could hear him as well, but even if he'd been silent she'd have known he was in the house. Every part of her was tuned in to him. She would swear she could hear his blood coursing through his veins.

Elyian knocked on her door and let himself in, holding a large tray laden down with the most delicious-smelling plates of food. She grinned up at him as he walked in looking sheepish.

"How are you feeling?" he asked as he laid the tray down next to her. "Sorry if I woke you with all the noise; the tray slipped."

She laughed. "You're only human. Don't worry about it!"

A huge grin split his face, as he appreciated the joke and revealed to her his now normal-sized incisors. "Can I see your arm, please? I want to make sure the bite is healing properly."

She held her arm out to him. He took it and carefully pulled away the bandaging that held a thick wad of gauze in place. "You were lucky that when the Grail bit you, I was close enough to get you to the infirmary without delay. Most victims die from these bites. You must be a lot stronger than you look. Or maybe your human DNA protected you. This has almost completely healed in just a few hours. Quite amazing."

"I felt like I was dying," she protested. "It hurt like hell at the time, but I feel just fine now, thanks to you for getting me help. Now, how about explaining how I got back here, please?"

"First," he chuckled, "you really must eat!" He picked up a piece of hot, juicy chicken and her mouth watered. As she ate, he gave a long and detailed explanation of the many puzzling things that had happened in the past couple of days.

"Let me tell you about Atlas first. I buried him for you right out there." He inclined his head toward the window that looked out over the rear of the house toward the woods. "He's under the first redwood at the edge of the garden. I marked his grave with a large boulder. Your phone is here, next to the bed. I charged it and I think you better get your messages. It's been bleeping at me all morning.

"Now, let me tell you what happened to you. To both of us."

Elyian told her that the ball of Leverium2 acted as a

fortune teller, letting him see her for what she truly was: a potential mate for him. He explained far-stepping, the act of moving from place to place with just a thought. Her eyes, already huge, turned into massive saucers of incredulity as he detailed how his body could move through space and how he could take objects and even people with him if he willed it.

Charlotte interrupted his monologue. "Do you mean to tell me you've been moving me around like some kind of chess piece whenever you felt like it?"

"Hardly that," he complained. "I only moved you when I needed to, such as from the river to Ranic when you refused to wake up, and to the infirmary when you were dying from the bite."

"Why do I keep passing out?" she asked.

"I'm not sure, but I think it must have something to do with your proximity to me. I feel strange around you, too. As if an unseen force is causing our bodies to react to each other. But something's not quite right. It feels like there's a missing link. I'm highly attracted you, but that's quite normal. Males of our species find almost all human females appealing. Humans are a constant source of frustration to our race. Much as we hate to admit it, Raniculan men find Earth women sexually riveting. We love their delicate features and the way they move. Your scent drives us mad with a frantic hunger. It is explicitly forbidden to engage in any kind of sex act with a human, under penalty of death. In such cases punishment is delivered fast and merciless. This fact alone has saved many human women from being taken from their homes and from the very planet on which they live. I am luckier than most, as being ruler has enabled me to circumvent convention, up to a point."

"Hmm," she snorted, "hardly the most flattering way to win someone over! You speak English very well. A strange accent but almost perfect." She pondered something and then asked, "Does everyone where you come from speak English? That would be odd."

"We have our own ancient language, but if needed we can speak in the native tongue of whomever we're near. It's something we're born being able to do. Like an automatic response. If we're questioned in a particular language, we answer in that language, until someone else speaks and then we can change again instantly. Very useful when several ambassadors from neighboring planets visit at the same time."

She realized her mouth was hanging open, so closed it quickly. But not before he saw her reaction and laughed.

Reaching down to his waist, he opened the drawstring on a pouch that hung on his belt and removed the small metal ball that rested inside. As the light hit its surface, it began to pulse and change color. Charlotte was mesmerized. Her head started to go fuzzy, like a warm wet blanket was enveloping her. Elyian saw her skin going pale and clammy and quickly returned the ball to the pouch.

"That ball," he said, preempting the question about to leave her lips, "is made of Leverium2, a metal found only on Ranic. It has many qualities, but the one that concerns us is its ability to read the future. It's normally solid and silver in color, but whenever I'm near you it senses your presence. It's telling me that you could possibly be the one person meant for me. It's not perfect at foretelling futures, though. And, I can also use it to send messages, like this."

He drew it back out, shut his eyes for a moment, then flicked the sphere into the air, where it hung for the briefest of moments before vanishing before her eyes. "I just it back to Ranic to tell my brother Jendal where I am," Elyian continued. "Think of it as an interplanetary cell phone if you like. It can do a multitude of things, very useful. I must admit, however, that it does worry me, the way it can manipulate your body's chemistry."

He pondered that for a while then said, "Does that answer some of your questions, Charlotte?"

She sat a long while not speaking, spreading the jigsaw puzzle out in her mind, sifting and sorting through the pieces, then letting them all slot neatly into place.

Something was missing. A stray thought drifted through her head, not wanting to find its place in the picture. She couldn't see exactly what it was, but she knew it was there. Eventually it would be the final piece that made the puzzle complete.

"I need to call Cam." Charlotte reached for the phone to make the call she dreaded but knew had to be made.

Cameron was very kind considering she'd let his dog drown. He said all the right things and insisted she stay at the house anyway as he wouldn't be returning for months. Eventually she agreed.

He's really a good person all 'round, she mused. She

loved her job. Cam was talented, and he paid her well to organize his business when he was in this country.

Charlotte showed Cam's work room to Elyian, who liked the paintings hanging in disarray around the light-filled dining room that had been converted into the studio. Many of them were fantasy pieces, as Cam was often hired to create the custom art work for speculative novels. Dragons and gothic towers vied for attention with other, traditional work that had been completed right there in the rolling hills of Sonoma County wine country.

Several pieces detailed a year in the life of a vineyard. Winter scenes with the bare, gnarled trunks of old vines sitting in pools of water, springtime views of buds bursting through the brown stems growing in fields dappled with bright, mustard-yellow flowers. The clear blue sky of high summer over vines heavy with ripening fruit, and beautiful oils of vineyards in the fall, a glorious riot of russet and gold as the leaves gave their final curtain call before winter's chill set in.

Charlotte and Elyian spent the day quietly talking through the million and one things that kept cropping up in her head. The one question she especially needed to ask, she kept ignoring, as if it would eventually go away. Of course, it didn't.

As the sun dipped behind the trees, they sat together on the porch swing, looking down the slope of the meadow ahead and watching the shadows creep across the valley floor. Charlotte handed Elyian a glass of a good pinot noir and took a large gulp of her own.

For courage, she told herself. Then, with a huge intake of breath, she launched into the question of the century.

"Fangs!" she blurted out. "You have goddamn fangs. Are you a Vampire or an alien?"

Elyian had been waiting for this moment, not wanting to push her but biding time until she was ready to hear the truth.

"Charlotte," his reply came out as a growl, low and animalistic. "I regret now that I showed them to you. It was too soon, but I have a hard time being patient and I needed you to know exactly who I am." He shifted uncomfortably in his seat and swiveled to face her unwavering gaze. The night fell around them like a cool blanket. He drew her in close to his side to keep her warm and talked again of his world.

He told her of how the Raniculans hunted on Earth for mother-of-pearl, and how they ended up drinking human blood. "We're not a violent race," he said. "We merely want to survive comfortably while we're here."

He told her that although Raniculans could far-step at will over short distances—indeed anywhere on the surface of the planet—they could only travel to Earth from Ranic once every few weeks or so, as it took that long for their internal strength to recharge enough to carry them safely in a dissolved molecular state and then reassemble them when they arrived at their destination. He explained how they could climb vertical surfaces and even levitate, and how they could stop a fall and lower themselves to the ground.

"Our people have lived on Ranic for an untold number of years. We didn't discover your planet until fairly recently. When we first arrived, man was still struggling to get beyond a quite primitive society. So we gave them a small kick in the pants.

"My many-times-great grandfather travelled to Egypt around 2630 B.C. He met a man named Imhotep, an architect and priest and by all accounts a very good healer. He stayed many months with Imhotep and they became fast friends. After an evening where a great deal of alcohol was consumed, he suggested that Imhotep design a great monument to honor Khufu, who ruled Egypt. As they sat on the dirt floor of the stone house where Imhotep lived, he picked up a sharp stick and drew the shape of a pyramid on the floor. That was the start of the great age of pyramids and truly the beginning of your civilized world.

"He was very careful never to show Imhotep his true identity, and didn't give humans everything they needed, just a cosmic nudge in the right direction.

"Then one night before he fell asleep at Imhotep's house, a lovely female crept into his bed. She was a thank-you gift from Imhotep for all the help that he had given. He took her blood, and she gave birth six months later. Gestation is 180 days on Ranic, so it seems safe to presume that the baby she delivered was the very first human hybrid ever seen on Earth.

"There is nothing written that tracks the lineage except for one thing. The baby had one very distinguishing feature: the shape of a tiny blue bird we call a Creck marked her head just behind her ear. Her mother tried to hide the mark, and fearing persecution she fled Egypt. There the trail ends."

Elyian stopped talking and looked to see if Charlotte was freaked out by his story, but to his amazement she seemed to be enjoying it. Her eyes had not left him and she smiled broadly. She seemed to be itching to say something so he gave her a nod. "Yes, Charlotte, what is it?"

"So, let me get this straight, Elyian. What you're telling me is that I've had sex with an alien Vampire king? To think my mother was worried about me going to prom with Carl Mathers and he wouldn't have said boo to a goose. My virginity was certainly safe in his hands."

She shook her head. "I'm a nervous person. I've spent my entire life afraid of what I can't see in the dark. I hate to fly—that's why I never go with Cameron on his trips abroad. Ants and other things that squeak or slither leave me quaking in my boots. Yet here I am, sitting in the dark with a tall, dark, and handsome Vampire who's not really a Vampire but a freaking alien! The strangest thing, though, is that tonight, I feel like nothing can ever hurt me again. When you're next to me I feel completely safe and protected."

As it finally sank in, she started to laugh, not stopping until tears rolled down her lovely face, leaving silvery streaks glowing from the light of the single moon that shone brightly over them both.

Chapter 8

in which life is culled

ESARELLE COMBED THE palace from one end to the other, until at last she found Elyian and his friend Agen sitting quietly on the floor at the far end of the vaulted library. They smiled as she approached and Agen, not wanting to be a third wheel, beat a hasty retreat.

Elyian was fond of Esarelle. She was a childhood friend and they'd spent many happy hours together. He still regarded her as a quirky friend, but she had changed her opinion of him. To her, he was a male to be conquered, and she was on course to pin him down as her mate. Elyian had other ideas.

He valued their friendship but was not attracted to her in that way. Sure, they'd enjoyed the odd night of sex, but their forays into the sexual side of their friendship had been brief. Though she was physically stunning with a petite but well-endowed figure and an ethereal face, he found her shallow and sometimes devious, which were not traits he found in the least bit appealing.

Today she was making her way through the library clutching a small animal not unlike a puppy, but with a little less fur and a lot more teeth. It wriggled in her arms trying to get down but she clung on to it with a determined grip that belied her small stature.

"Really, Mita, can you just stop that for one moment?" she berated the animal, which had taken up squealing like a pig in its determination to get free of her grasp.

"Well, now what have we here?" Elyian chuckled as he watched her efforts to control the little thing. "I'm not sure who's winning this battle, but one thing is for sure. Your tunic is ruined!"

"No!" she squealed and dropped the creature. It bolted away while she whirled around trying to see her garment from all directions. "Where? I don't see anything. Elyian, you brute! There's nothing there at all! Damn you, now you've ruined my surprise. He was going to be a pet for you."

Elyian threw back his head and laughed at Esarelle, who had turned an angry and unbecoming shade of red. She glared at him and stomped her foot in what he supposed was some kind of petulant huff, then turned on her elegant heel and left.

His duties escalated and took him away from home on an almost daily basis. When he was in residence he was surrounded by the court, who made it their all-consuming and primary purpose to continually hound him for favors and schedule his days to the minute with boring parties and state banquets, leaving him no free time for her. She was reduced to watching him from a distance and as the bitterness festered inside she plotted her return into his life.

Elyian was busy, yes, but no matter how many people surrounded him, he always finished the day alone. As a child he had basked in the glow of adoration that was a part of his life. He'd lost his mother while still very young, but he was loved unreservedly by his father and coddled by the many Frey that looked after his every need, so he'd never felt lonely.

Now, however, the loneliness ate at him piece by piece. He dreaded the hours spent with people who held no real love for him yet fawned over him. He felt a burning need to make a difference on Ranic and to prove to the Raniculans that he wasn't just a figurehead but an effective ruler. So he shut away the part of his soul that cried out for love and mechanically went about the business of being king.

His only source of freedom and the biggest joy in life were his hunting trips to Earth. Only his brother, the high court, and the few hunters he could trust with his life were privy to the fact that he left Ranic whenever he could get away. The trips were a bandage on his soul. He felt his spirit repairing as he sat on cliff tops watching the earth's ocean crash on the rocks below. He loved the ocean and never tired of watching its ebb and flow. Elyian found it totally absorbing.

From his vantage point high on the cliff, he could see hundreds of feet down into the depths. His eyes were able to clearly make out schools of fish swimming in great shoals and the Herculean blue whales passing by on their migratory swims from Alaska down to the warm oceans of Baja Mexico.

The hidden world of the ocean, normally closed to humans unless they were swimming underwater, was as clear to him as to a human at an aquarium looking through glass. On days when the water was exceptionally clear he could just make out the luminous glow of the deep-sea angler fish as they baited their prey.

When tired of merely observing, he would stand and, with a graceful arc of his beautiful, long body, launch himself off the cliff, hurtling down to the sea with the grace of a swallow. Once underwater he'd swim unaided and unfettered by the need to breathe, embracing the total freedom that came to him in that vast, wet, alien world.

Esarelle always knew when he had been on an off-planet trip. He came back with a glow in his cheeks and a ready smile on his lips. Convinced that he had an off-world lover, the fondness she had harbored for him turned to stone, and with a hateful grimace she turned away from the light in his eyes. She needed proof, but as a female she was unable to far-step, so off-world travel was out of the question. Esarelle was nothing if not stubborn, so she waited, for more than a hundred years, for Elyian to put a foot wrong.

Elyian's visits to earth kept getting longer. He couldn't seem to stay away. Of course the unfortunate side to this was that he sometimes had no other option but to feed from the human population. As technology increased, his ability to access blood banks had been compromised. So he frequented the seedier parts of large cities when the hunger grew unbearable.

On a hot, steamy night in New Orleans when the bars on Bourbon Street overflowed with college students living it up during spring break, a blonde girl in her late teens staggered out of a bar alone and swayed her way down the street, vomiting once in the gutter before lurching down a nearby alleyway. As she made her way down the darkened alley a shape moved in the shadows.

An old man who'd been watching her inside the bar stepped out and grabbed her by the neck, pushing her down behind a dented dumpster. Her blood-curdling scream rent the air, closely followed by a muted thump then a second, much lower scream. A few short minutes later Elyian appeared and wiped the last traces of blood from his mouth. He rose up to the rooftop and vanished into the night.

Behind the dumpster the girl stared in horror and disbelief at the ravaged neck of the would-be rapist who now lay dead at her feet.

It was all over Facebook within the hour.

Charlotte had been skimming the internet. *Someone certainly has an overactive imagination*, she mused, examining a blurry image of a man slumped in a dark corner of a filthy alley in what was purported to be New Orleans. Laughing at the girl's description of the handsome man who had saved her from a horrible fate, Charlotte had put the entire incident down to an excessively inebriated student who should, at the ripe old age of 22, have known better than to be alone at night in a dark alley, after an entire night of knocking back shots of Patron.

Only a few short weeks later Charlotte's own world turned on its axis, tilting her view of what was real and what was not and causing her to doubt everything, not just the stream of information that flooded the internet.

Chapter 9

in which a boy gets a toy

As THE STARS tracked their way across the Northern California sky, two beings from two very different worlds came to one conclusion and their lives began to move in unison. Elyian and Charlotte could not have moved from the porch swing had their lives depended on it. He brushed his fingers over the tracks of her tears then moved closer to her and gently kissed her sweet, full mouth. She yielded to his kiss and melted into his arms that crushed her against his hardening body.

"Elyian," she gasped into his mouth. She would have said more but his mouth was demanding and she never had the chance to utter another word. They would have stayed right there on the deck, but it was getting colder every minute and her breath made clouds around her face. Elyian saw and guilt engulfed him.

"I didn't notice that you were cold, sorry. The cold doesn't affect me so you must tell me if you need to be warmer."

She laughed. "Elyian, please stop worrying. I just told you, I'm fine. Never felt better, you're the best medicine ever! It is getting chilly out here, though."

He made love to her again that night, ignoring the niggle in the back of his mind telling him to stop. She did nothing to halt him and everything to encourage. Still, something seemed to be missing.

Much later, as they lay curled together on the bed, Elyian knew it was time to tell her his plans. "Charlotte, I need to talk to you."

Charlotte looked at him, puzzled. "We've been talking. I now know more about aliens than the combined knowledge of every human that's ever walked on this planet. But I'm still curious about those teeth of yours." She hesitated a beat before continuing. "Can I see them again, please? I promise I won't do the whole freaking out thing this time. I just need to be sure about what I saw."

The mere idea of her wanting to see his fangs was enough to make his gums throb with the need to let them drop. Hard as it was, he resisted the temptation to sink them deep into her carotid artery.

He turned her around to face him. "No, Charlotte, I won't. You were terrified and I..."

The sentence hung in the air unfinished as his voice trailed off into silence. "Shh!" He placed his finger to his lips in the universal signal for quiet.

In a flash he left her side and appeared next to the windows on the far side of the bedroom, where he gently pulled back the heavy drapes to see outside. Just behind the glass a small orb hung in the air, glowing and pulsing with a fluorescent green color.

"Shit, that's not good." Elyian cursed as he flung open the window and attempted to catch the orb. He almost wrapped his fingers around it but the orb shot skyward. He tracked its path and before Charlotte knew what had happened, he completely disappeared, stark naked, into the heavens above. Charlotte watched the entire stupefying event with her mouth open.

Good lord above, whatever next, she thought as she scanned the night sky for any sign of him. She paced the floor, made coffee, paced some more, then wrapped a huge, warm comforter snuggly around herself and revisited the swing seat for another couple of hours. Sleep finally overtook her just as dawn broke in the eastern sky. There was still no sign of Elyian.

When she eventually woke it was to the sound of car tires

screeching as a vehicle tore up the driveway. A sleek silver Audi, with windows tinted so dark she couldn't see the driver, snaked toward the house. Whoever was behind the wheel had no clue how to handle that much power. The Audi weaved from side to side, as though the driver was over-steering and then compensating for the lack of skill by over-compensating.

Charlotte's instincts kicked in and she knew she was in danger. Every hair on her body stood to attention and prickling adrenaline coursed in her veins. She shot to her feet and bolted inside. Once there she grabbed the loaded Glock from the top of the coat closet. With her heart hammering in her chest, she hunkered down behind the sofa and waited.

The door flew open and a gigantic figure stood backlit in the dawn light. A massive man of almost seven feet, dressed in black from head to foot, stood glowering in the doorway. His huge feet wore muddy combat boots and black leather encased massive legs. A battery of weapons hung from his waist. A long sword sat in its sheath. Various daggers and throwing stars seemed randomly scattered about his body. His head sat on a neck as huge as a tree trunk. The stranger turned to face her and smiled sardonically.

Charlotte raised her pistol and tried to keep her arm from shaking under its weight. The man stepped toward her and held out his hand. Her finger quivered and the Glock fired.

A deep red stain spread out from the bullet hole at the center of his chest and the man pitched forward like a redwood tree being felled. He hit the floor with a thump so heavy the glassware rattled in the cabinet down the hall.

Charlotte tried to breathe but her lungs seized up and her head spun as she tried to regain some control. She lowered the gun and gingerly went toward him. Reaching him, she put her hands on his shoulders and tried to roll him onto his back. He weighed a ton and her first couple of attempts did nothing. After a couple more tries she managed to get him rolled over.

"Ouch, that hurt!" he exclaimed.

"I thought I'd killed you," she gasped. "How on earth are you still alive? The bullet went straight into you. I know I didn't miss; I can see all the blood."

He growled his reply. "It wasn't for a lack of trying. Not a very friendly way to greet me. I was just trying to shake hands with you. My name is Jendal and I'm Elyian's brother."

His silky smooth voice seemed at complete odds with his

appearance. "I guess you have to be Charlotte. He told me you were beautiful, but whoa! He totally undersold you."

Charlotte grimaced. "Oh, my God, I'm so sorry. Elyian told me he had a younger brother but I wasn't expecting someone like you."

"So sorry to disappoint," he groaned. "And much as I would love to continue this riveting conversation, at this moment I'm more concerned with healing."

She leaned over him. "Here, let me see how bad it is."

Jendal grimaced as she pulled the sticky edges of his shirt apart, revealing the jagged entry wound. His voice low and a little weak, he asked, "Would you be kind enough to retrieve the small ball from the pouch on my belt, please?"

Charlotte pulled the suede bag open and retrieved the ball. As she held it in her hands she felt it move and pulse with a life all its own.

Jendal was amazed to see it reacting to her. It had never before reacted to anyone other than a native Ranic species. Intrigued to see how much influence she had, he told her to hold it over the wound in his chest. As she did they could both see the waves of energy rolling off the orb and bouncing off his bared chest.

He grimaced as the bullet pulled slowly but inexorably out of the wound until at last it rolled off him and with a satisfying plink landed in a pool of blood on the floor next to him. His skin rapidly returned from a sickly grey to the normal pale she'd gotten used to seeing on Elyian.

Within the hour the only sign he'd ever been shot was a slight puckering of the skin where the bullet had entered. When he was able, he filled Charlotte in on the reason for his hasty visit.

"I had a message from Elyian last evening. Someone's spying on you. He needed to catch the ball that had been recording the two of you here at the house. The chase took him off-world and he doesn't have the required energy to return yet. So he asked me to come and get you as fast as I could. Your life may very well be in danger here.

"We believe we know who's behind this. If we're correct it'll make Elyian's life very complicated indeed. I don't know all the details of his relationship with you, but judging by the state of high anxiety he's in, I can reasonably deduce that he's in way over his head. As we speak he's lying in a darkened room unable to speak or talk. He suffers mightily from migraines, so bad and now so frequent I fear for his sanity."

Charlotte took all of this in with a stoicism she didn't know she was capable of. She simply needed to do whatever was necessary to help Elyian. "I'm curious, Jendal, why the car? How come you didn't far-step like I've seen Elyian do?"

He grinned an impish, lopsided smile totally at odds with the massive hulking man he was. "I love to drive! Now, please, can you hurry and get ready to leave? We really need to get back to Ranic."

Charlotte nodded. "Give me a few minutes and I'll throw some stuff in a bag and we can go."

As she talked she made her way up to the bedroom. She retrieved her duffel from the cupboard and flung it open. Thrilled at the idea of returning to Ranic, Charlotte packed faster than she'd ever done before. She added some toiletries and a few other essentials before zipping the bag closed and hurtling down the stairs to where Jendal was waiting, impatiently tapping the car keys on the oak banister.

"Okay, I'm ready." Then she remembered one last thing. Pulling a manila envelope from the desk drawer, she wrote CAMERON in large black letters on the front. After locking the front door she slipped the key into the envelope and slid it back under the door.

They drove like the wind down Highway 101 toward San Francisco until they reached the rental agency. Jendal pulled into an empty parking lot at the rear of the building and parked discreetly next to a high wall that afforded them a measure of privacy.

One by one he handed Charlotte his many weapons to hold while he was inside. Weighed down with the armory, she leaned against the wall and hoped he would be quick. Inside the building it was a very reluctant Jendal that handed over the keys to his temporary toy.

As he came back around the corner Charlotte was struck by the lack of similarity between him and Elyian. They had identical eye colors, a vivid green rimmed in gold that was so distinctive. Other than that, and maybe the unearthly pallor of their skin, it was hard to believe they were related, so great was the difference in their build. Jendal had none of Elyian's easy grace and smooth, taut musculature. Jendal was all bulk and swagger.

That mountain of a man relieved her of the weight of

arms and took her by the hand. Before she had time to blink
she felt her body dissolve into a billion pieces.

Chapter 10

in which his destiny is fulfilled

As AMUN RELAXED at his home on Ranic, a series of earthly images flickered across his retina. As the first one clarified he took a deep breath, the first time he'd unconsciously moved his lungs for hundreds of years. He was totally unprepared for the shock delivered to his nervous system.

He watched entranced as the human sat on the porch swing with Elyian at her side. He kept the orb way back in the trees so it wouldn't be spotted and at that distance it didn't pick up their conversation, but the meaningful looks that passed between them were more than enough to show him what was coming next.

As the female stood he drank in her long, shapely legs and the way her skin shifted under her clothing. Little puffs of condensed air blew out around her face in the chill of the night and her hair shone like a burnished halo in the moonlight.

He watched spellbound as a spark flew out from the back of her head, unnoticed by either her or Elyian, and snaked its way toward the orb as if it was reaching for him. As Amun stretched his hand toward the orb it released the energy she'd unwittingly sent his way, shooting it toward him through the cool night sky and up into the cosmos.

When it hit his body he felt the release of a millennium of waiting. There she was. He couldn't believe he'd found her at last. Amun had spent so long alone that he hardly dared to move, in case she vanished, taking his heart with her.

As Elyian hugged Charlotte closer to his side, Amun wished with all his non-beating heart that he was the one next to her, breathing in her scent. He watched as Elyian scooped her up in his arms and levitated Charlotte upstairs. Amun's blood nearly boiled in his veins, but he couldn't blame his son; Elyian didn't know she belonged to Amun. But the passion he felt for this woman he'd never met simmered away, waiting until the time was right.

Later Amun used his mind to move the orb until it was suspended in the air outside the bedroom window. He watched her sleep and as she rolled over the sheet fell back, revealing the smooth planes of her hip. He tore his gaze upward until it rested on the ankh she wore around her slender neck, flanked by her perfect full breasts.

Amun groaned at the erotic form laid out in all her splendor for him to absorb. To clear his mind of her vision he paid a visit to the hunter training center he'd established many years ago.

His route took him through the seedier parts of Ranic, where the citizens who fell through the cracks in the social system scrabbled to make a living within the city limits. As always, Amun was saddened by the huge numbers of Frey that were unable to make a comfortable existence for themselves due to the limitations of their unfortunate disability.

A young woman hitched up her robe, revealing her unwashed and scabbed knees to a couple of men passing by. The look of scorn they shot her was a sad reflection of the way in which so many of Ranic's Greylings were treated. He gave the unfortunate woman some currency and reminded himself to talk to the court about setting up another feeding station to help cover at least some of their most basic needs. The planet's population was growing at a faster pace than many felt was sustainable, placing a massive strain on the already-insufficient resources he had helped put in place.

Gradually the narrow crumbling houses of the Frey gave way to the more affluent, polished-stone facades of the Raniculan homes. The winding passageways straightened and the roads became broad, straight and clear of all debris. Interspersed with the stone mansions were gleaming metal pyramids. In some places the points at their tips were joined with cables that formed an ethereal aerial cobweb over the streets. From these hung chains that dropped almost to street level, and at the tip of each chain were clusters of orbs that shone at night, providing even illumination over the city.

An extensive grid of canals connected every alternate road, with beautiful arched footbridges providing links over them. During the warm season the canals carried a huge variety of floating vessels that plied their way up and down the waterways, stopping at various points to load or unload cargo or passengers.

The entrances to the various merchants, bars and eating establishments were draped with a kaleidoscope of multi-hued banners and canopies that protected their clientele from the worst of summer's heat and winter's snow.

During the long, eight-month winter, huge clouds of hot steam rose ceaselessly from vents in the sidewalk. Next to each vent was a doorway leading to a public steam room where shoppers could warm up and exchange pleasantries with their friends and neighbors. If they were lucky an Ireculian would be inside taking the steam, so they could while away some hours reveling in the Ireculian's superlative singing voices.

In the summer many cafes placed seating outside under the shade of a canopy, and there the younger citizens would often lounge on thick cushions sipping long, tall glasses of chilled Yalon as they watched the sky darken and the cool of the evening set in.

It was nearly dark by the time Amun walked through the door and into the levatron that took him swiftly and soundlessly up to the top floor of the training center. In the main room a dozen or more males and females were engaged in various forms of training, hand to hand combat, martial arts and weapon handling.

Amun peeled off his outer layers of clothing and folded them neatly in a pile off to one side, unaware of the fact that several heads turned in his direction. One female hunter was so taken by his rock-hard abs and strong, broad shoulders covered in a taut layer of perfect skin that she lost her power of concentration long enough for her sparring partner to give her jaw a severe upper cut that spun her around in a circle before she fell unconscious to the mat. Amun turned around only when he heard the raucous laughter of the other females who had witnessed her demise.

Confused and a little embarrassed to be the center of attention, he moved quickly away and lost himself in a two-hour workout that he hoped would clear his head of the image of Charlotte that now seemed permanently tattooed on his brain.

Chapter 11

in which two worlds collide

CHARLOTTE AND JENDAL re-formed on a busy street in the very heart of the city of Ranic. Heat radiated in waves off the walkways. They were ignored by everyone around, who continued walking, talking and conducting business after a brief glance in their direction.

She tried to shake off the fog that surrounded her, but as she was unused to the act of far-stepping it took a while. Jendal held her upright while she took a few deep breaths. When she was steady he clasped her arm and led her down a wide avenue. The stark, pale purple sky above them shimmered in the heat of the day and the twin moons glowed low and beautiful in the clear morning light.

Jendal and Charlotte stopped outside a white stone building that was unremarkable apart from the small front door with a wobbly spiral symbol burned into the wood. In the very center of the symbol was a red droplet shape made of a gem of some sort. She later learned it was a large ruby and the symbol denoted the presence of an apothecary and physician.

They ducked inside. It took her nose a moment to adjust to the stench permeating every nook and corner of the room. So pungent was the smell that her nose wrinkled and her eyes smarted and teared up. Clamping her hand over her nose and mouth she gasped out, "Oh, that's horrible!" in a whisper, just in case the owner of the drugstore was nearby.

"Not nearly as bad as it'll smell a couple of days from now when it's applied to the festering leg of the man for whom it is intended," said a voice from somewhere at the very back of the room.

The voice then attached itself to a small, wiry man with the whitest skin Charlotte had ever seen. He was beyond wrinkled, his face like a crumpled map that laid out his entire life's journey in every fold of his skin. Dressed in a pale blue garment that seemed to float around his body as if a light breeze held it airborne, he moved around the room with an easy grace that belied his obviously advanced years.

He raised one bushy greying eyebrow. "So, we meet again, human." The old, cracked voice was at odds with the elegance of his attire.

Charlotte was bemused. She had no recollection of having met him and told him so. He smiled at her puzzled look.

"Ah, we most certainly have met. The last time I was privileged to look upon your lovely face, you were more than a little indisposed, having been rather badly bitten as I recall. It was I who tended to your wound when you decided to pet one of our local vermin. I trust you recovered quickly and are now fully healed. May I see the site of the bite?"

When she nodded her head in reply he walked over, did a quick examination, and determined that she would indeed live. He was just about to leave her side when he noticed something else and stopped. Leaning closer to her, he pushed her hair further back, enabling him to see the patch of skin just behind her ear.

He let out a gasp. "My word, that's something I haven't seen for a few hundred years." The old apothecary practically jumped back into the shadows at the rear of the room.

Jendal, who had quietly observed all this, suddenly moved like a viper. His arm whipped out and he caught the old man in his vice-like grip.

"What do you mean?" he demanded, shaking the old fellow as if the rattling of his bones would free information. It seemed to work. The apothecary pointed at Charlotte.

"Look," he said, "look behind her ear. She bears the mark of the originals."

Charlotte was shaken by this turn of events. She had no idea what it meant and there was no way Jendal was about to tell her, judging by the set of his jaw. Her birthmark, unremarkable to her, obviously meant something more than an accidental pigmentation of her skin to these men.

The apothecary grabbed a small, blue glass vial from a shelf laden with bottles and jars of all shapes and sizes. He thrust it at Jendal, then backed away.

Jendal took the bottle and dropped it into his pocket. "Come to the palace tonight," he growled at the old man, "and bring whatever you need to prove what you say." He dropped a small piece of mother-of-pearl onto the table. "Here is your payment for the tincture." Jendal kept his finger firmly on it as he added, "There will be ten times this payment if you can prove her to be descended from an original. Do not make a mistake or it will cost you your life—and I shall be the one who takes it from you." Jendal snarled and his fangs snicked down to prove his point. Vigorous nodding of his head showed the old man had listened well to Jendal's threat.

Jendal didn't give Charlotte a moment to ask any of the multitude of questions bouncing around in her head. In a flash he far-stepped them straight into Elyian's bedroom. He expected to find his brother in much the same state as when he'd left for Earth, groaning on the bed in a darkened room, clutching his head as if it would fall off without help from his supportive hands.

Now the room had the windows flung wide open and Elyian was in the process of doing up the last pearl buttons on a silky black shirt that skimmed over his biceps and hung perfectly on his wide shoulders. He beamed at the sight of Charlotte standing there in her wildly inappropriate clothing for a hot Ranic day. She was practically steaming in her "Earth on a winter's day" outfit. At the sight of her, he bounded across the room like an excited puppy and flung his arms around her, trapping her against his chest.

"I've never been so happy to see anyone as I am to set eyes on you right now," he mumbled as he buried his face in her flaming hair and breathed her in to his very core. "I am so very, very sorry I had to leave you alone and without explanation last night. I hope Jendal has explained the reason

I had to do that."

Charlotte hugged him closer and shook her head. "He didn't really have time to do that much explaining, but I got the abbreviated version," she laughed. "He was far too busy trying to control his toy car. It's the strangest thing; no matter what planet the male of a species hails from, they still seem to have this burning desire to prove their manliness by burning off as much fossil fuel as possible in the shortest amount of time."

Elyian laughed at this very true analysis of his brother. "Yes, you would think being the size he is would give him a sense of stability but apparently not. He's always lived life as fast as he possibly can and I don't think that'll change anytime soon."

Charlotte looked up at him. "We brought you a medicine from the apothecary but you look fine to me. Did the migraine go away?"

"Yes, it vanished about ten minutes ago. I don't know why, but when you're in my vicinity they get better. Most curious."

It was then that Jendal caught his brother's attention and beckoned to him. Elyian excused himself and left Charlotte's side so they could speak privately. As Jendal conveyed the findings of the apothecary to Elyian, she watched his face change as astonishment, doubt, worry and a multitude of other feelings passed over him. His lovely face turned, if possible, even more ashen than his normal milky complexion.

An exasperated Charlotte yelled, "Okay, enough with the cloak and dagger stuff, you two. I need some explanations here. Just what exactly did the old man see and what does it mean to you, and more importantly to me?"

Her voice rose even louder as she spoke, her fury turning her face quite pink. Wasn't it bad enough to be shuttled from one existence to another without having all this to deal with as well?

"You're right, Charlotte, and though I'm not sure of the details, I'll attempt to make sense of this," Elyian said. He thanked Jendal for acting as an off-world chauffeur then told him quite imperiously that he could wait outside until the apothecary showed up. Jendal dipped his head in acquiescence to the man who was not only his brother but also his king, and with a final smile in Charlotte's direction he left the room.

Elyian went to Charlotte and tipped her head to one side, moving her hair back to look behind her ear. His finger traced a short line that went way up into her hairline. He looked closer and there on her scalp, hidden by her luxuriant locks, was a small birthmark shaped like a tiny bird in flight. He gasped as the realization hit him like a freight train. No doubt about it; Charlotte was a human who also had the blood of his ancestors running in her veins. She had the right to know about her heritage.

"Charlotte, let me explain a little of our history and where I believe you fit in. The first time a Raniculan impregnated a human, he bequeathed his offspring a genetic and visual marker, exactly like this one, in case he ever needed to claim the child. My father told me that his father never did return to Earth, but he left a written account in the Library of Souls. Scholars through the ages pondered the question as to whether the child had survived and then gone on to reproduce, but inexplicably they never researched it on Earth. As time crept by the whole event became buried in mountains of dusty tomes and eventually the book was lost."

Unknown to Elyian or the scholars, the book had fallen backwards off the shelf. A young female Frey found the book and realized by one of the marks on the cover that she was holding her very own family history in her hands. Knowing that the earliest record of her lineage had been lost a considerable time ago, she eagerly scrambled out from behind the shelves and curled up on a stone bench at the very end of the cavernous space that held the history of every race on Ranic since writing had been invented.

As she read a world of possibilities opened up. Then her little gamine face changed as she read the account of the Earth baby. There on the page was a very clear description of the mark which showed that she herself was also of Royal blood. She certainly wasn't considered Royal; from the time she'd come of age she held a fairly lowly position as keeper of the palace nursery.

Afraid this knowledge would endanger her life, she squirreled the record away, back behind the very same shelves it had dropped from so long ago. Every so often she would secret the book under her robe and take it home with her, where she could sit and read without fear of discovery. She never forgot what she read; she cataloged it safely away in her head, ready for use whenever it was needed. A gem of knowledge more prized than an entire ocean of mother-of-pearl lay in wait for the right moment to resurface.

Elyian regarded the lovely woman standing before him. His heart nearly stopped when he thought about the ramifications of all that had transpired. He knew without a single shred of doubt that he had fallen in love with her, but he was also under no illusions of the difficulties that lay ahead if he were to continue this path with her.

It would have been hard even before this discovery; now the situation was untenable. Something momentous was rocking the very foundation of life on Ranic. He felt it in his marrow. For now he wanted her with him, and as he held up a mirror behind her head to show her the bird that marked her skin, he watched her face, waiting for the sky to fall.

A knock at the door interrupted them but not before Charlotte had a good, long look at the mark. Jendal appeared with the apothecary beside him. The old man bowed respectfully to Elyian. "Sire."

Elyian nodded his acknowledgment. "Physician. I see we have the need to meet again."

"Indeed, Sire. I will not waste your time but will tell you in haste what I have discovered. When I saw the mark upon the woman I knew I had seen it before. My daughter Esarelle brought a book from the Library of Souls into my house and read it late into the night. She tried to hide the fact from me but I grew suspicious, and so I too have been turning the pages when she was busy at the palace with her duties. When I read of the mark that was left on the skin of the infant on earth, I knew instantly that I had seen it before. On the day Esarelle was born, on the very the same day that her mother passed on, I saw the mark on her head shaped much like a small blue Creck in flight.

"As her first year passed, her hair grew long until the mark was no longer visible. I forgot it even existed, until I saw this young woman today. I have no doubt, no doubt at all, that she bears the identical mark as my daughter. I even get the same feeling running through my body when I stand near this woman that I get from Esarelle. A strange feeling that prickles at my extra sense. I knew instantly the two women, although both from different planets, share a link by blood.

"Esarelle is not of my blood. Her mother was already pregnant when I met her. Her mate had been mortally wounded on Earth and never made it back to Ranic after a dive went horribly wrong and he got entangled in the trawl net of a fishing boat. He was dragged for hours behind the vessel and eventually the wounds he suffered were too much for his body to heal. His hunting companions found him washed up on a beach but they were too late to help.

"But I digress; my apologies. Your brother Jendal asked me to bring proof, and proof I most certainly have, right here on my person." At that he stopped and, cautiously looking up at Elyian, added, "For a price, Sire, as promised by none other than your own kin."

With that he unwrapped a large, tattered, leather-bound book from its canvas wrapping and revealed it to Elyian, who looked at the book as if it was going to bite him. Curling his lip in distaste at the greedy apothecary he nodded curtly once and then took it from his hands.

"Pay him, please, Jendal," he growled to his brother, who was already in the process of counting out a large amount of pearl buttons and threading them onto a cord.

"Here." Jendal handed over the long necklace of currency. "We trust that this will also buy your absolute discretion on this matter. That of course also includes your daughter Esarelle, who must never know that her ruler now holds the book. As far as she is concerned, it was stolen. Are we completely clear on this matter, Apothecary?"

"I was never here, Sire," the apothecary stated blandly. He bowed low and left the room, followed by Jendal.

Elyian turned back to Charlotte, who had been standing off to one side trying to take everything in. With a movement so swift she failed to see it, he'd dropped the book and wrapped her in his arms again. A mere shadow of time later he untangled himself and stepped back from her. She felt the loss of his presence and, as usual, felt very alone again.

"Charlotte," he said with a catch to his voice, "I feel as if you should be mine. I can see your soul's unwritten messages drifting through the air, waiting for me to pull them in. My body seems linked with yours; but no matter what we believe our feelings are for each other and no matter how urgent our cravings to have each other, this cannot ever be. You see, I know what's in that book." His gaze drifted down to where it lay on the ground behind him.

"What is it? Please just put me out of my misery and show me what it is," Charlotte pleaded.

He retrieved the book and laid it down on the table next

to them, then pulled her onto his lap. They sat together and looked at her ancestral history.

Of course Charlotte could not understand a single thing written on the pages. The language was a mystery to her. She watched Elyian scan page after page with lightning speed until suddenly he stopped, and there on the last page, right at the end, was a pictogram. A small bird winging its way across the final piece of paper.

Charlotte leapt up, pointed to the picture, and hopped up and down like a demented rabbit. "That there!" she yelled. "I have that on my head. What's that bird doing on my head? I know it's the same, they both have the same spiky bit sticking up from their heads. Elyian, why am I in this book?"

"What it means, Charlotte, is that you are a direct descendant of the Royal house of Trainor. You're human, but you also carry Raniculan blood in your veins.

"What's more, it means that you and I are related, albeit very distant relations. It also means you must leave here. I wanted to ask you to stay, but if anyone were to find out you're half Raniculan, your life would be in even more danger than we thought at first.

"I knew someone found out we'd been together, and that one fact is a huge issue here, but possibly one I could have overcome given a bit of time and a lot of fortune. This is altogether different.

"As the ruler here I'm expected to keep our bloodline pure, and even though you bear the mark, I'll never be allowed to have another species as my mate." His voice cracked and the strain was etched on every inch of his chiseled features. "I honestly don't know how I'm going to let you go."

Charlotte had long since stopped bouncing up and down and now sat stock still and cold as ice. "No!" she cried, panic raising her voice a full octave. "I just found you. I can't leave you now. This is the first time in my life I've felt whole and like I truly belong somewhere. Now I know why I spent my entire childhood feeling so different from the other children. I am different." A thought flashed through her mind "I'm a hybrid human, so does that mean that I'm also a Vampire?"

Elyian laughed shakily. "No, not at all. You'd only be a Raniculan Vampire if you had a pair of these." With that he growled deep in his throat and his long, white, gleaming fangs exploded down. His arms rocketed around her and with no pretense at being a gentleman he pushed aside her lovely ruddy locks. With another growl he plunged his fangs deep into the pulsing artery at her neck.

Charlotte's eyes widened in shock as the first sharp stab of pain hit. Then a warm, sensual wave washed over the pain, her eyes went hazy, and her pupils dilated as she got lost in the amazing images that flooded her mind.

She saw the planet Ranic and memories that obviously belonged to Elyian. His entire life flashed through her head until she knew every place he'd ever seen, every person he'd met, and felt all the passion he had for her. She took in everything until her mind could not hold another single image, and as the last one faded away so did her present reality.

The last thing that she saw was Elyian's face as he licked the twin punctures closed and held her face in his hands, locking their almost identical green eyes. As hers closed, his misted over and a single tear rolled down his cheek. Then he set her gently down and far-stepped her back to Earth.

As she slept he moved around the cabin readying everything for when she woke. When he bit her, his venom stopped her heart, then coursed through her veins changing her cells at a molecular level, embracing her Raniculan side.

He wrote her a letter, a long and detailed account of everything that had happened and why. It included a heartbreaking apology for losing his self-control. He would never forgive himself for what he had done to her.

He told her that now it was known that she was a hybrid, and she could not return to Ranic. He promised to leave her to live her life peacefully out of danger here on Earth.

Elyian tried to tell her how to handle her new, strong body that would crave blood above all else. The truth was, he didn't have a clue what happened when a full-blooded Raniculan mated and then bit a human hybrid. He suspected it would be spectacular, but who knew for sure?

He carefully tied the letter to her wrist so she couldn't fail to notice it when she first opened her eyes. On the kitchen table he left a large envelope with her name written in bold letters on the front. Inside was a vast amount of cash, a small pile of beautifully cut gemstones, and a bank account opened in her name with a balance that would keep her in the lap of luxury for the rest of her life. It also held the keys to a beach house and to his fabulous penthouse apartment on the marina in San Francisco.

He would never need either one again, but he did need to be sure she'd be well taken care of, as she was now homeless and unemployed, thanks to his carelessness. He needed to give her the financial freedom to start over.

He also left a charged cell phone with a single number saved into the memory. It linked to a voice mail account from which he could get the recordings. Whenever he sent hunters to earth to collect mother-of-pearl, they would be able to access the voice mail and bring him her messages. He couldn't risk returning to Earth. If he did, staying away from Charlotte would be impossible.

A trip to the local blood bank stocked the freezer with enough units to feed an army. With that done, the very last thing he did was remove a mother-of-pearl pendant from his pocket and tie it gently around her neck, settling it carefully next to the ankh she always wore over her heart. Her now dead, still heart.

With tears falling unheeded, he croaked out a final goodbye to the woman he'd believed would be his mate.

Elyian watched as the sun played over her eyelids, which were fluttering awake for the first time as a Vampire; then, blinking slowly to clear his eyes, he far-stepped away from Charlotte and toward the dawning sun.

Chapter 12

in which a page is passed

ELYIAN WAS BACK in the court. He pleaded, cajoled and bribed, and when that didn't work he resorted to threats. But they weren't working either and he was getting more frustrated with every passing month.

He hadn't told the court about Charlotte being part Raniculan. They considered it a travesty for him to ask permission to take a human as his mate. They steadfastly refused him every day for months. He may be the ruler but he had no ultimate authority over the high court.

As the court ended its daily session he left dejected and with yet another screaming headache. On the way to his quarters he saw Esarelle lurking around a corner.

"Elyian," she whispered to him so the Frey just ahead wouldn't overhear. "Please stop, I really need to talk to you."

Elyian wasn't in the mood to deal with Esarelle so he turned and walked in the opposite direction.

"Elyian!" This time she was louder and the insistency in her voice made him stop in his tracks.

"What do you want, Esarelle? I'm not feeling well but I'll

listen as I walk back to my room, so come on."

"Fine, I can do that," she pouted. She matched his pace for the first few yards, then had to nearly run as her tiny legs were no match for his gigantic stride.

"Elyian!" She grabbed his arm and pulled him to a stop. "Enough of this. I have something to say and I can't do it while running." He relented and she pulled him over to sit at a window seat overlooking the central courtyard.

"Please," she gently cajoled. "I'm so tired of this animosity between us. Can we not go back to being friends? I miss our times together. I've come to accept that we will not have a life as a couple, but I cannot accept losing your friendship. So in the spirit of friendship I have something to give you."

She held out her hand to reveal an orb.

"How generous of you Esarelle," he said sarcastically. "I've never seen one of those before." He nevertheless took it from her and held it out in front of him.

Esarelle raised her eyebrows and in a scathing voice said, "You may want to see its center before you throw it away. Sometimes the most interesting things are seen by the smallest and most insignificant of objects."

Suddenly he knew what he would see when he looked into the core. Sure enough, as his gaze passed over it, it shimmered and waves of color passed over the surface before it cleared and a moving image appeared at the very center. It was Charlotte, pacing the floor of his beach house on Earth.

At first she had her back to the orb camera so he couldn't see her face; but then she turned around and what he saw nearly brought him to his knees. Peeking out from under her upper lip was a pair of delicate white fangs.

Her lovely face was a picture of total devastation. Her tears fell unrestrained and the sadness in her eyes broke his heart. Her arms wrapped tightly around her body as if the mere act of holding herself was the greatest comfort she had. As they watched, she left the cabin and went to sit on the porch swing. She curled up and sat there, alone, looking up as earth's single moon rose into the darkening evening sky.

"Why are you showing me this?" Elyian groaned to Esarelle, his headache becoming far worse in an instant.

"I know," she said. "I know who she is."

It was his turn for the eyebrows to shoot up.

She continued, "I felt her presence. It clung to your skin when you came back from Earth. That first time I saw her, lines threaded through the air from her to me. She and I are connected and that connection is through our blood. We both carry the same mark left with us because of our common ancestry.

"I read the book, Elyian; I know my mother had human blood in her and that she passed it to me. The mark of the Creck bird is also on me. I first saw it a few years ago when I braided my hair as an experiment. When I found the book I realized I'm part human. Possibly in a quite diluted form but still there. My fangs are very small and now I know why. Charlotte and I are related.

"She now has fangs because you." Her voice trailed off before she concluded, "You must have bitten her, Elyian, but even so she wouldn't have fangs unless she also had some Raniculan DNA inside her."

He sat very still and mulled her words over in his mind. Elyian had been waiting for the coup de grâce, the final fall of the sword. But Esarelle seemed quite calm and devoid of animosity.

Elyian stood and paced in front of Esarelle as he spoke. "You and Charlotte are both hybrids!" As her words sank in he began to understand the implications. It meant Esarelle was also in hiding from the high court, as she had no desire for her lineage to become known.

She looked at him and a world of hurt showed there. She knew that with her next revelation she would lose him forever. "I can help you bring her back, Elyian. There's a page missing from the book. I tore it from the binding when I saw it."

"Why? What does it say?"

"It details how any offspring from our line can cure the birth defect that causes so many Freys' brains to be damaged in utero. We each carry a microorganism in our blood that, if passed to a newborn Frey, would heal that fetus from brain damage suffered in utero."

"Why would you not make this known? You'd be allowed to remain on Ranic with that ability."

"When I found out, I was worried that if someone knew that I carry that ability within me, I'd become a test subject. I know that makes me weak of character and for that I am truly sorry. I wish I could help more, but in a small way I can by telling you this.

"Charlotte also has this ability, but she'll be able to heal others faster and better than I can, because she's also the holder of the key. I don't know what the key is or where it's located. The page says that each generation will pass to the next the key of Ranic, and that it will give them the power of life over death. I'm afraid the rest will be up to you to discover." She held up a folded square of weathered paper which he took from her.

Elyian took the page and scanned it quickly, grasping the enormous significance of what it said.

"Esarelle, I thank you profoundly for the gift you've given today. It won't go unrewarded, of that you can be very sure." He bent and kissed her forehead. "I must go and find a way to use this information as quickly and as wisely as possible. Again I thank you and bless you for coming forward with this."

As Esarelle watched him far-step away, she prayed that she'd done the right thing for once in her life. Her heart cracked in two as he vanished, but another part of her felt as though it was a new beginning. She would mend as never before, so it was with a smile on her lips that she left the palace to start her life over with no secrets to plague her tormented soul.

Chapter 13

in which the earth moves

CHARLOTTE AWOKE TO sunlight pouring onto her face. She pulled the blanket up over her head and tried to will herself back into oblivion. When that didn't have the desired effect she rolled out of the bed, slathered on a large handful of sunblock, and shuffled sleepily across the uneven reclaimed wooden floor to make some coffee. She'd been here since Elyian brought her back to Earth.

She finished making coffee and went out the back door and onto a pathway that led directly to a wide, sandy beach. The Pacific Ocean was the only balm to her broken spirit. It was the first thing she craved every morning and the last thing she saw before the sun went down in its final blaze of glory.

The first week had passed in a haze of shock, grief, denial and outright horror at the situation. She tried the blood but hated it even though her body craved it. As weeks turned to months, she drank less and less until she didn't need it at all. As a hybrid she'd been able to do what Raniculans could not. Her body had adjusted to being both human and Raniculan.

She could eat regular food and never need blood.

Now coffee, that was a whole other ball game. She could drink it endlessly, and with no one around to berate her for imbibing far too much caffeine, she did just that. She poured gallons of the stuff down her throat, her thirst for it never ending.

She also developed a love of chocolate. Never much of a candy eater before, now she always had a little piece of it stashed somewhere on her.

But the jolt of caffeine from the chocolate and coffee did nothing to ease her inner turmoil. The anger she felt toward Elyian was a slow torture for her, as every day she relived the destruction of her human life. Even so, there was still something in her that craved the Raniculan. An unseen cord tugged at her psyche, pulling her back toward the world that had abandoned her.

Time passed in a slow progression of foggy mornings followed by clear, warm days and cool nights. She discovered Elyian's cliff, where he'd scanned the waves for the ocean creatures far below. She took up the watch and grew to adore it as much as he had.

Now, as the long, hot summer ended, she was restless. She'd resisted the urge to go out in public much, just venturing out late at night to pick up groceries when essential. Everything else she did over the internet, which reduced her exposure to other people to virtually nothing. With all the resources Elyian had left for her use, the need to expose herself to the outside world had been radically reduced.

Not once had Charlotte used the phone to leave a message for him. She was too hurt by his abandonment, and too overtaken by the fierce determination to be bravely independent of him, even though every cell in her cried out for his company. There was nobody she could talk to, no one who could possibly understand what she was, and how it felt to be so very different from everybody else.

She decided to leave the beach house. On the last day of September she called a cab, and with a couple of suitcases in hand, moved herself from Salmon Beach to the city. As the car passed over the Golden Gate Bridge, she gazed out the tinted windows at Alcatraz, perched on its massive rock in the middle of the bay. Alone and isolated, just like her. She nibbled on a piece of Ghirardelli dark chocolate and pondered what to do next.

That evening she turned the key in the lock of the penthouse apartment situated on the thirtieth floor of the most prestigious address in the city. She had arranged for a housekeeper to open the place up and get it ready for her visit; as a result, the fragrance from an abundant arrangement of cream and yellow roses wafted from the hallway as she entered the foyer. The housekeeper had given her some idea of the apartment's size and quality when Charlotte negotiated her exorbitant pay, but the reality of what she saw upon entering was stunning.

The understated casual elegance entranced her. It was decorated in a sophisticated palette of grey and cream with touches of acid green, giving it a modern sensibility. The floor of palest Carrara marble reflected light from the line of scones that flanked a wall of mirrors, framed in chrome on dark grey walls. The entrance hallway was starkly beautiful. The entire look would have been too cold if not for the velvet drapes that hung from poles fourteen feet high, puddling on the floor in great creamy lakes.

The rest of the apartment was, if possible, even more gorgeous than the entrance, and she spent the remainder of the day exploring the huge rooms and enjoying the comfort in which she was now ensconced.

Her bedroom boasted a wall of windows that looked out over the marina. Charlotte fell into the bed—and what a bed it was. From there she was able to see the ranks of madly expensive yachts gently bobbing up and down at their berths; and in the distance beyond the bridge she could see the golden hills of Southern Marin County as they rose and fell toward the Pacific Ocean. The four-poster frame was hung with sheer silver drapes that billowed gently as the ocean breeze lightly played over them. Snowy linens and a cloud of a duck-down comforter cosseted her body so well that before she knew it, she had fallen asleep.

It was the deepest, most untroubled sleep she'd enjoyed for many, many months. When Charlotte woke she felt almost human again. After a large cup of very strong coffee she pulled on a pair of shorts and her favorite well-worn T-shirt.

It was a warm fall day even by California standards. Hundreds of white sails dotted the bay and the last of the summer tourists could be seen parading on the piers and riding the cable cars up and down the impossibly steep city streets of San Francisco.

After looking longingly at the twin moons that she had painted on her cell phone cover, she stuffed the phone in her pocket, threw some chocolate and a water bottle in her shoulder purse, and hailed a cab. The cabby dropped her off at a little-known cove where abalone divers could be seen on weekends bringing up their allotted haul.

Today the cove was empty, the only living creatures being a pair of raucous seagulls fighting over the rotting carcass of a crab. Charlotte sat on a salt-encrusted rock, watching the waves crash endlessly onto the boulders that scattered the beach close to the tidal line. The city center seemed a world away, but it was only a mile from where she sat.

She strolled further down the beach but stopped when she saw a net fishing bag tucked next to a large boulder close to the base of the overhanging cliff. It was lumpy so she presumed there were a few abalone tucked safely inside. A neat stack of clothing sat next to it.

The wind was blowing strands of hair across her face, so she nearly missed seeing the large and almost naked man who stood turned to the cliff as though he was about to get dressed. She averted her eyes to give him some privacy.

Brave man, she thought. *The ocean here is frigid all year.* It was hard to believe he could dive in those icy waters for abalone without the protection of a wet suit.

At first it was almost imperceptible, just a cold feeling that crept up her spine and made all her hairs stand to attention. Her heightened senses flew into overdrive. Her pupils dilated and adrenaline flooded her system, giving her already amped-up body an extra boost of speed, perception, and strength. She heard a low and distant rumble, combined with the barking of a multitude of dogs way off in the city.

The first tremor hit the beach, followed by several more in quick succession. Charlotte looked wildly around to see what was happening and realized with shock that it was an earthquake. Then several more large jolts shook her off the rock and she fell tumbling over and over in the freezing surf.

Underwater she kicked her legs and her super-charged body raced back up to the surface. She ran out of the sea and up the beach. The sound was now like a freight train passing through. Huge tremors and violent, jolting shocks hit the beach again and again.

She ran toward the cliff, away from potential tidal waves. The man she'd seen at the cliff had been struck by falling rocks and lay with his leg trapped under a massive boulder. She watched with horror as a huge section of the cliff began to tear away at the top edge. The trapped man looked up as the entire section fell in one enormous piece down to where he lay.

Charlotte hurtled toward him with preternatural speed, reaching him as the last of the boulders were still falling. She threw some of them to one side before they hit the ground, but most of them now covered his body. One arm stuck out of the huge pile of rubble with fingers extended. She grasped his hand and squeezed it gently to let him know he wasn't alone as the shaking finally stopped.

"It's okay," she said, hoping he was still alive under all the debris. "I'm going to help you." She let go of his hand that had gone limp and tore at the pile of rocks that lay at her feet. Her extraordinary strength kicked in as she lifted, rolled and pushed tons of dirt and rocks away from his body, slowly uncovering the limp body beneath.

Finally she was able to see his head. He hardly looked like a person any more. Dirt and blood covered his face. Blood poured from several large, nasty gashes on the sides and back of his head, and the skin had peeled back in places revealing his skull. At the sight of all the blood her fangs snicked into place, but by now she was able to quickly retract them. The poor man had been shocked enough. The sight of a Vampire kneeling over him would surely put him into cardiac arrest.

As Charlotte gently placed his head into her lap his eyelids flew open and she found herself looking into the green and almost carbon copy of Elyian's eyes. "Jendal? Oh my God, Jendal!"

He opened his mouth and tried to speak but his mouth was full of dirt, so she pulled the water bottle out of her purse which had miraculously remained slung crosswise over her body, gently cleaned out his mouth, and gave him a drink.

"Charlotte, what the hell?" he croaked out.

"Shh, don't try to speak yet," she said while she gently cradled his head, "and please don't move. I have no idea yet how badly you've been injured."

"Charlotte, I'm not going to make it. Every bone in my body feels like it's been broken."

He tried to move his head but lost the battle to stay conscious. She ran her eyes frantically over him, trying to figure out what the hell she should do next. His body was twisted at a very unnatural angle and she suspected his back was broken. As she sat there on the deserted beach, sirens started up in the devastated city.

Chapter 14

in which teeth are tested

THE HUNTER FLEW through the palace as if on wings. The orb clutched in his hand was nearly jumping out of his grasp. Charlotte's voice was nestled inside it, ready for Elyian. The orb seemed to sense Elyian nearby.

"Your Majesty." Panting with exertion, the hunter fell to his knees at Elyian's feet. Elyian inclined his head toward the hunter.

"Thank you, Mallan," he said politely, "but tell me, what brings you here at this hour and obviously with such haste?"

Mallan thrust the ball unceremoniously towards his ruler. He had far-stepped from Earth and made his way to the private quarters of his king in record time.

"I was told to immediately bring you any message from Earth. From the way this damn thing is bouncing around, I'd say it needs to tell you something important."

Elyian tore the orb from Mallan's hand and raced to his quarters with it. He slammed the door shut, commanded it to speak by slowly blinking twice, and tossed it into the air.

The orb hung there pulsing with light, then Charlottes'

silky voice filled the room. It was edged with panic, but also a determination that Elyian had not heard before.

"Elyian, we need you. It's Jendal. There's been an earthquake and you need to get here. I don't know if he's going to live much longer. His body was crushed by a cliff falling on him. Please hurry. I'm going to take him to your apartment in the city. I ..." At that the phone went dead.

Elyian called an emergency meeting of the high court. They could deny him no longer. This time instead of asking if he could return to get Charlotte, he informed them of his decision. They were all fond of Jendal and were aghast when they heard his news. They told him to make haste.

"But take note," they admonished, "you bring back Jendal alone. Do not bring the human here."

After they'd approved his travel plans, Elyian far-stepped right into the home of the apothecary. This was considered an outrageous act, as privacy was zealously guarded, but he was the king, and as such and with circumstances being what they were, he didn't much care for protocol.

Esarelle was in the room when he appeared. Startled, she whipped around, sending the bowl of food she'd been mixing flying through the air until it hit the opposite wall and fell with a resounding crack, oozing a sticky mess onto the floor.

"Damn, Elyian, couldn't you have knocked?" she exclaimed as she picked up the broken bowl.

"No time," he said, and asked for her father. She waved her hand toward the door of the clinic behind the main room and huffed contemptuously at him as he left.

Five minutes later Elyian had filled a bag with bandages, ointments, and weird smelling herbal remedies, and had far-stepped from the apothecary's house directly into what looked like a war zone.

San Francisco had suffered the worst earthquake in memory, in a city renowned for the shaking ground on which it stands. The Coit Tower on Telegraph Hill had managed to survive intact, but most houses and apartments for miles around suffered some degree of damage, which ranged from a few broken plates to the destruction of buildings down to their foundations.

Elyian stood and watched for a moment as humanity raced around him like frenetic ants trying to rebuild a lost colony. The noise of the city was amplified into a cacophony of sounds. Fire engines and ambulances competed with police cars and burglar alarms. Dogs, rumored to be highly sensitive to earthquakes, barked endlessly, and the sounds of children crying and people screaming drifted upward into the sky, following the soaring embers of the many fires roaring out of control on the city streets.

Smoke hung in the air around him, choking and thick as he ran into the apartment. If he had cared one jot for his personal possessions, what greeted him as he reached the top floor would have devastated him. As it was he barely registered that the grey marble circular table in the hall, on which had sat a priceless Tiffany vase, now lay on its side, cracked clean in half with the vase obliterated on the floor around it. The picture windows in the sitting room now decorated the pavement far below. Wind whistled through the rooms, lifting papers from desks and swirling them in eddies on the floor.

In the kitchen, cabinet doors had been flung open and the contents ejected so that heaps of broken china, pots and flatware scattered across the floor. In the bedroom he looked wildly about, praying he would see her safely there, but no. The room, although devoid of broken china, had water underfoot.

A piece of the ceiling had come crashing down in the bathroom and a cracked water pipe was flooding the entire space. He squelched his way across the carpet to the bed where a diary lay half covered by the comforter. Recognizing her handwriting, neat and feminine on the title page, and to save it from being ruined by the water, he picked it up and stowed it safely in his pocket.

Elyian sank down onto the bed and let out an anguished howl of frustration. He'd left in such a hurry he hadn't brought an orb with him, so now he had no idea where to look for them.

While Elyian searched the apartment, Charlotte and Jendal were in a small house near the ocean. She'd managed to persuade a man with a pickup truck to help her, and together they pulled Jendal off the beach and got him into the abandoned house. Her Good Samaritan had his limits and once they got Jendal out of the truck and into the house, he'd left them to take care of his own family.

Charlotte could have wept when she finally got Jendal onto a bed and cleaned up. The once-powerful Raniculan was reduced to a broken pile of bones that writhed and moaned and bled from a multitude of cuts and abrasions. His handsome face was puffy and swollen and his right foot had been almost completely severed at the ankle.

She thought about calling an ambulance but quickly realized that even if she could get one to come—which was highly unlikely in an emergency of this magnitude—he couldn't be treated by a human doctor. They'd know instantly that he wasn't human if they listened for a heartbeat and found none. So it was all up to her and she had no idea where to start.

By the following day, his extremities were turning grey and his moments of lucidity were getting farther apart. She was losing him. She had bathed and cleaned him, given him large doses of Advil and some antibiotics she'd found in the bathroom. They were out of date, but beggars can't be choosers. She'd wrapped him in every gauze bandage she could find and when she ran out of those, she shredded sheets until he closely resembled an Egyptian mummy. Now she sat there alone with no power and no water, and numbly came to the conclusion that she was a useless doctor.

The answer to her dilemma came most unexpectedly when she was in a small upstairs room that had obviously belonged to a little boy with a love for collecting bugs and crawly things. Pinned up on his wall was a "Reptiles of North America" poster. Lizards and snakes took up most of it, but in the corner an alligator grinned.

"Yes, of course! That's the answer!" she exclaimed to nobody in particular. When she thought about what it would mean to sink her fangs into flesh, her stomach heaved. But her new stronger, determined attitude took over and she willed it to settle. She didn't know what force compelled her, she only knew she had to help.

Charlotte leaned over the dying man, offered up a quick prayer to any god that might be listening, and with a lightning-fast motion sank her teeth into her wrist, tearing two large holes straight into the vein. As the skin broke, thick red blood poured out. She held the wound over Jendal's mouth, watching as it oozed past his parted lips and trickled over his tongue for several minutes.

She'd seen all the Vampire movies and figured she'd better close the twin punctures, so she poked out her tongue and tentatively licked it over her wounds to close them. That seemed to work, as the skin quickly re-formed over the holes.

Within minutes she could see a difference in Jendal. His color changed back from a cool grey to a healthy complexion. He screamed as muscle, bone and tendon realigned. She could hear the bones in his body moving around and knitting back into place.

When his skull became covered with new skin she knew he was going to be fine. Jendal opened his eyes, twitched his neck, and stretched like he'd just taken a long and very satisfying nap.

"Well, Missy Charlotte," he drawled with his idea of a Southern accent, "y'all certainly know how to make your guests feel welcome here on Earth. Dropping a few tons of rocks on them certainly puts a whole new perspective on the joys of travel. Just do me the favor of reminding me to find a new planet on which to vacation, would you?"

Charlotte laughed. "You do know that you're in the west and not in the deep south, don't you Jendal? The one thing you definitely won't hear in California is 'y'all' used in any sentence!"

Jendal smiled then, showing that his previously cracked and broken teeth had been repaired to their normal state of pearly perfection. "I happen to be quite partial to the southern accent, Charlotte. I'm nearly as fond of that, as I now am of you. Thank you, for doing whatever it was you did to save me on that beach. I don't remember anything after a rather bumpy ride in what felt like the back of a truck. Things just faded in and out for a while there." He started patting down his body like a DHS agent at the airport security line.

"What...where are my clothes?"

"Too late to be modest, Jendal. Sorry, but I've seen it all during the past day or so. You have nothing to hide from me now."

Jendal looked suitably abashed and rolled over to preserve what was left of his modesty. Charlotte blushed like a schoolgirl and beat a hasty retreat to the kitchen, where she hoped to find something that resembled coffee beans.

That night sirens howled continuously throughout the city and the sky turned orange from all the fires still raging in many districts. As dawn broke, Elyian was still searching for Charlotte, but the only clue he had as to her whereabouts was her diary. She'd written a few times about going to the beach. He decided to methodically search every one.

Fate stepped in. At the very first one he spotted it. Lying at the base of a partially tumbled-down cliff, half hidden under a large pile of rocks, was a cell phone in a case that sported a hand-painted image of a pair of blue moons in a purple sky. Only one person could possibly be the owner and that would be Charlotte.

His joy at finding the phone was quickly tempered by the knowledge that it wasn't going to help him find her or Jendal. He knelt on the sand and let his eyes drift over the rocks. He stared unblinking and horrified when he saw what else decorated the sand: pools of congealed blood in pockets all around. It covered the piles of seaweed that were above the tide line and lay in sticky puddles in the hollows. A connection to the blood rang in his veins.

He stretched out his hand and touched his fingers to the nearest rock, stroking the spilled blood. He raised his hand to the sky then pulled it down his face, streaking the blood from forehead to chin. As it touched his lips he flinched, then his eyes flashed emerald green and his fangs snicked down as he recognized the taste on his tongue.

It wasn't Charlotte's blood; it belonged to his brother. As he knelt there, devastated and worried and at a loss as to where to look next, an orb suddenly appeared in front of him, pulsing with light. He blinked twice through the foggy air and waited.

It changed color a few times and then her voice came through clear as a bell. "Elyian, we're at Sunset Street, number—"

Jendal's voice interrupted her. "Brother, you need to get your ass in gear and get over here. Pronto."

Elyian didn't need to be told twice and before Jendal had finished speaking, he was there.

As he appeared in front of her, Charlotte felt sweat break out on her upper lip. If she'd still had a heart it would've pounded uncontrolled in her chest. She felt as though the world stopped when his eyes met hers.

Elyian gave his brother a quick, appraising look to verify he wasn't going to expire anytime soon. When that was done he locked eyes with Charlotte yet again. They stood unmoving and silent as time stopped.

After a while Elyian growled, "Jendal, I'm delighted that news of your demise has been grossly overstated. Now go away and do some good with the contents of that bag." He raised his chin to indicate the bag full of medical supplies he'd brought with him. "There are nearly a million humans in San Francisco and I've seen many that would benefit from some help today. Try not to eat any of them, please."

Jendal grabbed the bag and, smirking to himself, left by the front door, shutting it quietly behind him.

Chapter 15

in which plans are made

"TU MIHI ANIMAM meam pro qua centrum." The words were whispered gently in her ear and although she didn't understand them, they had an echo of something familiar. She'd heard a language like that before, but where?

"What does that mean?" Charlotte asked.

Elyian stroked her cheek and translated for her. "It's our ancient tongue. It's no longer spoken on Earth but it was known as Latin. What I said to you, roughly translated, is this: You are my reason for being, the center of my soul."

Charlotte sighed. "That's so beautiful." In awe she added, "So was it the Raniculans that taught humans to speak Latin?"

"Yep," he replied, in a decidedly human way.

Charlotte chewed on that a bit and then, smiling, pulled Elyian to his feet. "Is there no end to the things I'll find out from you?" she said to change the subject.

Elyian was getting dangerously close to her emotionally. Although she enjoyed him physically, she didn't quite feel the connection to him that, she was now very sure, he felt for her. She continued, "I feel like a child exploring the world for the first time. Everything has changed for me. It's all going to take me a while to absorb."

"I'm going to enjoy showing you more of the truth," he said as he buttoned up his shirt. "However, dearest Charlotte, for now those truths will have to stay dormant. There are many more pressing things to attend to, such as you explaining to me how Jendal, who according to your message was dying, is now parading around like the cat that got the cream?"

Charlotte filled him in on everything that had occurred since she arrived in the city. She didn't go into the details of the devastating time she'd endured after she woke up alone and sporting fangs. That could wait, as apart from everything else she was still mad as hell at him for that.

When she got to the part where she'd given Jendal her blood, Elyian stopped her. Tension showed in little lines around his mouth and a muscular twitch in his jaw. His eyes flared with sparks of yellow and green and his fangs shot down.

"Wait a minute. He obviously needed your blood to fully recover, so it's good that you did that. But did you drink his blood?"

"Ugh, hell no!" was her vehement reply. "That would be beyond gross."

She watched a slow transformation as jealousy and fear left his face and it returned to the gentle features of the man she was coming to know quite well. As his demeanor changed his fangs retracted and he licked his lips in a nervous motion.

"I don't know how to handle the feelings I have for you," he said, as he walked stiffly away to put some distance between them. "My whole body falls apart whenever you're away. The only way for me to keep it together is to have you with me; but if I bring you back to Ranic the high court will have you summarily executed. They've never knowingly allowed a human to walk among us. The last time I took you there I wasn't in my right mind. I never should've risked your life like that. I even threatened the Frey that work in the palace with a swift death at the end of my sword if they let slip their knowledge that you were in the palace."

Charlotte paled visibly at that but then asked him to continue. "Keep going, Elyian. I need to know it all."

He nodded. "Okay. As I was saying, we're lucky they were mightily afraid of that threat and nothing was said in the wrong ears. If there's any way to get around the law, I promise I'll find it. I have an inkling of an idea that may just work. You've just managed to heal Jendal, pulling him back from the brink of death. It's not easy to kill us, and although we don't get sick or mortally wounded easily, when we do it's difficult for us to heal."

She frowned at that then asked him, "How, after all these centuries of coming to Earth, have you not figured all this out on Ranic, Elyian?"

He started pacing around to help him concentrate as he talked. "The physicians on Ranic do their best, but something in our bodies seems to constantly defy their best efforts to heal us. What you did is amazing. You say his bones knitted together by themselves? Staggering! If a bone gets broken on Ranic the physicians tie the poor person down, cut them open over the broken bone and try to not listen to the screams as they use Leverium2 wire to bind the broken pieces back together. They use a special glue made from the skull of our beasts of burden to hold the bone in place, but it's rare for a bone to return to full strength.

"There's something special about you, Charlotte. I knew that from the first moment I saw you, but now there's something else. I think you hold the key for wonderful things on Ranic, and that's what we'll use to get you back there!"

Suddenly the land around them quivered in a violent aftershock. Elyian grabbed hold of Charlotte and covered her body with his as great hunks of plaster came tumbling down from the ceiling. The dust in the room became so thick they could barely see each other. They didn't need to breathe but the gritty air wasn't pleasant so they stumbled out of the house and into a blisteringly hot fall day.

Elyian and Charlotte both winced at the brightness of the sun and flung themselves back against the shadow of the building where they were protected from the worst of its rays. Although Raniculans did not, as popular culture would have humans believe, burst into flames when exposed to UV light, they were more sensitive to it than humans. Sunburn was easily come by, as the purple sky on Ranic filtered out the burning rays of their sun. On Earth, a liberal coating of sunblock normally protected their delicate skin from frying.

Staying on the shady side of the street worked in their favor as they made their way up to Telegraph Hill. Before them the city lay in ruins, but Elyian had seen the aftermath of so many disasters it hardly had an impact on him. He knew life went on, that the city would, as it had done a hundred years earlier, rebuild stronger than ever. It was part of life, the circle of birth and death, of war and peace. It was merely Earth's glacial progression toward whatever lies beyond the universe.

He sensed his brother's presence nearby and pulled Charlotte unceremoniously into the seclusion of a dark side street. Jendal was sitting on top of a building looking down at the alley below. As they approached Jendal dropped off the roof and lowered himself slowly to the ground, landing silently before them.

It seemed impossible for a being so huge to be so quiet, but stealth was an integral part of Jendal. He was a warrior through and through. The men slapped each other across their backs in greeting, just as humans do.

"So, you managed to find time to come and look for me, then!" Jendal stated with what Charlotte recognized as his usual slightly sarcastic tone of voice. "You two seem to have trouble keeping your hands off each other. Don't know what the high court is going to think about that little turn of events in the life of their ruler."

The cordial manner in which they'd greeted each other was suddenly lost as Elyian wrapped his hands around Jendal's throat and squeezed it so hard the veins on his forehead stood out in stark relief. As Jendal choked, Elyian growled out a warning to his baby brother.

"Never joke about that, my ever-flippant sibling, or you'll again find yourself in dire need of Charlotte's blood. Except this time I'll tell her not to help you so you'll bleed out and fade into nonexistence."

He dropped his hands and Charlotte was amazed to see Jendal shrug it off. "Good grief," she admonished. "Boys never seem to grow up, no matter how long they live. After five or six hundred years surely you two could have learned to get along."

They both turned to look at her and when she saw the great, wide smiles that split their faces she grinned back at them, happy to see it was just male posturing. The next minute they were hugging and slapping at each other's backs again.

The three strange beings spent the remainder of the day wandering the city, helping out wherever they could.

They used their preternatural strength to lift fallen beams and uncover victims of the quake. Great care was used to be stealthy. Very few of the humans saw them, and those who did were far too distracted to notice the pallor of their complexions or to recognize anything in them that could be remotely considered as alien.

Charlotte was becoming familiar with her new abilities and she reveled in truly being able to help. Not only was she now almost as strong as a Raniculan, but she also had far superior medical knowledge. Compared to a human doctor she knew virtually nothing, but compared to her companions she was a veritable Florence Nightingale and Louis Pasteur rolled into one.

In the chaos that was now San Francisco, they were able to go into empty houses and find enough bandages, painkillers, and antibiotics to stock a cottage hospital. They roamed the streets until well after dark, helping wherever they could, until eventually fatigue forced them to call it a day and they retreated back to the house near the beach.

That night the three forged a plan to get Charlotte back to Ranic. Only a few small details remained. As Charlotte lay in bed she was more at peace that she'd ever been. At last she felt needed, useful and excited about the future and whatever it might bring. Sleep came quickly that night, for the first time in years.

Elyian watched her sleeping. He wanted to wake her but knew she needed rest. This time he was patient and he merely kept watch until dawn, holding a vigil over the precious female. As the hours passed he memorized every curve on her long, lean body, the line of her jaw down her throat, the way her back arched and those two adorable dimples just over her hips. His hands had roamed every inch of her until he knew her body better than his own. Her glorious mane of russet hair glinted and shone, and as the sunlight shafted through the edge of the drapes she began to stir. His body responded to her instantly.

She woke to find him inches from her face. "Charlotte," he said, "there's no way I can leave you on Earth again. I would be so honored if you would consent to be my mate. I will love and protect you, and allow you the freedom to live your life exactly as you choose, as long as you can find it in you to come and live on Ranic with me. I would come here to live, but as ruler of Ranic I have no choice unless I abdicate...

That's it! The plan, Charlotte, I've got it!"

"Elyian, you certainly don't need to abdicate for me! When I saw you drop out of that tree I knew that my life had just irrevocably changed. When I woke up after you changed me and you weren't there, it felt like someone had ripped my heart out of my chest. Each day I was here, alone, seemed to last an eternity. It was so confusing; I wanted to drink blood all the time but hated the taste. Everything I touched broke in my hands. I wanted you there to guide me. Why weren't you there when I needed you?"

As they argued, kissed, made up and made love, the alien in the room next to theirs rolled over, yelled, "Get a room already!" and tugged a down-filled pillow over his ears.

Chapter 16

in which glass ceilings are breached

Havvol Vax stood slowly and faced the other one hundred ninety-nine members of the Raniculan Interplanetary High Court with a dour expression. His long gown of office swept around his slipper-clad feet and glittered in shades of lilac and gold. It was heavily embroidered with scrolling motifs and sported a high collar made from the white winter fur of the Ajil, a rare and beautiful mountain creature much like an Earth goat. He looked quite splendid, but his mean countenance spoiled that splendor and an air of menace floated around him like a stinking cloud of sulfur.

Elyian's uncle was a vile man. He thought nothing of having someone incarcerated for the most minor offense, and any crime worse than that was given the harshest sentence available to them under Ranic law. When he didn't feel that the punishment fit the crime, extra charges would magically appear, along with a witness or two of sterling repute.

The high court decided on matters of state as well as overseeing the day-to-day running of the planetary fiscal system. Unfortunately, although the court decided guilt or innocence for criminal matters, Havvol Vax alone was responsible for meting out the sentences. On this day his mood was as black as the blood that ran through the Manos, those unfortunate creatures that lived in the caves under the Shoulen Mountains. He'd heard enough.

Vax bellowed at the gathered dignitaries. "We cannot allow him to do this. King or not, he cannot be above the law. We are all here to see our laws enacted without prejudice."

He took his seat again, yielding the floor, and his place was immediately taken by Agen Trace. The polar opposite of Vax, his position on the court was a constant thorn in the side of Vax, who didn't agree with anything Agen said or did. If it had been within his power he would've thrown him off the court, but Agen's position was by royal appointment and Vax had no say in that.

The two males jointly held the highest office in the court and they balanced each other well. Whereas Vax was aggressive, Trace was passive. When one man demanded more taxes the other would hold out for a tighter rein on court spending. They had nothing in common other than the usual Raniculan fine looks.

Agen Trace was a classy man. He was adored by the populous and respected by his fellow jurors on the court. His knowledge of the law was complete and flawless and he had the keenest mind Elyian had ever seen. He took care of the people he cared about, which meant he took care of every man, woman and child that walked on Ranic; but he was especially careful about keeping safe Chimara, a Frey who was carrying his child.

She was now almost at term and every day he prayed to the gods that the child would not suffer a brain injury at birth. It wasn't unheard of for a ruling class Raniculan to be with a Frey, but it certainly was unusual. Because of the high regard in which Agen was held, the affair was largely ignored by everyone he met.

Agen turned slowly in a circle, meeting the eyes of as many court judges as he could. When Agen spoke he held them entranced. His melodious voice rang out clear and true, with all the conviction he could muster. "Your king, Elyian Trainor, has ruled this planet well since the abdication of his father and predecessor Amun. We have no reason to doubt his ability to be a person we can all count on to be honest and true to his convictions. He has proved his love for this place many times over; his courage in battle and the fair and honest way he handles the trying issues that form the bulk of his job, have been irreproachable. So tell me, why now, when he tells us this human holds the key to our future health as a nation, do we doubt him?"

Murmurs of agreement rumbled through the vast hall. Vax was one of the very few dissenting voices.

Agen went on, "Elyian is a truthful being. I have been his friend for the entirety of his life and a lie has rarely passed his lips. He has been here again and again, begging us to let him bring the human to Ranic, and he has been turned down so many times that a lesser male would have given up long ago. Not so Elyian; he will keep coming back, because he has promised that he would fight for her.

"He believes she knows how to cure many ills, including the birth issue with the Frey, the one thing that has plagued our planet for as long as anyone can remember—and you all want him to ignore that! Are you insane? It is in the best interest of all who are gathered here, indeed of all the citizens of this planet, to find a cure for the wretched affliction that causes so much pain for the Frey and those who love them!"

Nobody was murmuring now. Loud shouts of support mixed with a few of dissent were heard until one voice rose above the others.

"VOTE, VOTE..." called out the juror, joined by others until all were calling out with single accord, as they banged the long wooden poles they held onto the stone floor in a rhythmic thumping.

"Well now, Trace," Vax said with a sneer, "it would seem to appear that other members would like their voices heard."

As Vax was sure they'd never agree to let any human onto the planet, he was all for the vote being held quickly, so he could go back to his house and that well-endowed female he'd been bribing to come to him every night for weeks now. He thought about her and the court uproar faded into the distance as he dreamed about the perverted sexual fantasies roiling around in his head. As Vax daydreamed the court went into full voting mode.

Agen Trace held his Leverium2 orb high in his hand, blinked, and with an enormous swing of his arm let it go. The orb left his hand and flew in a circular motion around the gathered assembly. As it reached each of the jurors in turn, it stopped and hovered over their heads. They cast their vote telepathically, and the orb registered the vote and moved to the next member. When all the votes were gathered, the orb stopped in the very center of the room where it settled itself on a crystal pedestal and opened up like a flower. At the very heart of the orb lay a massive pearl-like gem, which shifted color from red to blue and back again. Eventually it stopped, with the red glowing and pulsing insistently at its heart. The entire room fell silent as they stared at the pearl, until the orb slowly closed up and with a speed that defied description shot into the air and disappeared.

Agen turned from the court and with a smile playing on his lips he winked at the small female hiding near one of the massive pillars at the edge of the room.

Esarelle felt slightly queasy when she saw him winking at her. She thought she was well hidden in the shadows, but apparently not. Lately, since she'd turned her attentions away from Elyian, she'd begun harboring strong feelings for Agen but had not acted on them. "One day," she thought, "one day I will tell him how I feel, but that day is not today."

Agen left the palace and headed out into the street, eventually stopping outside a modest house on the outskirts of the city. He sniffed appreciatively at the large Yalon plant growing against the wall then knocked gently on the door and went inside into the warm embrace of his pregnant lover.

In a far larger house on a distant planet, another couple were arguing the finer points of how to make a decent cup of coffee when the sound of breaking glass from a nearby window made them whirl around in shock. The glass rained down, revealing a spinning orb inside the gaping hole. It flew inside the house and hovered overhead like an insistent bug. It was the voting orb from the Ranic high court, and it instantly sent the results of the vote to Elyian then took off again through the large hole it had created in the window.

"Don't they ever knock?" Charlotte said, exasperated, as she shook shards of glass out of her hair. "What was that about?"

"It's been decided, Charlotte!" Elyian was so elated he was barely able to contain himself.

"Whoa, there, calm down, big guy." She laughed and tried to get him to tell her what the hell was going on, but he just kept laughing and kissing her. "What's been decided, Elyian?"

"The high court has passed a vote. They're going to allow

you on Ranic. Without me having to hide you. We'll have to prove you can help us but that shouldn't be a problem."

She paused a beat too long. Elyian misunderstood her hesitation and blurted out, "I'm sorry, of course you don't have to do this. I hoped that by now you would have come to the same realization as myself, that you are meant as my mate, that we are meant to be together." He looked so devastated that she hugged him and kissed his generous mouth for so long that in the end it was he that broke the kiss and pulled away.

"Of course I'm going to Ranic!" she said vehemently. "Nothing on Earth can keep me away. I was just shocked that it's been decided. It seems too easy somehow. And I'm not sure what it means to be your mate, either; you'll have to explain the finer points of that little arrangement to me soon. So when are we going and what will I need to take with me?

Elyian laughed then with palpable relief.

"Wonderful!" he said. "Let's go back to the apartment and see what, if anything, we can salvage. I can ask Jendal to help to bring some of your personal possessions as there's a limit to how much we can take with us when we far-step."

The three of them made their way back to the apartment, which by this time was in really bad shape. Major flooding had wrecked at least half of the rooms and the rest were getting badly damaged by smoke and the thick dust that poured in through all the broken windows. Charlotte had, luckily, shut the door to the massive walk-in closet and most of her clothes were salvageable.

She stuffed photographs, her makeup, and various books that had belonged to her late father, a world-class surgeon, into her bag. Elyian had told her of the lack of skills that existed on Ranic in the medical field and she was sure some of the books could be useful.

Last of all she raided the larder for as many bags of coffee as she could fit in the extra duffel Jendal produced. Then she took a last look around.

This is it.

This might very well be the last time she'd stand on planet Earth. Tears welled up in her eyes as the reality of her situation hit home. "I'm ready now," she said as she wiped the last traces of tears away.

Elyian had been watching her carefully, trying to asses just how fragile a state she was in. Her teary eyes had done little to alleviate his concern for her well-being.

"I'll make sure you can come back and visit Earth as often as you wish," he said quietly as he stroked her flaming hair, letting the waves fall through his fingers. "You can't far-step alone but I can bring you back. I'll arrange to have this place restored when a builder's available. It may take a while, but this apartment is now yours for whenever you need it. I want you have a home here. And of course there's the beach house; I'm sure it weathered the quake just fine."

At the mention of the beach house Charlotte's entire demeanor changed. She smiled at him fondly. "I love that little place," she said. "Even though my darkest days ever were within its walls, it felt safe. And being close enough to the ocean that I could hear the waves crashing on the shore at night was just magical."

Jendal chose that moment to appear, stumbling slightly since he'd far-stepped onto a soggy rug that was trying to escape his big feet. "Arrgh, damn!" he said as he righted himself. Then he grinned lopsidedly at Charlotte and held up a large plastic bag. "Guess what fell out of the back of a passing truck?" he said, holding it open for review.

Inside was a small mountain of every variety of chocolate currently in production at the famous Ghirardelli Company at Ghirardelli Square. Charlotte squealed in delight and Elyian groaned. "Let me at that, I'm starving."

Jendal teasingly held the bag aloft, grabbed Charlotte's duffel and vanished back to Ranic.

"It's a good job we're related," growled Elyian as he took her hand and they followed Jendal, appearing again under the pale purple sky of a Ranic dawn.

Chapter 17

in which an army moves

THE MANO RAISED its head and bared fangs oozing with slimy venom dripping in long, viscous strands. Its head was almost humanoid, with many of the same characteristics as both Raniculans and humans including a nose of unremarkable shape and size and a regular-looking mouth—until, that is, it opened. Long, brown, matted hair hung over the eyes.

It was their eyes that really set Manos apart. Devoid of anything that resembled humanity, the creatures' cold, hard eyes glittered with a menace that was palpable. The pupils were vertical slits in a neon orange iris.

Their bodies had the scaly look of a reptile armed with multiple spines eighteen inches long that ran the length of the body. Vicious talons tipped small forearms but their back legs boasted the powerful thigh musculature of a born runner.

Manos lived their entire lives in caves that dotted the Shoulen Mountains, seven day's ride from the city. The beasts resided in scattered pockets all over the planet, but the largest population by far dwelled here. Musty-smelling lichen lined the dank and dark caves, covering almost every surface except the places Manos had scraped out sleeping places in the dirt.

True omnivores, Manos lived on anything that grew, walked, or flew within their grasp. Nothing was off limits, including the many creatures that slithered under the rocks inside their cave. But like most creatures, they preferred some foods over others—and their favorite walked upright on two legs.

The Raniculans were both prey and hunter. When they captured a Mano, the creature's venom was rendered useless by the daily infusion of a special herb that neutralized it and had the added benefit of calming them to the point of domesticity. As long as this herb was administered to them on a regular schedule, Manos were not a threat, and indeed were quite useful when put to work pulling carts around the city.

On occasion a Mano would wander into the city from the plain and manage to circumvent the security of the hunters who secured the perimeter. Wandering at night, stealthily and silently through the empty city streets, it hunted for its favorite prey. If it happened to meet an unarmed lone Raniculan, the Manos would always win the argument and the unfortunate victim would be skewered through his body by those dreadful talons and held aloft as the Manos injected the paralytic venom straight into the poor person's brain. Death was instantaneous.

On the very day that Elyian brought Charlotte to live on Ranic, the Shoulen Mountains spat a hundred or more newly formed Manos into the hot, dry expanse of desert and scrublands that separated the city from their habitat. They formed a line across the width of the plain. After five hundred yards they stopped and sat down.

Sometime later another hundred appeared, then another and another. By the time the sun sank low behind the mountains, an army of nearly a thousand Manos sat in uniform ranks on the dry, cracked ground.

When darkness fell they rose together and with single-minded intent faced the valley that led toward the largest city on the planet. As one they slowly moved off, their long tails swishing behind them kicking up a dust storm of gargantuan proportions.

The last being to exit the nearest cave to Ranic was a small, wiry man who watched from the shadow of the cave as the dust storm shrouding the army moved off into the night. He gripped a large goblet of Yalon tightly in his hand, from which he sipped slowly as he watched the massive shapes grow smaller as the distance between them increased.

When he could no longer make out anything except the night sky, he downed the last red drops, and as the added liquid silver filtered into his system he dropped to his knees and wept like a child for the force he'd unleashed on an unsuspecting world. As his life was swept away in a sea of pain one vision remained, an image burned into his retina: his daughter Esarelle

As the image faded the apothecary crumpled to the ground, the goblet rolling away. His body was soon devoured by a female Mano that had stayed behind to tend her young.

The creatures were a lot smarter and more wily than the Raniculans believed them to be. The assault on the city would be quick and violent. Manos did not discriminate between Raniculans or Frey, male or female, adult or child; they were all going to die.

Their leaders had been biding their time, waiting for the perfect moment to take advantage of a rift in the fabric of Ranic society. Since their bodies had severe limitations, such as the lack of an opposable thumb and forearms essentially useless for anything except grabbing, tearing, and holding onto prey, they weren't able to build cities or develop their culture beyond a very basic level.

Their lack of physical attributes did not in any way alter their ability to reason. For centuries they'd endured the forced slavery that made pack animals out of them. The Manos who ended up in the cart harnesses wanted to help the resistance movement. Among the Ranic they learned everything they needed to know to one day take over the planet and destroy the Raniculans.

What they failed to understand was that it was a single entity that they should target. One being had single-handedly forced the apothecary to conduct the experiment that led to the abomination that was the Manos species.

Through the preceding months, Havvol Vax delighted in visiting the lab where the apothecary had been forced to work in secrecy long after his day at the clinic was over. He cooed over the babies that hatched from the rubbery eggs lying in neat rows on rack after rack in the deepest recesses of the caverns deep under the castle, hidden from public knowledge. As they hatched they were placed in baskets and smuggled out, a dozen or so at a time in carts pulled by the babies' sires.

Under cover of darkness the Manos hauled them overland to the shadows of the Shoulen range. Some nights two or three carts rattled through the streets. When enough creatures had been raised he let them procreate naturally, resulting in a huge population of hungry Manos itching to enter the city and take as many Raniculans as they could.

They were kept in control by the calming herb, administered in minimal doses—enough that they didn't attack the men who handled them, but such a small amount that missing one dose would let them return to their natural bestial savagery within a few hours.

Vax felt overjoyed at the realization that every generation brought him one step closer to being the ruler of Ranic. He wanted it all, to be not only head of the interplanetary high court but also king. He didn't need the love or respect of his people. The only thing that drove Vax was a burning desire to rule the world with the iron fist that he could use on only a limited basis now.

His experimental program was funded with the extra mother-of-pearl he'd stolen from the citizens that he had tossed in jail or sent off-world for every offense he could think up. He had threatened the apothecary with a swift but violent death—after being forced to watch his daughter die slowly and painfully at Vax's hands.

When Vax saw the orb render the result of the vote which allowed Elyian to bring the human to Ranic, he knew that the time was right. He couldn't afford to waste another day.

Although abundant herds of animals roamed the verdant valley on the other side of the mountain pass, the Manos were lazy creatures and did not enjoy the steep, arduous trek over the high passes. An easy walk across the flat arid desert was far preferable to them. They didn't need much liquid to survive; much like a camel, they could drink large quantities and store it inside their bodies to be used when necessary. The hot, dry desert to them was like a walk in the park.

Vax glanced up at the sun that normally shone relentlessly. Clouds passed overhead and Vax's brows drew together when he saw them. Unusual for this time in the planet's cycle but not unheard of. Deciding it was the perfect time to indulge in a few large meals and some female company before he sought shelter to ride out the carnage that would happen in a week's time, he donned a light garment and a wide-brimmed hat and strode out into the noonday sun toward the nearest tavern.

Once inside the cool interior he spotted a familiar figure sitting alone in a corner hunched over a half empty tankard. The apothecary did his best to sink lower in the chair in the vain hope that somehow he would vanish and Vax wouldn't spot him.

Alas, today is not my day for peace and quiet and respite from that odious man, he thought as he sank even lower, crunching his spine painfully against the chair back.

"Ah, Apothecary!" Vax sidled up to him and dragged a bench out from under the table to join him. He peered down his nose and sneered at the little man. "Today is a fine day to drink to what is to come, do you not agree? My little plan is almost at its conclusion and so far you have done everything you were told to do. My plan does not change and you know what to do now. Be sure that you remain silent or... need I continue?"

The apothecary swallowed visibly and nodded his head in acquiescence before realizing that he should be answering the question in the negative; he then shook it vigorously.

"Good, good, I'm glad we're seeing this from the same perspective." He dispatched the apothecary to the Shoulen Mountains with instructions for him to let the army loose on the city.

Vax suddenly swiveled in his seat as a beautiful female sashayed past him, her perfume wafting in the air.

The apothecary was quite forgotten as his libido took center stage and without a backward glance he followed her across the tavern, leaving the apothecary to fulfill his dastardly commission before taking his own life in heartbreaking regret and grief.

The Manos made good progress on the first night and spent the following day lounging under scattered trees making half-hearted attempts to catch a few tasty morsels. As the sun sank they rose again and with a unified roar stirred the ground into a thick dust storm as they continued the long march towards Ranic.

What Vax still had not comprehended, but the apothecary

was all too aware of, was the immutable fact that the two of them had created monsters. The creatures' brains were superb, and fast reflexes and enormous strength gave them the ability to hunt and kill like machines; but their complete lack of any emotion meant no one could truly control them.

So as the army marched toward the sleeping city, Vax was out enjoying himself, unaware that the force he'd unleashed was not going to stop at killing the ruling class, but would, given the chance, wipe out every last Raniculan that walked the planet—and that, of course, included himself.

Chapter 18

in which the circle continues

THE TINY FREY thrashed about on the pallet, laboring to bring her child into the world. Agen Trace, all pretense at calm having fled hours ago, was now in a state of complete panic. The midwife had banished him to the enclosed courtyard where he alternately sat and paced around the fountain at its heart. When he had flattened the greenery in the path around the fountain, he turned his attention to counting the bricks that lined the walled garden and separated it from the street beyond.

The water in the fountain shimmered in shades of purple, reflecting the sky above. Floating in the shallow pool were large lily-like flowers and little glass bubbles that drifted in and out of the streams of water falling around them. Tall trees laden with fruit and rows of gleaming vegetables vied for attention with row after row of Yalon plants sporting their strange, blood red, bulbous fruit.

All around the perimeter a tall hedge of spine-covered plants towered above the walls. It was a beautiful, magical place that Chimara had spent the past eighty years turning into a haven for them both. The walls of the courtyard gave them the privacy they needed in a world where their relationship was not met with complete acceptance.

Sometimes they needed to escape, to leave the condemnation of narrow-minded neighbors far behind them. Agen loved this garden almost as much as she did. In this place he was able to think and calm himself after a day of dealing with Havvol Vax.

Chimara screamed again and then all was quiet. Agen waited for what felt like a century, listening for the next scream, but heard only silence. Suddenly the door to the house flew open, revealing the sweating midwife who was wiping her hands on a less-than-sterile apron. Blood smeared up her arms and her face bore the lines of stress that extreme fatigue brings.

"Fetch the physician, Agen," she said, wearily but urgently. "There's nothing more I can do. She's losing blood too fast and I can't stop it. I fear there's no hope for Chimara or your child without his skill."

Agen pushed past the midwife and ran to Chimara's bedside. Her damp hair matted to her face. Drenched in sweat and clutching her belly, she hardly noticed he was there; she was so entrenched in the pain that nothing else could permeate her consciousness. He wrung out a cloth and wiped the face of the tiny, precious person of whom he was so fond. He knew she was not meant to be his mate or his life's partner and love, but they did share a great and close relationship and had decided that they wanted a child together as neither one had children.

"I'm going to fetch the court physician. Hang on, Chimara, please," he begged. She turned her head, her lovely violet eyes glazed over with pain. Another contraction hit and her face paled even more.

She gripped his arm. "No time," she gasped, then screamed again. Agen watched in horror as the blanket beneath her swam with her blood.

Agen fled the room and far-stepped to the apothecary's house. Hammering on the door he yelled, "Let me in! I need a physician. Please, let me in!" The door opened a crack and one eye looked out at him, widening with surprise.

"Agen?" The door opened and Esarelle nearly pulled him into the room.

"Esarelle," he said breathily, "sorry to disturb you but I really need your father. It's my...it's my..."

"It's your what?" she replied impatiently. "Spit it out, Agen!"

"Chimara! She's in labor and she's losing so much blood! By the gods that watch over us, there's so much blood. The midwife is with her, but she doesn't know what to do. I'm afraid for her, Esarelle. I don't want her to die having my child. We need your father now!"

Esarelle looked tense as she replied, "My father hasn't been home in several days. I'm worried about him, Agen. He does sometimes leave for a few days to tend to people in the outlands, but he never stays away long without letting me know when he'll return. This time there's been nothing. Not even an orb."

Agen listened to her with growing concern and at her words he felt like his body was flying apart. "No, that can't be!" he snapped.

"I'm afraid it is, Agen. My father is gone and we'll have to think of something else."

He slumped to the floor and dropped his head into his hands. "You know as well as I, that the apothecary is the only person within reach with any knowledge about medicine."

"The palace!" Esarelle pulled on her shoes and gathered some items as she talked. "Someone there will be able to help you. Come on."

Hand in hand they ran through the few streets that lay between her home and the palace gate. They arrived at Elyian's door at exactly the same time that Charlotte and Elyian arrived from Earth. The four of them collided in a tangle of bodies. Guards quickly arrived at the scene and looked aghast at their ruler, squashed but laughing under Charlotte, Esarelle, and a very embarrassed Agen Trace.

Jendal appeared as Agen helped the two women and Elyian to their feet and quickly explained the situation. Elyian gripped the shoulder of his dear friend and spoke with concern. "I'll go find another physician, Agen. I heard of a new one that's started an apothecary and clinic in Saul. I'll be back as fast as I can."

Elyian vanished. The other four made their way across town to Chimara's house, Charlotte praying all the way that she wouldn't faint or anything really embarrassing like that. Since she'd been turned she'd become much stronger emotionally but she still hated the metallic taste and smell of blood. "I guess this is a little different," she muttered to herself.

Bracing herself, she stepped through the door and into the little house. The poor little Frey lay deathly still, her face grey and her lips blue. The midwife looked up and shook her head.

"I'm sorry, but she's gone," she said to Agen, who had run to the bedside and was cradling Chimara in his arms. It was a horrible thing to see the devastation on his face as he rocked her and wept for the life that had been lost.

None of them noticed the little bundle in the arms of the midwife until it let out a disconsolate wail that filled the silent room. As one, they all turned to look at the bundle in amazement.

"Here, Agen Trace, come and hold your new daughter," the midwife said. She carefully passed the baby to the new father. "She's fine, and didn't turn grey, so I do believe you will have an intelligent little daughter there."

Agen gazed down at the new life that squirmed in his arms and through tears watched the baby stare back at him with huge, unfocused, but startlingly violet eyes.

Charlotte looked at the new baby, cradled and warm in her new father's arms, and wished she'd arrived in time to give the child a mother's arms to hold her as well. It was a sad little group that left the house later that day, after arranging for a wet nurse and helping the wretched Agen as much as they could. Elyian still hadn't shown up so Charlotte and Jendal returned to the palace alone as Esarelle went home.

In the solitude of Elyian's quarters Charlotte sat and took stock of her situation. Her new strength and heightened senses delighted her. She still had accidents almost daily, but with less frequency as she learned to pick up delicate crystal without reducing it to tiny shards; and her hearing was sensitive enough to discern distant conversations, but now she was able to filter out the sounds she didn't want or need to hear. Like the snoring emanating from the hall and the Frey servant down in the kitchen using a knife like a drumstick.

She put her ears on filter mode and lay down on the big bed with hopes of getting some rest before Elyian returned. She'd presumed he was going to get back quickly, but hours had gone by with no sign of him. Her worried stomach clenching returned. Her gut was the best indicator of trouble; she could rely on it absolutely.

A gentle knock on the door woke her several hours later and she groggily staggered to open it. Standing on the other side was a little man, holding a tray almost as wide as he was tall. She could barely see him, the tray was heaped so mountainously high with various dishes of food and a large steaming goblet of Yalon. Charlotte gagged at the smell of the drink and pinched her nose shut in a futile effort to keep the revolting smell out.

"Good evening, Mistress, my name is Arun," the Frey said, nodding his balding head at her. "I received a request from His Majesty to make sure you were brought sustenance."

The tray tilted precariously to one side and as he fought to regain its balance the food and goblet slid down the tray and with a massive crash tumbled to the floor. Warm, dark red Yalon spilled on Charlotte and the fur rug spread out by the door. After multiple apologies and muttered words that to her sounded like he was swearing up a storm in his native tongue, Arun backed out of the room and ran down the corridor like his life was in danger.

He was back quite quickly with a small army of servants who swept, mopped and dabbed at her, the rug, and everything else that had been within range of the contents of her dinner tray. When at last they were done she was invited to come down to the kitchen so they could give her something else to eat.

She eagerly agreed as she was quite taken with the Frey. They were generally happy souls who delighted in the jobs they held, be it the lowliest of kitchen help or the lofty position held by Arun, who was the Ranic equivalent of a butler. Some of them could barely talk, their mental acumen so severely damaged that on Earth they would almost certainly have been institutionalized for their entire lives. Here on Ranic they lived happy, productive lives in the service of Raniculans.

Arun was fairly bright, more than capable of running the household, and he had the other servants running around like chickens with their heads cut off, making sure Charlotte's every need was met in a timely manner.

Before she knew it she was seated at the long, wooden kitchen table with an assortment of extremely strange fruits and other unidentifiable things that may or may not have been meat, laid out on platters before her. Charlotte cautiously picked at the food, finding some of it to be quite tasty. The yellow slimy stuff with little grey bits floating in it looked too gross for words so she pushed that around the plate a few times and then rubbed her stomach as if she was full to bursting.

Arun looked delighted that he'd managed to get her fed well. As a young maidservant cleared the plates, Arun surprised Charlotte by sitting down next to her.

"I trust the meal was to your satisfaction?" he inquired politely.

Charlotte smiled at him and thanked him profusely, which seemed to render him speechless, much to her amusement. "Can I ask you something, Arun?"

"Of course, anything you wish, Mistress. I will endeavor to answer any question I am asked."

"Do you know where Elyian, sorry, I mean His Majesty, may be? I expected him to return a long time ago but there's no sign of him."

Arun shook his head vigorously. "No, sorry, Mistress, I do not know. I have not seen him since yesterday. He has not taken any of his personal possessions with him so I am sure he will be back shortly. You could always ask his brother Jendal to find him; he is able to use a seeking ball and that would be the fastest way of seeing where he may be. Be aware, though, that the King can render himself unseen to the ball if he so desires. He also cannot be anywhere very dangerous as I saw his favorite sword on top of the chest in his room. He wouldn't normally go anywhere without it. Certainly nowhere too far away. So I am sure there's no need to worry."

Charlotte nodded and asked if he would accompany her back to the room as the palace was so huge she was worried she'd get lost if left to her own devices. They were just about to leave when the world around them exploded.

Charlotte found herself flying through the air and she smacked into the stone wall on the far side of the kitchen, closely followed by Arun, who was pushed against her by the force of the explosion.

Good grief, she thought as she picked herself up and helped Arun to his feet. *I'm beginning to feel as though disaster is just one step behind me all the freaking time. What on earth did I do to deserve all this?*

"Arun, are you all right?" she asked the servant, who was brushing himself off and although somewhat annoyed didn't seem to be injured as he patted his clothing down and adjusted the few tendrils of grey hair that still grew from his smooth white head.

"Yes, Mistress," he said, "I am fine; but I will have to go and check on Cook. He tends to blow up the kitchen on a regular basis. He tells me that he has no idea how it happens but I know that sometimes he cooks up a stew made from some Grail that he finds in the attics. They are vermin and their venom is not only deadly but can explode if it gets too hot. The meat is good eating but you do have to be careful to remove every last trace of poison from their little bodies or Kaboom!" at that he threw his stubby little arms up in the air to drive the point home.

Charlotte laughed. "Really? That huge explosion was caused by one of those tiny little things?"

They laughed together and Charlotte knew in that moment that she had an ally in Arun. It felt good knowing that there was another being she could talk to in this land so far from home. She wasn't homesick—there hadn't been time for that—but it was all so strange and tiring.

Suddenly she didn't feel so good. Her head was swimming and she was having trouble keeping Arun's face in focus. *Damn*, she thought. *Tell me I'm not going to faint again.* A voice was coming to her but it sounded a long way off.

"Charlotte, Charlotte!" Her vision cleared and there in front of her, shaking her shoulders for all he was worth, was a very worried-looking Elyian. "Good lord, Charlotte, would you stop all this passing out? It's really disconcerting!"

"It's not like I have any control over it. Where do you get off telling me what to do, anyway?" she snapped at him.

"I am the ruler here, you know," Elyian hissed back, his fangs poking out just to show her he was boss.

"You may rule Ranic, but you do not, and you never will, rule over me!" Charlotte showed her fangs, too.

They looked at each other, a hint of a smile twitched at the corners of his mouth, which made him look kind of dorky and adorable, and before she knew what was happening he'd scooped her up, to the accompanying whoops of delight from Arun and the other Frey who'd gathered in the kitchen to see what had exploded. With a few long strides he had her out of the servant's hall and was making fast progress toward his bedchamber.

Chapter 19

in which the battle begins

His long, elegant fingers thrummed restlessly on the metal tabletop, the only outward sign that Elyian was feeling anything other than cool, calm and collected. With an impassive face, he looked inscrutable and elegantly casual in an immaculately tailored, pale grey linen shirt and a great-fitting pair of black jeans he'd obviously picked up on Earth.

Charlotte's heart would have done a flip in her chest had it still been beating. As always, just being in the same room as Elyian did the strangest things to her body chemistry. He was sexy as hell, but she definitely had the feeling theirs would be a passionate but short-lived relationship.

Right now, though, looking at him standing in front of the assembled high court, she was proud to be associated with this man. He listened attentively as various members postulated that he'd been taking them for fools and many wondered what he considered to be so special about this particular human. Time crept inexorably by, the hours turned into days and still they kept up the charade of a court process. Until at last on the fifth day of deliberations they eventually allowed Elyian his chance to talk.

In the intervening days he and Charlotte spent endless hours with Jendal and, on occasion, Agen Trace, when he could excuse himself from his court duties for an hour or two and when he could pry himself away from his new infant daughter, whom he named Violette at Charlotte's suggestion.

They solidified their plan. Agen had grown to respect and like the human with whom his friend was so besotted. Her keen, creative mind was a breath of fresh air after the stupefying conversations he was used to hearing by members of the court, male and female alike. Gossip about the latest court scandal and endless pontificating on the finer points of fashion seemed to be the primary focus of their narrow-minded world.

Charlotte had knowledge of things most Raniculans could not imagine. Raised in a technologically advanced world she'd picked up a diverse wealth of knowledge. She didn't consider herself above average intelligence, but to the average Raniculan she was Mensa material at the very least. The Raniculan hunters who went to Earth had learned a fair amount in their visits over the centuries, but she had lived it on a daily basis. Her mind was like a sponge and all they needed to do was allow her to stay on Ranic and her years of learning would be theirs for the asking.

The Raniculans had moved their civilization to roughly the same level of advancement as the general populous of late Victorian England. They had beautiful homes, gorgeous fabrics, great castles, and a great many mechanical machines, but they had yet to build any kind of gas-powered vehicle or anything that could fly other than the mind-powered orbs. There was a basic sewer system, but no plumbed showers; for that they diverted water from the canals into wet rooms. There were roads with no cars and rooms with no electric lights.

She could possibly help them come up with fairly complex things like internal combustion engines, but could definitely help them design simpler things like zippers and matches. She was no engineer but she'd read enough books and helped her father fix his ancient Oldsmobile enough times that, with her skill at drawing, she could render a workable plan of a simple engine.

Of course she was also a hybrid, and when her blood had mixed with Jendal's it had altered everything they knew about her. Elyian now felt she was capable of giving a restorative antibody straight into the circulatory system of any injured being to help with the healing process.

He began to detail to the court all the ways in which Charlotte would benefit and not hinder the development of the species.

It's going quite well, she thought as she noted the nods of approval around the great hall. All of a sudden she felt a prickling along her spine and her fangs descended as she instinctively registered a threat. But not to her. She knew with absolute conviction that the longer Elyian stood in the hall the more danger he was in. She was about to call out his name when someone else called it before her.

"Elyian Trainor, bring forth the human." The man behind the snarling voice that thundered through the cavernous room was none other than Havvol Vax. He strode forward clutching his cane as if his very life depended on it.

Questioning murmurs made the rounds of the court members as they watched with interest the drama unfolding before them. Shaking with anger, Havvol raised the cane high over his head and brought it down on the metal surface of the table, which shuddered and buckled under the impact. The court gasped and held its breath, waiting for the inevitable reaction from Elyian.

Elyian did not, however, so much as flinch. He stood his ground and snarled back at Vax. Both men had dropped their fangs and to Charlotte it looked for all the world like two dogs about to rip out each other's throats. The air was thick with testosterone.

"What's wrong now, Vax"? Elyian hissed the words out through his fangs.

"I need to see the female human for myself. Something here isn't right; in fact, I believe it's decidedly fishy." Vax turned on his boot heel and strode to the very back of the room where Charlotte was sitting half hidden behind a pillar with Jendal next to her for moral support.

Elyian watched him go with a worried frown creasing his face. He got to Charlotte's side just after Vax took hold of her head and pulled her hair away from the back of her neck, revealing the unmistakable image of a bird in flight. Vax dropped her hair as if it burned his hand and smiled half-heartedly at Elyian and Jendal, who was pulling her away from him.

"Maybe I was a little hasty." He back-tracked as fast

as possible out of the sticky situation. The instant he saw the mark, he knew she was a direct descendant of the very first ruler of Ranic, and as such she was entitled to claim the throne if she so wished. That would put a rather large spanner in the works for his plan to become ruler after he had staged his coup to replace Elyian.

Elyian pulled Vax away from Charlotte and with a movement too fast for her to register he drew his sword and placed the edge right at the center of the judge's stomach. Vax's laryngeal prominence bobbed up and down as he swallowed audibly.

Elyian did not mince his words as he threatened Vax. "You so much as breathe on her again, and I'll make sure your very last meal is one that consists solely of your own intestinal tract," Elyian said as he slowly and carefully drew the sword up Vax's body ending at his mouth.

The judge moved backwards, away from the blade's tip and Elyian's tongue, and continued backing even further put more distance between himself and his angry monarch.

"Of course, my mistake, Sire." Vax said the words with a decided lack of conviction and respect.

Charlotte stood and flung her arms around Elyian. "What now?" she whispered to him. "Will they vote? What happens to me if they decide I can't stay here? Please don't let them send me back; I feel at home here."

Elyian wished with all his heart that he could hear her say she wanted to stay with him. He didn't know why she held back from including him in her reasons for wanting to stay.

"Hush now, try not to worry. I've almost finished telling them everything, and then they'll have to let you stay. It would be the height of ignorance to banish you merely because you began life on another world. You have Ranic blood in your veins, although most of them don't know that yet. There's something else you need to know, but now isn't the time." He kissed her and watched as she sat back down on the wooden stool, a worried expression haunting her pretty face.

Elyian took his place again in front of the assembled dignitaries and cleared his throat. "As I was saying, before I was so rudely interrupted," he glared at Vax as he said this, "you are all well aware that I intend to claim the—"

His speech was brought to an abrupt end by a disturbance at the end of the hall. People were standing, staring and pointing out of the long wall of gothic-looking windows that flanked one side of the room. He turned his head and horror spread over his features as he saw what was bearing down, with lethal intent, on the city he loved.

Elyian turned. His entire demeanor changed to that of a sure and steady ruler.

"Everyone out! Spread the word, all the women who are not hunters, children and the elderly or infirm are to get down into the catacombs. All hunters get armed and to the defense points." He noted with relief that Jendal handed Charlotte into the safe keeping of some Frey, who hurried her away. Then he turned his attention back to the window.

An impenetrable wall of dust was hurtling towards them, led by a line of beasts a hundred wide and heavens only knew how deep. He saw with a deep, sinking dread that it was no regular army come to rout the city. This force had bodies fifteen feet long and arms sporting talons that could rip a man to shreds in an instant. They came with a steady pounding beat that grew louder by the minute. He clutched the hilt of his sword, that had been resheathed so soon before, and far-stepped to the battlements.

Chapter 20

in which the streets run red

VAX WAS NOTHING if not startled by the appearance of his mutant army. He'd badly miscalculated the timing of their arrival.

"*Damn*," he muttered to himself as he watched Charlotte being led quickly away by the Frey.

He followed them until they were in a quiet place, then he sidled up beside the Frey and told them not to worry, that he would see to her safe keeping and that they had to go quickly and make sure that their own families were helped.

As soon as they left he took her by the arm and pulled her backwards into a recess in the wall. Wasting no time, he stabbed a loaded hypodermic needle straight into her neck. He kept one on him at all times, loaded with a small amount of paralytic venom, in case he happened upon a female who didn't succumb to gentle persuasion.

Charlotte dropped like a stone. He hefted her over his shoulder and walked away with her limp body draped over his back.

Actually, he thought to himself as he descended the stairs, *this is perfect. Everyone will be so busy keeping themselves alive that she won't be missed for hours.*

A series of small doors at the bottom of the stairs led through a tunnel and eventually to his secret room. His own little piece of heaven, that's how he liked to think of his private, dark, dank underground room that housed the instruments of torture which were his most precious possessions.

Long, curved blades in graduated sizes with beautifully crafted handles of mother-of-pearl, and heavy iron clamps lined with spikes that bit into flesh as screws were tightened, were laid out in neat rows on a highly polished slab down one side of the room. A large, black metal machine that was all cogs and wheels whirled quietly away in a corner, providing power to a constantly turning stone he could use to sharpen dull blades.

At the side of the machine, a dozen small furry things ran around the inside of a large metal basket, turning it constantly, like hamsters in a wheel, providing the source of power. Bowls made of the finest porcelain, meant to hold spilled blood, were lined up along a shelf and vied for room with long needles tipped with various poisons and small buckets of ground glass that were tipped down the throats of his many victims.

It was a house of horrors that Charlotte saw when her eyelids eventually managed to open of their own accord. He had raised them a few times to see if she was awake and eventually had left the dungeon with the intention of returning when he'd dispatched updated orders to the attacking army.

Her eyes took some time to adjust to the low light. A single taper in one corner left much of the room in deep shadow.

Charlotte tried to move but found to her dismay that she was firmly shackled by her ankles to a stone wall. A groaning to her left made her whip her head around.

A small, dark-haired woman sat in a corner, hunched over with hair falling over her face. As she raised her head Charlotte was staggered to see Esarelle, although her face was almost unrecognizable.

"Why are we here? What's happening?" Esarelle just managed to speak through swelling lips. Dried blood coated the side of her swollen face and a black eye was beginning to show. She winced as she spoke, obviously in tremendous pain.

Charlotte tried to assess the cell to see if there was any

possible way they might escape. She spotted the table as the gleam of metal from the burning taper caught her attention. The unsettling sight of the shiny weapons of torture caused her stomach to heave and release the contents of her last meal.

I will not cry; I will not cry. She repeated the mantra over and over in her head until she felt calmer.

To take her mind off the table she told Esarelle of the events in the high court and of her abduction at the hands of an unknown assailant. Vax had been behind her when he spoke to the Frey, and then had pulled her so fast into the shadows that she hadn't been able to see his face.

It was when she described his foul breath and described the color of his gown that she'd seen when she was slung over his shoulder that Esarelle nodded and confirmed the identity of her captor.

Some small rat-like creatures scuttled around, and Charlotte was relieved not to see another creature like the one that bit her the first time she was on Ranic. A more urgent problem was the huge, black spidery thing the size of a teacup crawling insidiously in her direction.

She wiggled her foot and managed to get the manacles lifted a few inches above the floor. She waited until the disgusting thing was right under her satin-clad foot before she stomped down on it, turning both the gargantuan bug and her slipper into a foul, oozing mess.

"Ugh, gross!" she exclaimed, which would have raised a smile out of poor Esarelle, if she had been able to smile. By now her lips were so contorted that speaking was impossible. Charlotte wanted to ask her why Vax had taken them but questioning have to wait.

Both women were desperate for water but there was none within reach. A bucket of some kind of liquid was fairly close to Charlotte, but even if she lay on the ground and stretched out towards it, with her ankle manacled to the wall she was still not quite close enough to reach the handle.

The miserable reality of their situation was apparent to both women and a cloud of despair settled around them. They could hear commotion over their heads. Muffled sounds of banging and screams of agony filtered down to where they were incarcerated and Charlotte went into full meltdown. Every time they heard a scream or a howl of pain she cringed and ended up with her hands over her ears trying to cut out the awful sounds. She hunkered into as small of a ball as she could and sat there shaking with fear, praying Vax would stay away.

The hours passed slowly, with nothing to do except sit and contemplate their fate. Slimy green algae that covered the cell walls soon mucked their clothes and hair. Thirst was quickly becoming unbearable and sleep evaded them; but as dawn broke the next day exhaustion finally overtook them and they both slipped into blissful unconsciousness.

Jendal had swung his sword so many times it felt as though every tendon in his arm was about to tear loose from its anchor. At first, the wave after wave of Manos had seemed insurmountable. They tore through the ranks of hunters, tearing off limbs and biting into tender flesh with their venomous bite, killing the men in seconds.

Fierce as they were, they were no match for the well-trained hunters, who managed to coral groups of them in interior courtyards where they were better able to mow them down with volleys of arrows shot down from the battlements. The ones who managed to scale the walls by digging their talons into the soft sandstone blocks were treated to vats of boiling oil tipped over their heads. Even so, a few broke through the ranks of hunters and stalked through the palace in search of anything on two legs.

Elyian was on the ground floor holding off a Mano, aided by a couple of fairly young hunters. They were being pushed steadily backward toward the top step of one of the many stone staircases that led down to the catacombs. He'd plunged his sword into so many Manos so many times the floor was running with their blood.

This one was not giving up without a fight. It bellowed at him like a cow in heat, its spiny reptilian tail swooshing from side to side, splattering the tiring men with warm, sticky blood. The hunter on Elyian's left took a moment too long to readjust his sword arm and the beast plunged its head down and gripped the poor man by the throat, thrashing him violently to one side and then the other like a rag doll, before tossing him aside. The man hit the opposite wall head first, cracking his neck on impact and landing in a broken, unceremonious heap on the floor.

As the Mano was distractedly examining his kill, Elyian

and the remaining fighter plunged their swords deep into the animal, finally dealing it the death blow. Elyian stepped backward, pulling his sword free of the body. His foot slipped on the blood pooling on the floor and he fell backward through the open doorway and down the stairs to the catacombs. Excruciating pain coursed through him as he hit the first few steps, but he was oblivious to the rest.

Havvol Vax watched the battle rage through the night from the relative safety of his upstairs quarters. Housed in a separate tower from the main part of the castle, it had an iron gate at its entrance, which he had ensured at the start of the battle to be securely bolted shut.

His initial glee at the wholesale slaughter of so many of Elyian's people was turning to apprehension as he watched the tide turn against his army. By the time the last Mano had suffered the removal of its head, Vax was in a blind rage. Someone was going to pay for this, of that he was certain. Tonight was the night he was supposed to be sitting on the throne, head of all he surveyed. Instead, the castle was in ruins, hundreds of people had died, and Elyian was still king.

Where is that bastard Elyian? Vax wondered. The last time Vax saw him was hours ago, battling half a dozen Manos at the rear of castle with some of the palace guards and several hunters at his side.

He peeked cautiously out the door of his tower, ever the coward for all his brutality. When he was quite sure he wouldn't be run through with a sword or, worse still, be made a meal of by a hungry Mano, he hightailed it to the main building and shot through the door and out into the main courtyard.

The sight that greeted him defied description. Mountains of Mano corpses lay in grotesque piles all over the main square. The ground that a few hours ago had been stone of a lovely pale golden color was now a sticky brownish red. Pieces of Raniculan, Frey and Mano flesh lay scattered all over, a leg here, a head there. Dying men and women lay groaning and crying out for help.

Several Frey and some Raniculans ran around trying to help as many as they could, but the task was monumentally overwhelming. As the morning wore on they gradually cleared some of the dead and started to burn the Manos in great bonfires all over the city.

Vax tired of looking for Elyian; the ruler was nowhere to be seen. Deciding that finding out the fate of the king could wait, he returned to his outpost, clanging the gate closed behind him, and made his way downstairs to his secret quarters.

Charlotte looked up as the sound of someone coming towards the cell shook her out of her light sleep. Vax unlocked the door and almost slithered his way toward the women, a look of sheer menace glittering in his cold grey eyes. He took in the unconscious Esarelle and quickly dismissed her as of no use to him since she could no longer feel pain.

He focused on the human glaring at him with utter contempt. He picked up a particularly nasty-looking curved blade and used the tip to pick at his filthy teeth as he eyed her lasciviously from head to toe.

"So we meet properly at last, little human." He spat out the word human like it was something particularly nasty stuck in his throat. "Time for us to play, I think."

Charlotte's screams would haunt the nightmares of the little bald Frey who was hiding in the hallway outside for a century to come. Arun blanched at the sounds emanating from the cell. He knew the best way to help her was to get Elyian, and fast, so he high tailed it out of the tower and went to find his master.

It wasn't easy to find a needle in a haystack, and between the gore-saturated courtyard, palace rooms that were almost destroyed, and the many people desperate for help, he got caught up in the general mayhem. Then he saw his mate dragging a badly injured leg as she attempted to reach his sheltering embrace.

In the midst of everything, Arun temporarily forgot about the human woman in the cell.

Chapter 21

in which earth reels

Planet Earth. December 2019

CAMERON GRANT ARRIVED back late one evening to his cold and empty house. It had been so long since he'd last been there that the garden was totally overgrown and the house was overrun with dirt and bugs.

I should've hired someone to come in and clean the place up. That's something he'd have had Charlotte do if she'd still been around. Just one more of many things that didn't get done since she left his employ.

He lit a fire, filled the house with smoke, and then remembered to open the flue. While he sipped a hot cup of coffee, he pressed the play button on his house phone answering machine and listened to a year's worth of missed calls. Luckily most people called his cell phone, so there weren't many messages he'd need to deal with.

Next on his to-do list was the home monitoring system. He'd installed it before he left for Europe.

And shit, I forgot to tell Charlotte. Hope she didn't do

anything she wouldn't want me to see. It was set to record all movement.

Cameron's heart raced when her image filled the screen as she padded about from room to room, petting Atlas when he pushed his wet nose into her palm. As her face re-implanted itself into his memory, he sadly recalled that message that had severed her ties with him.

He didn't blame her for Atlas's death. That dog was determined to get into trouble. He hoped her leaving wasn't from guilt—although that would be better than the alternative he feared. No matter how many avenues he tried, he hadn't been able to locate her since the night she told him about Atlas. She'd vanished off the face of the earth right about the time of the San Francisco earthquake. What if she'd been lost in the quake? Would he ever know?

As he watched the early video images flash across the screen he realized Charlotte looked upset and distracted. Then there seemed to be a long lapse of time without her.

Cameron sat bolt upright as the playback showed an unknown man in his kitchen. The man was dressed in leather, and he was extremely tall and slender. He had his back to the camera as he stood at the range frying up what looked like bacon and eggs...and chicken. The man placed the cooked food on the tray by the side of the range and picked it up.

As he turned he dropped the tray. All the flatware tumbled to the ground, and the food began to slide from the plate as it, too, dropped. The man cursed loudly, but managed to catch the falling plate in mid-air. He moved so fast that Cam couldn't tell how he'd done it. He picked out new flatware from a nearby drawer so quickly Cam didn't see the drawer open or close. Then, as if that wasn't enough to scare him witless, the stranger lifted his bloodless face in the direction of the camera, showing a perfect pair of white fangs before he closed his mouth and levitated up the stairs.

Cam didn't move for a long, long time. His heart beat so fast he was positive he was about to have a heart attack. Eventually he hit the replay button. When he still wasn't convinced he watched it a dozen times more.

The White House got the call three weeks later, after the video had been reviewed by dozens of high-ranking government agents. They'd passed it from one agency to another until it finally reached the desk of the head of homeland security.

The film had been analyzed so many times it was a

wonder it was still intact. Everyone that viewed it tried to find some kind of digital meddling with the photography to explain what they saw. After many tests they all came to the same conclusion, and it was with extreme trepidation that the agents watched the film one more time in the company of the President of the United States.

The president held his breath, knowing with a dreadful certainty that the country over which he presided and the planet on which they lived had just irrevocably changed. Planet Earth, as the human race knew it, was changed forever. Everything previously held as fact might now be fiction; and fiction became a terrifying new reality.

Chapter 22

in which threads are spun

Arun EVENTUALLY FOUND Elyian lying at the bottom of a flight of steep stone steps, clutching his head and moaning in pain. The Frey crouched next to his ruler and spoke in a quiet voice. He knew only too well the signs of Elyian in the midst of a full-blown migraine.

"Master, are you all right? Can I help you?"

Elyian moved his head very slowly from side to side and whispered back to him. "Charlotte. I need to find Charlotte."

He was dizzy from the fall which, apart from giving him a mild concussion, had also broken his femur clean in half. The jagged bone poked like an iceberg out of his torn leather pants.

"I fear you will not be going anywhere," said Arun. "Not until we get that leg set. I don't know where the physician has got to; he hasn't been seen for days." He wished that was the worst of the news, but was compelled to tell Elyian the rest. "I do, however, know where Charlotte is, and you're not going to like it."

Arun told Elyian what he'd overheard, and long before he finished Elyian was trying to stand. He collapsed, of course, as his leg couldn't bear any weight upon it.

Elyian held his sword hard against his thigh, pulled the wide belt from his waist, and cinched it tightly around both his leg and the sword, pushing the bone back into place. He added Arun's belt below the knee so that his leg had been effectively stabilized. Pain, beyond excruciating, made him see stars.

Raniculans were nothing if not stoic, and as a race they had a pain threshold far higher than any human could begin to tolerate. Still, Elyian felt nauseated as he climbed the stairs, unable to far-step again that day. Every time he put weight on his leg he felt the stab of the broken bone as it mashed the flesh around the edges of the wound to a bloody pulp.

Once at the tower he used his master key to enter the private quarters of Havvol Vax. With two palace guards as back up, he drew his sword, and moving as silently as possible they made their way to the tunnels below.

Screams of terror and pain reached him long before he found the room where Vax held the women. As Vax plunged a short, curved dagger deep into Esarelle, Elyian was shouldering the door, and before Vax registered that Elyian was in the room, Elyian had pinned him to the wall and held his dagger up tight to the side of Vax's throat.

Elyian tore the keys from Vax's belt. His voice dropped, deep and menacing as he growled, "You bastard, Vax! I would slit you from ear to ear but it would be far too quick and easy a death for a monster like you." He raised his voice again. "Guards, take him away. Make damn sure he's as uncomfortable as you can make him, but don't kill him."

As the guards levered Vax out of the room Elyian whirled toward Charlotte, his long hands roaming frantically all over her, checking for injuries. In the dark he couldn't see the missing piece of flesh behind her ear.

He released both women from the heavy iron clamps that had bitten into their ankle bones. Charlotte was shaking but she tried not to let Elyian see how badly she was injured. She knelt next to Esarelle and Elyian dropped down with her.

"Oh, Elyian, he stabbed her, I think she's dead." Charlotte cried with great heaving sobs as she felt for a pulse and then realized she didn't know if Raniculans had a pulse to begin with.

"She's not dead, she can't be dead," he growled as he lifted Esarelle up from the floor and with his preternatural strength managed to get his own broken body into an upright position as he held her supine body in his arms. "We'll take her to her home. Her father has disappeared, but there should be supplies we can use to help her."

They fought their way through streets strewn with the detritus of war. Charlotte was horrified at the carnage that resulted from the battle she'd heard while held captive in the cell. Nothing she'd previously experienced could have prepared her for what she witnessed.

The sun was high in the sky. A multitude of people were dragging the Manos to massive pyres outside the city, where they'd be burned. Swarms of flies and various birds of prey descended on the feast laid out for their taking. Already the rancid stench of brutal death permeated the air, and it was only going to get worse.

The dead hunters, guards and civilians were loaded onto wagons and taken to a giant amphitheater where they were laid out in long rows and draped respectfully with fine shrouds. The next day, after Elyian honored the dead and thanked them for their service to Ranic, survivors would be able to claim the bodies of their loved ones and take them away for private burials.

It was with great relief that Charlotte closed the door behind Elyian when they got inside the cool, dark interior of the cottage. She drank several large goblets of blessedly cold water and started to feel somewhat better.

Esarelle was still alive; they could see a tiny muscle twitching on the side of her face. A huge gaping wound in her belly oozed blood and didn't show any signs of stopping.

Once again Charlotte found herself the primary caregiver in a trauma situation. She found clean bedding and tore it into strips, which she wadded and pressed over the injury. Elyian took over holding the compress while she raided the house for anything that could be of any immediate help. Shelves of glass bottles filled with various liquids, powders and one that contained dead bugs, were sporting labels that did nothing to clue her in on their contents.

"What the hell is this?" She pulled the cork on one that held a thick, cream-colored liquid and sniffed. Her head snapped back in disgust. The noxious odor reminded her of a pair of socks that had run a marathon but had yet to see the inside of a washing machine.

Then she saw it, tucked at the very back and covered

in a layer of dust, a white plastic bottle, looking oddly misplaced among the old glass bottles and vials. The label read ACETAMINOPHEN. In astonishment she grabbed the bottle. Damn, her head hurt. She struggled with the stupid childproof cap, shook out a couple and downed them in one swallow.

"Elyian, you'll never guess what I found," she said as she headed back to him. "Someone must have brought this back from Ear..."

She stopped dead in her tracks at the sight of Elyian with his fangs sunk deep into Esarelle's neck. The look on his face was one of pure lust and she was stunned into shocked silence.

He stopped and licked Esarelle's neck with one swipe of his tongue. He turned his head toward Charlotte but his eyes remained downcast, unable to meet her eyes.

"Charlotte, I...I'm sorry, I had to...I couldn't help it..." he trailed off, quite unable to continue.

Charlotte's eyes burned with unshed tears. It wasn't that he bit Esarelle; Charlotte should have thought to heal Esarelle that way herself, but she was so new to this whole Vampire thing that it didn't enter her mind. No, what hurt was the salacious desire on his face.

That settles it. We're through. I've done enough crying over this man. Enough is enough.

Esarelle stirred. The huge wound in her stomach already closing, and her face was almost restored to its usual state. When she recognized who was leaning over her she smiled, a long, seductive smile. Her hand rose from the bed and she held Elyian's face captive as she cooed his name. "Elyian, I might have guessed it would be you who rescued me."

Charlotte turned and ran from the house, from the man that kept breaking her heart...and right into trouble.

The man in her path buckled as she hurtled into his body, her tears now flowing in unending rivers down her cheeks.

"Are you all right, Mistress?"

She looked up, then up some more, into the face of a god. Words failed her. He was similar in build to the infuriating and fickle Elyian. This man had the very same emerald eyes with long, dark lashes that framed them so beautifully they looked almost feminine. His age was hard to determine, considering the extreme longevity of the Raniculan race.

A few very faint lines creased his face. She reckoned by Earth standards he'd be in his late thirties, maybe at a push early forties, but in amazing physical shape. He had perfect skin with the shadow of a beard along a strong jaw, and thick, dark hair.

Obviously a hunter.

An arsenal of weapons hung from his body at various points. These included a quiver of arrows, a bow, a sword, and a matching set of daggers tucked into long, leather boots. Bits of dead Manos had stuck to his clothing but that did nothing to diminish the impact he had on Charlotte.

She sniffed, reined in her rampaging libido that seemed to kick in at the most inappropriate moments, and swiped away the tears on her face. As she removed herself from the front of his jacket, odd little static threads danced around her clothing and landed on the man. She barely gave them a thought, just another Ranic oddity to figure out later.

"No, I'm not all right," she replied, "but I'll get over it."

He looked her over carefully and winced. "Your head looks badly hurt. Here, hold still a moment." He moved her hair back and gasped when he saw the missing flesh. "How did you get that injury? It's not from a Mano, far too neat. Someone carved an exact circle of skin away."

She'd felt okay up to that point. Upset and mad as hell, yes, but not ill. But hearing the description of what that mad man had done to her, she knew without a shadow of a doubt that she was going to throw up.

He waited with her until she stopped heaving and then helped her get back to the palace. On the way he introduced himself.

"My name is Amun, Amun Trainor."

She stopped dead in her tracks. "Please tell me this is some cruel coincidence and that you're only very distantly related to the king," she said hopefully. He looked vaguely familiar; she was almost certain she'd seen the image of this man flash through her mind when Elyian bit her. How were they connected?

He laughed then, showing his pearly whites and of course perfect fangs. "Long story, and it can wait until we're much better acquainted," he said, changing tack just before they reached the palace entrance. He gave her arm a tug, led her down a long, narrow alleyway, and pulled her inside a tavern that in the best traditions of alcohol-serving establishments across the galaxy was the very first business to open after the battle.

"I'm parched, how about you?"

She nodded, happy to be out of the heat and to be anywhere Elyian wasn't.

She had another try at drinking fermented Yalon. Hated the first one, tolerated the second, and was drunk as an earthly skunk by the third. Her drinking was nothing compared to the amount downed by Amun, who managed to empty a cask by himself. The fiery liquid licked at her core, heating her blood and rendering her legs almost useless.

She found Amun to be a very accommodating drinking partner. He seemed nervous at first but they quickly relaxed in each other's company. He was attentive and quite amusing, and by the time she poured her fourth drink he was sitting very close to her and she did not dislike it at all.

Amun helped her stand when the barkeep threw them out. It had been a long day and she was well past the point of total exhaustion, but the Yalon helped her remain awake if not particularly lucid. They staggered down the street with Amun's arms around her waist, propping her up.

She giggled inanely when he tripped on a stray Mano leg that had escaped the cleaning crews. Eventually he managed to get her to the palace entrance. The sight of the towering structure had the same effect as a whole ocean of freezing water being dumped on her head.

"I don't think I can go back in there again," she slurred as her head slumped against his shoulder.

"No problem, you can stay with me!" Amun declared, delightedly.

So it was that during the night of the battle with the Mano army, Elyian spent the entirety of the time between dusk and dawn trying in vain to find Charlotte. His orb had been broken during the battle and he was in agony from his leg that wasn't healing, as it was broken clean in two. His head was pounding, and he was mad and frustrated as hell. She'd fled before he could explain why he bit Esarelle.

"Why didn't she understand? Oh, that's right; she's a damn human!" he steamed to himself as he stalked the empty streets and peered down all the dark alleys in the hope of finding her.

As dawn broke, lack of food and a massive migraine forced his return to the palace. He hadn't eaten in nearly two days and he knew he needed sustenance to continue the search. It was with relief that he spied Arun in one of the receiving rooms, crawling under a large table retrieving books and paperwork that had been scattered in the confusion the day before.

"Arun, I need food. Now, please," Elyian said as he peered under the heavy table.

Arun, unable to bow, nodded his head vigorously. "Yes, of course, Sire," he said, then his brows creased as he noticed the grey pallor of Elyian's skin.

"Shall I also get a headache remedy for you, Sire, and maybe something for that leg?" he inquired solicitously, staring pointedly at the sword still strapped with blood-soaked belts to his ruler's thigh.

"Yes, that would be good, Arun, thank you. I'll be in my quarters. Bring it there, please. And Arun, have you seen Charlotte anywhere? She seems to be missing."

Arun looked worried and more than a little puzzled. "You did find her at the high court judge's tower, did you not, Sire?"

"Yes, Arun, I found her and Esarelle. Esarelle will be fine, but Charlotte is now lost on a planet that she knows almost nothing about. The danger here…" His voice trailed off and his frown deepened before he continued. "I don't need to tell you what dangers she could face. If you hear anything, anything at all—"

"Yes, I will find you at once, Sire. Now please go and rest. You look as if you are about to collapse."

Elyian dragged his body up the stairs, lacking even enough energy to far-step to his room. Arun checked on him several times over the next few hours and each time he left the room he was more concerned.

He summoned several junior physicians but none of them wanted to set the leg of a king. What if they killed him? Their own lives would be cut short for sure by the high court. So all they did was apply hot compresses, which did nothing except cause him further agony.

At the apothecary's house he had drunk Esarelle's blood and given her some of his in exchange, so that they would both start to heal. But evidently her blood couldn't set or heal his leg, though it did repair the other injuries he sustained during the battle. Those wounds were minor compared to a broken bone. On this planet a deep stab wound was easily fixed; bones, however, were not.

A night of deep sleep thanks to a potent sleeping draft Arun procured helped Elyian recover his strength, but his leg was still a major issue. If left untreated an infection could end up taking his life. He needed care and he needed it fast; and so far, there was none to be had.

Chapter 23

in which life is a circle

"DEAR GOD, WHAT was I thinking?"

Obviously, she hadn't been. A hangover on Earth was bad enough, but this one had Charlotte wishing someone would swing a mighty sword and sever her head from her body, thereby ending her misery conclusively.

She tried to open her eyes but they seemed stuck shut. After another attempt she managed to get them to move, a little. As the first shaft of light hit her retina she winced in pain and squeezed them closed again. After a few more attempts she got her eyes to cooperate and she slowly scanned her surroundings.

Well, this is different. Don't often wake up in a forest. Actually looks a little more like home.

The leafy ceiling above her was interspersed with patchy bits of purple sky. She slowly turned her head to the side. Her cheek hit something which impeded further movement. The something was warm against her skin and a little rough. Charlotte came fully awake that very second and shot upright, turning to stare at her companion.

Amun lay on his side next to her, with a look of beatific

serenity on his sleeping face. Under them both was a thick layer of ferns that had formed a very comfortable bed. They were ensconced in a natural bedchamber, of sorts. A wall of towering trees with trunks at least eight feet across formed a circle around the pair, so close together that anything larger than a rabbit wouldn't be able to pass through.

She stared in wonder at the beauty and serenity around her. Exotic birds of every size flew in and out of the overhead branches, weaving a tapestry of color among the forest of green and blue leaves that sprouted from the living canopy. Silver droplets of water cascaded down from the leaves, glittering as they caught the light. A tiny stream entered the circle then formed a spiral that wound around the bed and left on the opposite side.

Each tree in the circle had symbols burned into the trunk a few feet up from the forest floor. The higher branches swayed gently in the wind, but it was still and calm within the circle. Charlotte had never seen a more lovely place.

Unfortunately, her pleasure at waking up here was tempered by the knowledge that she was not alone. On the forest floor beside the bed was a neat pile of weapons and an even neater pile of clothing—his only, none of her own, as she was still fully dressed, if a little dirty and rumpled. She groaned aloud at the sight of the very naked and gorgeous man sleeping soundly by her side and resolutely shook his shoulder.

He woke quickly, stretching his muscular arms and then shaking his head so that a thousand droplets of water flew in every direction. His smile as he caught sight of her was so dazzling she forgot to be put out by the fact that he was wearing nothing else but that smile.

"Good morning, Mistress Charlotte. I trust you slept soundly?"

Charlotte gaped at him, her power of speech temporarily frozen. A dozen questions zoomed around her poor, over-stimulated brain, but only one seemed to be of paramount importance at this time. She dragged it forward.

"Did we…did I…you know…did we? Damn it, Amun, did we have sex last night?"

He smiled languidly at her and her blood froze in her veins. "No, tell me we didn't!"

He smiled again but this time laughed as well and shook his head vehemently from side to side. "We were both drunk—

no, that's not altogether accurate, so let me clarify. You were falling-down drunk and I felt a little happier than usual. I would never again have sex with a drunken woman. I did once and was quite ashamed of my lack of morals. Apart from that, I've heard they tend to throw up on you and then fall asleep. Anyway, you kept muttering something about being 'once bitten, twice shy' or something like that. Figured you were stewing over something to do with Elyian, so I left you alone."

"But, you're naked, apart from that pendant!" she exclaimed, pointing to the golden Ankh that hung around his neck.

"I always sleep nude," he stated, completely impassive. "What would you have me do, sleep with all my daggers poking me? It's much more comfortable to sleep without any clothes."

"You could've at least kept your pants on!" she retorted.

"Stop fretting, Charlotte, your virtue is intact. That," he pointed up at an orb of Leverium2 that had been hovering unnoticed by Charlotte a few feet over her head, "will ensure that I keep my hands off you. See the way it sparkles over you? It's sending your location straight back to Elyian. I summoned it so we could get a message back to the palace. I can't take you there myself as I used up my energy far-stepping us both here last night. I figured Elyian was probably worrying himself over your disappearance, so I decided to let him know where on the planet you are."

"And where on the planet am I, exactly?"

Amun stood and picked up his pants from the neat pile on the floor. He tugged them on as he spoke. "You're at my summer home," he replied, seemingly surprised by her question. "I told you last night you could stay with me. So I brought you here. This is my haven away from everything on Ranic that I detest. Unfortunately I have to spend much of my time in the city, but I escape here whenever I'm not needed at the palace."

His explanation was interrupted by a loud buzzing sound that seemed to be surrounding the circle of trees.

"What's that?" Charlotte whirled around, frantically trying to find the source of the noise.

Amun didn't reply, but instead drew one of his swords from the scabbard that was by now safely secured on his person. He put one finger up to his lips for silence.

Charlotte's eyes widened, and she moved quickly off the bed to stand at his back. His free arm crept behind him until he found her waist, and he pulled her tight up against his buttocks. She would have protested but it did seem a safe location.

The buzzing grew steadily louder and was now accompanied by an occasional cracking sound. She peeked out from behind the safety of Amun's broad back and saw little bits of what looked like sawdust falling from the trunks of the trees.

A thin, black, wisp of a feeler stuck out of a hole in the trunk, closely followed by a second one. Then Charlotte saw the eyes, huge, saucer-sized orange eyes with hexagonal shapes all over their surface.

An insect that closely resembled a bee, but was the size of a house cat, was hatching out of the tree. It dragged itself out of the hole in the trunk, pulling its long, translucent wings free. The insect flew down to the forest floor and turned to look directly at them.

Its huge head swiveled back and forth as it stalked toward them, its body covered in long, dark fur that half hid the four pairs of legs down each side of the long, hairy body. The legs were black and shiny with multiple joints. It bore more than a passing resemblance to a cross between a bee and an enormous hairy spider.

Amun swung his sword high over his head and with a massive swing brought it down on the creature's back. He cleaved it into two neat halves that twitched a couple of times and then fell neatly apart.

"Yum, breakfast," he said. Still hiding behind his back, Charlotte quivered and gagged slightly.

"Seriously? You're not going to eat that." She tried to act nonchalant but it came out more of a squeak. Would she ever be able to wrap her mind around the constant new realities? She cleared her throat and gamely tried again. "How does mutant ninja bee taste when fried?"

Amun skewered one half of the bee on his pointy stick. "They're really quite good. Taste better boiled than fried, so let's get a fire going and we can discuss your present delicate condition over a hearty breakfast. How are you at skinning?"

He tossed a small knife at her and laughed when she caught it in mid-air. "Well, full of surprises aren't you?"

"My father used to take me on long camping trips in

the Sierras," she said, an air of wistful remembrance on her face. "He loved to teach me how to fish and hunt. By the time I was a teenager I was good at helping him skin the deer we hunted."

Amun jumped over the small stream that separated them from the trees and gave Charlotte a helping hand. As they approached the circle she saw a tall but narrow wooden door she hadn't noticed before. It was cut right into the center of a massive tree trunk.

He opened it and she was amazed to see through the doorway a stunning view. The circle of trees stood at the very pinnacle of a steep hill. Devoid of other trees or shrubbery, it afforded anyone standing there a three hundred sixty degree view of the land around them.

In front of them lay a green and lush valley dotted with lakes, rivers and gently rolling hillsides. It reminded her of the valleys of Sonoma, minus the vineyards. To the west the land changed to a rocky, jagged landscape; at her back was desert. She could just make out the foothills of the Shoulen Mountains as they shimmered in the haze, far off on the rear horizon.

To the east, land was heavily forested and it was in this direction that Amun led her as they started down the hill. He slung the dead bee over his shoulder and whistled as he strode down to the tree line.

They stopped at a large hollow in the ground where a circle of rocks marked the outline of the remains of a cooking fire. Sitting nearby were some pots and a few utensils. Amun was obviously totally at home in the great outdoors. He had a fire going and the creature cooking by the time she returned from a fast but necessary trip down to the river that ran next to his camp.

A small cabin nearby housed a few other items that made life in the wilderness a bit more comfortable. Some blankets and, somewhat surprisingly, a dog-eared copy of the collected works of Edgar Allan Poe. A long, slender, blue feather held the place of his poem "The Dream." While Charlotte waited for her meal to finish cooking she read the well-worn page.

> *In visions of the dark night*
> *I have dreamed of joy departed-*
> *But a waking dream of life and light*
> *Hath left me broken-hearted.*

Ah! what is not a dream by day
To him whose eyes are cast
On things around him with a ray
Turned back upon the past?
That holy dream- that holy dream,
While all the world were chiding,
Hath cheered me as a lovely beam
A lonely spirit guiding.
What though that light, thro' storm and night,
So trembled from afar-
What could there be more purely bright
In Truth's day-star?

Charlotte clutched the book to her chest. A sudden wave of loneliness swept over her. She was so very far away from home and anything familiar.

"It's a lovely poem, isn't it, Charlotte?" Amun was stirring the pot and watching her as she finished reading. He continued, "I met him, back in 1836. I'd been invited to his wedding, acting as an escort to a very fine-looking female friend of his. His new wife, Virginia, was only thirteen years old. She died ten years later of tuberculosis. Very sad; she was an entrancing young woman by then and he loved her very much. We kept in touch and he sent me this collection of his work many years later."

Amun took the book from her and opened the frontispiece. There in a faded, spider-like scrawl was the signature of the Victorian poet Edgar Allan Poe.

Charlotte lightly traced it with her finger. "I wonder what he would've said if he'd known about Ranic."

"Oh, but he did," Amun stated. "We had many long discussions over a glass or two of fine port. He knew exactly where I came from and who I am. I like to think I had some small influence in his choice of subject matter. He was sworn to secrecy, and to the best of my knowledge he never divulged my identity. Although I did catch Virginia watching me with a strange look in her eyes more than once."

He finished cooking the bug, hacked it into bite-sized pieces, and served it up to Charlotte on a large wooden platter. "There you go, see if you care for this."

As Charlotte ate she had to admit it tasted delicious. A tad fishy, which was strange for an insect, but very satisfying.

Amun watched her, crouched down on his haunches

several feet away. His eyes never left her face. Long, wavy strands of her lovely red hair were blowing freely in the wind and she had a slight flush to her pale complexion.

As she licked her fingers to rid them of the grease from her meal, he felt his groin tighten in response. His fangs, which he'd been fighting to keep under control all morning, slammed down into his mouth, which he opened slightly to accommodate them. Then he could taste her scent on his tongue, as the breeze wafted it toward him. It was driving him wild, but he knew he couldn't let it show. He stood suddenly and stalked off, unable to remain close to her any longer.

Charlotte looked up, bemused. "Where are you going, Amun?"

When he didn't reply but kept walking, she shot to her feet and ran to catch up. He stopped and looked at her, and when she raised her bottomless green eyes to his, he was lost to her. She saw those threads of connection tighten between them again and her body screamed to be with him. Elyian was forgotten.

Here, in the wilderness, she couldn't deny the attraction she instantly felt for Amun. Although Elyian's brother Jendal was handsome in a brutish kind of way, she was not attracted to him at all. But this man exuded a confident, vibrant and primal energy along with something else she couldn't quite put her finger on. He seemed familiar, but she'd certainly never seen him before last night.

The way he was looking at her made her stomach clench and she felt heat rising in her until little beads of sweat broke out on her brow. Her fangs ached and she turned away from him so he couldn't see how she was responding.

"That won't help you, Charlotte. I can smell your scent. I can tell with every fiber in my body, that you want me." His words came out like a caress, spinning in the air before landing, soft as silk, against her mouth.

He clutched her arm and pulled her toward him. She groaned as they met, his body like steel against her soft curves. He kissed her hard and long and she melted under him, until as suddenly as he'd taken her in his arms, he released her, pushing her gently away.

She felt bereft, as if a part of her had been ripped asunder. Tears filled her eyes as confusion and sadness replaced need and desire.

"Elyian isn't the man for me," she sobbed at him, "and

apparently I'm not appealing to you. I feel so very alone."

A long, low sound rumbled up from deep in his throat. When he answered, there was no doubt that he was being truthful.

"By the gods above, I would have you, Charlotte. But you belong to Elyian, and I will not take what is not mine to have, though you are without doubt the single most lovely thing that has ever walked upon this planet. Sadly, even though Elyian has not shown up, I have no right to keep you here."

She wasn't able to take in everything he said, as a blur of movement caught her attention, followed by a crashing, splintering sound. The world around her became a tumbled chaotic mess of arms, legs and cussing males, rolling around on the forest floor.

"Damn right, you can't keep her here," and, "Shit, that hurt!" were interspersed with grunts and yells. Every creature for miles around would have fled in panic at the bedlam in the camp.

When the two men rolled into the fire and the flames licked at their clothes, she decided enough was enough. Picking up a large wooden bucket she flung the contents at the pair, dousing their male egos considerably. As the pair of smoldering, bedraggled men pulled themselves together, she looked at them with not a little amusement.

"Why are you two fighting? Elyian! Get your hands off Amun. What are you doing here, anyway?"

She glared at Elyian, trying not to let him see just how funny she found the sight of him, with his hair sticking up all over and decorated with bits of twigs and leaves. And Amun, who had his pants on but hadn't gotten around to donning a shirt, standing there with his entire chest covered in wet rivulets of soot from the doused fire and a liberal coating of grease, courtesy of the remains of their meal which was now scattered on the ground.

Charlotte asked sarcastically, "Do you two know each other, or is this the Raniculan idea of being gallant?"

Elyian grunted out a terse response. "You could say we know each other. Didn't he tell you? No? I suppose he had other things on his mind. He's my father, Charlotte!"

"He's your *what*?" she yelled back.

"My father, Charlotte. May the gods above preserve us, he's my sire."

"That can't be possible. Elyian, I slept with him!"

Charlotte's voice was now several octaves higher and she prayed she'd heard him wrong.

On hearing that last interesting little tidbit of information Elyian's face went as dark as thunder and he turned on Amun like a person possessed. Amun saw him coming, deflected the strike and caught Elyian in a head lock, easily flipping him onto his back. He then sat astride him with his leather pants stretched to the point of tearing. Amun was getting a little tired of the conflict by now so he let Elyian have a piece of his mind.

"You great oaf, Elyian, have you absolutely no idea how to treat this wonderful woman? When I came across her last night she was devastated, and even though she respected you enough not to give me all the gory details, I gathered enough to know you've made one poor decision after another. I really thought after the first five hundred years or so, you might have gotten the hang of how to have a relationship without derailing it every single time. Apparently I was wrong. When Charlotte said she slept with me, she meant *sleep* and that's all, you idiot!"

Elyian looked into his father's eyes and saw he wasn't lying. But he could also smell Charlotte's unmistakable scent all over Amun's body, which did nothing to calm him down. It was obvious that Amun was exceedingly attracted to her; and knowing the Raniculans' predilection for human females, he also knew he couldn't trust his father to stay away from her for long.

The only way he could turn off the powerful pheromones she exuded around males was to claim her as his mate and go through the ceremony that would bind them irrevocably together. Elyian would've told her why Amun was acting like a lovesick teen, but he was in no fit state to have a long, drawn-out conversation as he couldn't stand upright, let alone have a coherent conversation.

Elyian's leg crumpled under his weight and he fell heavily against Amun, who lowered him to the floor with concern etched on his face. Once Elyian was horizontal he quickly lost consciousness.

"Charlotte, what's wrong with his leg?" Amun asked as he noticed for the first time the wrappings tightly wound around the break.

"I know he was injured in battle but I didn't get a chance to look at it," she replied, more than a little shamefaced. "Let me help.”

Amun and Charlotte worked together to unwrap the huge bandage encasing his thigh. They let out a simultaneous gasp when they saw the now truly gruesome injury. One jagged end had slipped back under his flesh and the other end still protruded a good couple of inches from his thigh. The entire area was red, swollen and starting to ooze.

“That looks really bad.” Charlotte cringed away from Elyian. She wasn’t particularly squeamish, but this was a step too far. Elyian let out a deep growl in his throat as he surfaced again and she saw a sheen of sweat on his skin. It had taken on the same nasty grey color she’d seen on Jendal when he was buried in the rock slide.

Amun nodded and looked grim. “There’s nothing we can do for him, Charlotte. Fever has set in and we have no way to fix this.”

She smiled at him, her eyes dancing. “Oh, but we do, Amun. When I was on Earth after Elyian changed me, Jendal was badly injured and I cured him. With these.” She delightedly bared her little white fangs at him.

Amun shook his head and couldn’t help but smile at the childish enthusiasm of the newly turned. “Did Jendal have a fever, Charlotte? If he had, he wouldn’t be alive today.”

“He did. Enough talking,” Charlotte said. “Time for me to help your son.”

She knelt next to Elyian’s head, swiftly plunged her fangs into her wrist and watched as the healing blood dripped from her body and raced into his bloodstream.

Nothing happened. They sat and watched and waited. Elyian lay still as a statue. His skin remained pale as the ashen Carrara marble that graced the lobbies of a thousand hotels on earth. His hair lay thick, long and jet black against his cheek and she gently moved it away from his face. The world seemed to slow to a crawl and then stop as the pair waited in silent vigil over the king.

Hours passed and Charlotte grew sleepy as she sat next to the silent Amun. He hadn’t said a single word to her since he watched her try to heal Elyian. The silence between them was a chasm that seemed to be too vast to cross. Even the most minuscule thread of conversation would have been enough to start, but neither one could bring words to the surface.

Eventually Charlotte broke the barrier.

"Amun," she whispered, "why is Elyian the king? Surely you as his father should be the one ruling Ranic?"

He turned to face her, his features composed but profoundly sad. "He is king because I am not in line for the throne. Our line of succession is not by birth. When my mate, Queen Nefertia, gave birth to Elyian, she passed to him the mark of a Creck, a small birthmark in the shape of a flying creature much like an earth bird. She was the queen on Ranic and it was her mark that decided who would rule after her death.

"Alas, she lived only a short time after his birth. So Elyian became the ruler of the third house of Ranic while still a child. I guided him as best I could and acted in his stead until he reached adulthood. Then I abdicated all my duties to him.

"The members of the high court also influenced almost all of his early decisions. He's still not permitted to make laws of his own volition. That will change when he finds his mate. Then she will be his consort and they can instate whatever laws they wish as a couple. The court will enforce those laws but will no longer make any."

She furrowed her brow as she absorbed and analyzed what he said. "Hang on a minute, Amun. The mark, what does it look like again?"

He smiled at her and held back the hair on Elyian's head so the mark of the Creck was visible. Her hand shot up to the side of her own head where her mark had been until Vax carved it away.

"I used to have the mark," she said touching her now-healed head. "Havvol Vax took a hunting knife to me the night you met me. He took away my mark. Why?"

Cold hard anger crept like ice through Amun's veins. Anytime the name Vax was mentioned he had a visceral response. Vax was the madman responsible for more death and suffering than any other being on Ranic and Amun detested him.

"Easy question, Charlotte. He wants the throne. If you bear the mark you could become queen. But now that it's gone, I'm not sure what will happens next. Vax's profound immorality surely won't lie dormant for long."

"Elyian had him jailed. I don't think he'll be a problem anymore." Hope rang in her voice.

Amun was certain Vax wouldn't go quietly into the

abyss. There was no need to add to Charlotte's worries today, though.

They turned back to Elyian, but as the twin blue moons rose in the sky, the king lay still and silent, looking for all the world like death not warmed up.

A long time later, much to Amun's amazement, Elyian began to stir. With loud pops, pieces of bone slid back under the skin and the gaping, infected wound knit back together. His color improved, and slowly Elyian woke up. As soon as he was able, he said a curt goodbye and far-stepped back to his rooms at the palace.

Chapter 24

in which the flagon is half empty

AGEN TRACE WAS out walking with his new daughter, Violette. As she lay in his arms, he marveled at the perfection he had helped create. He looked adoringly at the gentle swell of her rounded cheeks and the soft downy hair that curled in fair ringlets on her head. She kicked her strong legs free of the swaddling cloth, then with a sigh of satisfaction she lifted her fat little foot, stuck it firmly in her rosebud mouth and sucked contentedly.

Agen had finished with the high court for the day so now his time was free to indulge in his joy at spending time with the new woman in his life. True, she was only a few weeks old; but already the bond between father and daughter had been forged and was unbreakable. He wandered down the broad avenues, occasionally taking a break and walking through the doorways of one of the many small stores that lined the street.

At the first, he bought a soft blanket spun from the wool of a mountain Ajil. The storekeeper wrapped it carefully in paper and tied the package closed with the silk from a chule spider before tucking it under Agen's arm.

At the next store the doting father added some dried milk and some very precious salt, an off–world, imported commodity that was as expensive on Ranic as saffron is on Earth. His next stop was the Yalon repository, where he attempted to buy a gallon of the liquid but was told there was none left on that day.

A little annoyed and more than a little hungry, Agen decided to try the other Yalon dealer in town. The second storekeeper said his supplier had brought in only half the usual order; and what's more, tomorrow he wouldn't get a delivery at all.

Puzzled by the drink's sudden scarcity, Agen took Violette to the palace nursery and dropped her off to be cared for by Esarelle and the other girls while he went off in search of his evening meal. The bar nearest the palace had a line that snaked around the building. Upon questioning the waiting people, he discovered they were in line to purchase enough Yalon to take home for their families, as they had also been unable to find enough for their needs at the stores.

Agen eventually reached the palace and went down to the kitchens. As a lifelong friend to both the Frey servants and the king, he was always welcomed in the warm, inviting space. This evening was no exception.

He was greeted at the door by the cook Tianala, who ushered him in as she clucked around him like a mother hen.

"Come now, Agen Trace." She smiled warmly, showing off her multiple dimpled chins. "Sit yourself down right here and you can tell me all the gossip while I find you some sustenance." She waddled over to the larder, rummaged on the shelves, then came back and ladled a good portion of Yalon into a large flagon and placed it on the table along with a slice of meat and some cheese.

"Tell me, Tianala, are you having trouble finding Yalon for the palace kitchen?"

"Some trouble, Master Trace, but they always seem to find an extra cask for the palace." The homely woman was now sweeping the floor and kicking dust up into the air in great clouds. "Can I get you some Yalon, Master Trace? We certainly have enough to spare here."

"Thank you, but no, Tianala. See, you've already poured some for me." He held up his still-half-full flagon for her to see.

As with so many members of her race, her short-term

memory was severely damaged. Agen was always patient with her—and all the others that had the same issue. She nodded to show she understood and then turned back to her sweeping with a determined and energetic air.

He sighed. It upset him to see the Frey who had been so compromised at birth. They were such wonderful, kind people and he was saddened by the knowledge that they'd been denied so much merely because of the circumstances of their birth. He finished his meal quickly, thanked Tianala and was about to leave when Arun entered.

"Ah, Master Agen Trace!" He beamed at Agen and then touched his shoulder in greeting. There was little formality between this Frey and the lofty high court judge. Arun had been a vital and constant presence while Agen, Elyian and Jendal were growing up. The three boys had been very close and Arun had been a constant presence, helping Amun raise not only his two sons but also their mutual friend Agen, who spent so much time in their company that he may as well have been related to them.

Agen asked Arun about the Yalon, as the supply situation was beginning to worry him. The butler told him the fields that supplied the city with most of the liquid had been stricken with a plague of sorts that caused the plants to wither and die before the fruit could be harvested. The plants growing outside most houses seemed to be healthy for now and were supplementing the supply. However, there were not nearly enough of them to cover the needs of all the hungry Raniculans in the city. The problem had struck suddenly and was getting worse by the day.

Agen thanked Tianala and Arun for the help and for the meal, collected Violette from the nursery and made his way home pondering the issue at hand. He wanted to ask Elyian his advice but nobody knew his whereabouts.

Jendal rounded the corner as he left the palace and almost ran smack into Agen. "Hey, Agen!" He patted his friend's shoulder in greeting.

Agen grinned. "Jendal, good to see you. It's been a while! Come back to my house, will you? I have a matter I'd like your opinion on. Here, take her for a while." He practically threw Violette into the arms of Jendal, who held her out at arm's length and looked askance at Agen.

"I have absolutely no idea how to hold an infant, Agen, take her back!"

Agen threw back his head and roared with laughter. "It really isn't that difficult, you dolt. Anyway, you need to get in some practice. One day, my friend, it will be you changing the dirty rags on some mewling baby."

Jendal grimaced at the thought, and thrust poor little Violette, who smelled as sweet as spring rain, back into her father's waiting arms, where she cooed and gurgled at the wonderful world into which she had been fortunate enough to have been born. "Try giving her to Elyian instead," he said, smiling at Agen.

As they walked together, Agen recounted his difficulties in obtaining Yalon. They paused outside a home and inspected the Yalon plant that grew in a large pot outside the door. It had a sturdy trunk with long, feathery leaves and stood about four feet high, covered in cauliflower-like protuberances that were dark red in color. These were the fruits of the Yalon. If the owner of the plant needed some of the liquid, he'd boil the fruit until soft then mash it down and leave for a few days in a dark room. Left to its own devices it bubbled away and smoothed out in texture and became extremely thick. It was then strained and watered down until it was of the preferred viscosity.

When drunk within a few days of harvesting, it was highly nutritious and provided Raniculans with every mineral their bodies required, including, amongst other nutrients, massive amounts of iron and large doses of protein. If left for a longer time it fermented and formed the liquor of choice on the planet, as its alcohol content was considerable. Cheap and easy to obtain, the Raniculans relied upon it heavily.

The crop had never failed; indeed, much of the time there was a complete glut and farmers ended up throwing the Yalon away or reburying it as fertilizer. Yalon's down-side was that it didn't store or travel well, so they were unable to take it to Earth as sustenance on hunting expeditions.

The two men examined it closely but didn't find anything wrong with the plant. It appeared to be in robust health and was sporting multiple florets ready to expand into full-sized fruit.

Jendal puzzled over the problem and decided they'd better take a field trip out to the flatlands to see the growing fields. Perhaps they could discover why there was a lack of supply. Jendal was head of the hunters and as such he was ultimately responsible for the food supply for Ranic.

They agreed to meet the following morning after Jendal had conferred with Elyian on the matter.

Later that day the pair of brothers were deep in discussion. It was the first time since Elyian was injured that Jendal had been able to spend any time with him, as he'd only returned that morning with Charlotte and Amun. Elyian told Jendal, with quite a bit of caution, as he suspected that his brother's reaction would be intense, that he and Charlotte would not be mated.

He saw the light in Jendal's eyes as hope sprang up, so he doused it with the news that their father had taken his place.

Jendal was furious. He paced and cursed, the air turned blue and his ranting could be heard far beyond the boundaries of Elyian's lavish quarters. There was no love lost between Jendal and his father. Somehow that bond had been broken and neither man could say exactly when or why. With so many centuries behind them the reason for the original strife was lost to the sands of time.

Amun had tried on countless occasions to spend time with his youngest son, but Jendal always managed to be in another city, or off the planet entirely, whenever Amun suggested meeting for a drink or going hunting or training together.

It took him many centuries to accept the fact that he and his younger son would never reconcile, but in the end Amun gave up. It hurt him too much to keep being rejected by the son he loved so much. It was the main reason Amun had decided to have his summer quarters in such a remote area of the planet. His soul was at peace there and he had nature to keep him company on the countless long nights he spent alone in his circle of trees.

Elyian tried to explain to Jendal that he was resigned to what had transpired but Jendal would have none of it.

"Where is he now, and where is Charlotte?" he demanded of his brother. Elyian didn't know and frankly didn't particularly want to know. He was still healing, both physically and emotionally, from the events of the past week.

Jendal left the palace with his blood still at boiling point and followed his sixth sense, which told him Amun was at his winter house in the canal area. The canal system was an immense grid of waterways that spread out over the southernmost part of the city. It was here that the wealthiest and most influential of Ranic's citizens had their homes. The winter palace had been Amun's city home ever since Elyian had taken over as monarch, and it was to that palace that Jendal made his way. He wasn't quite sure what he would say to Amun but he guessed it would come to him by the time he got there.

Chapter 25

in which humans debate

INSIDE THE OVAL Office a dozen men and women, each the head of some government agency, stood in a semi-circle around the president's desk. Once again they watched the video of the pale-faced man with the long white fangs, and they held their collective breath as they watched the slowed-down video and saw him rise silently and majestically up the staircase at the little house in Sonoma County.

The house had been examined so thoroughly that there wasn't one square inch that hadn't been scraped, dusted or photographed. Several things seemed questionable about the place.

A recent grave at the rear of the house had been exhumed, and revealed the remains of a dog with a broken neck. Dogs don't often die that way, so the skeleton was taken away to the Smithsonian for further analysis.

The garage was the most revealing. A large chest freezer contained bag after bag of human blood of every type. They all bore labels that connected them with a blood bank in San Francisco that had reported the theft of hundreds of units.

The president rose from behind his desk and grimly

turned to address the men and women standing before him. With a solemn and concerned face he said, "I don't need to emphasis to everyone assembled in this room the importance of this discovery.

"For thousands of years, there have been stories of a race of beings known as Vampires that drink the blood of humans. The folk lore goes back to well before the written word was even invented. So we can't blame the long-since deceased Victorian writer Bram Stoker for the invention of Vampires. Everyone thought it was just that: a story about a mythical creature.

"Now we must question everything we once believed to be fantasy. This single piece of evidence could mean the end of everything humankind holds dear.

"Conversely, it could be a new beginning. None of us knows what this really means. If there are truly Vampires walking among us, could there also be ghosts or werewolves? We don't know; but there is one thing of which we can be absolutely certain.

"This being," he pointed at the paused image of Elyian baring his fangs at the camera, "is not of this world. We cannot begin to imagine what else he can do. He can move his body at such great speed that even when we slow the film down as much as possible, he's a blur.

"He defies everything we know of physics—and that's before we address the issue of how a fully grown male of about six and a half feet can ascend a flight of stairs without moving his legs.

"Gentlemen, we must decide how to continue from here. We will confer here for an indeterminate time. These meetings, it goes without saying, are so confidential that your cell phones and other items will be removed immediately."

At this, four heavily armed guards entered the office and took away every device that bleeped, rang or vibrated. They confiscated everyone's wristwatches, car keys and every piece of identification.

The president was taking no chances. He needed the think tank kept in total seclusion, with no possibility of any of them leaving the White House.

Not one of them left the building for the next week, and when they finally emerged, blinking in the sunlight, it was to a world that was about to be changed forever.

Chapter 26

in which the snow falls

AMUN'S WINTER PALACE was a study in elegant beauty. Multiple massive, hollow obelisks, each the size of a large house and made of pale grey granite, rose majestically around the central building. Massive shining orbs, each crafted of a different material, topped the pillars. There were orbs of gold, silver and Leverium2, some of marble and others crafted of the finest wood available. Most astounding was the one crafted of clearest crystal that shone and sparkled in the moonlight, reflecting the stars and the twin moons on its shimmering surface.

Summer was at its tail end on Ranic. There were no intermediate seasons; it was either summer or winter. The weather changed almost overnight so the populous had to be well-prepared for the change. During Elyian's recovery, the sun put in her final hurrah and on this night the chill in the air was palpable.

Amun was guiding Charlotte through his home, showing her how his mate, Elyian's mother, had decorated the palace to her taste and not his. Charlotte was entranced with it. The woman had obviously been blessed with exquisite taste—

and the nearly limitless funds needed to bring her vision to fruition. He led her through room after room that took her breath away.

The entire palace was built around a central courtyard. A large lake in the center reflected both the moons above and the orbs that encircled the courtyard high above on the tip of each obelisk. Several trees with feathery leaves in a silvery hue dripped their arching branches into the cool water.

Covered walkways encircled the courtyard lake and bridges with graceful flying buttresses crisscrossed overhead, providing passage from one side of the palace to the other, with astounding views down to the lake below.

Each obelisk had a different purpose. One housed the kitchen and larders and the quarters of the kitchen Frey. The Golden tower held a library and the offices of both Amun and his butler. The Crystal tower in the center of the lake was Amun's private quarters, accessed by a high, arched bridge. Only one Frey housekeeper, his butler, and the three boys, Elyian, Jendal and their friend Agen, had ever been inside. Amun was maniacal about his privacy.

Charlotte was becoming more agitated with every passing minute. He'd shown her almost every inch of the palace, but had yet to crack the door to his rooms. She'd seen the inside of what seemed like every closet and bedroom and had even admired his collection of rare local birds that were housed in an extraordinary aviary of such a size that they were flying freely around within its boundaries.

When the sun dipped down in the evening sky and he was still playing tour guide, she was beside herself. The tension between them rippled and stretched the threads between them.

He had yet to really talk to her about what would happen next, now that Elyian had stepped out of the picture. As they stood on a bridge overlooking the garden, she bit her lip and a tiny bead of blood appeared.

She heard the low rumbling growl that welled up from deep in Amun's throat, then she saw his eyes. Those lovely emerald eyes had changed color and a circle of shimmering intense violet now rimmed the green. They were stunningly beautiful pools of color that held her captive in their gaze.

He grasped her face and drew his tongue over the bead of blood that sat like a red pearl on her lower lip. That very first taste of her was like nectar on his tongue; her blood was sweet as honey with the merest suggestion of spice. He would vividly remember that initial taste for the remainder of his long, long life.

Amun groaned. "More, oh gods, I want more!"

Charlotte's knees buckled at his words and she was grateful to feel his hand press against the small of her back, giving her support. But the whole interlude was tinged with unspoken guilt over Elyian. Neither one had been able to banish the feeling. Charlotte shook her head, and suddenly the words she'd been holding back all day flooded from her mouth in a verbal torrent of angst.

"I can't do this, Amun, it's not right. I look at you and you're so gorgeous I can hardly breath; but then I remember that you're Elyian's father and I really can't think straight. It's just plain weird. You look like you're his brother and a part of me isn't able to accept that. You're as ancient as the hills, yet you look like a Greek god. If I was to paint the perfect specimen of a man, I would paint you.

"I don't know how I can live on Earth now, because I'm not just a human any more, but I do know that I've got to try. This isn't my life, Amun! The city of Ranic is a bizarre fantasy world that I somehow stumbled into, no thanks to your freaking son. I'm still not totally convinced you want me, Amun. I think you're as intrigued by the idea of me as I am with you, but it would be smart to allow some time to pass so we can look at this with some perspective, please?

"So, that being said, I really need to go back to Earth. I want my old life back for now. I know it's stupid, but I miss coffee so much I could scream every time I open my eyes in the morning and all I can smell is warm Yalon!" Her emotions were so raw and unbridled that as she finished talking her fangs dropped, and she swiped at her face in a useless attempt to dry the tears that were falling like a river.

Amun looked so devastated she almost caved, almost kissed that full mouth that was so temptingly close to hers. Instead she lowered her lashes and turned her face away from him and into the wind, which lifted her hair and whipped it from side to side.

He swept one gentle hand over her forehead and encircled her hair behind her neck, effectively holding her captive. Then with a movement so decisive and swift she couldn't track it, he held his other wrist up to her mouth and dragged it across her fangs.

The razor-sharp edges caught his flesh, slicing a neat, straight incision that welled with his blood. If her resolve hadn't fled at the moment he grasped her hair, Charlotte would have moved away. As it was, she was putty in his hands. His blood dripped between her lips and her head exploded with sensation as the first taste of his warm, rich blood hit her tongue.

It was instantaneous, a connection so vital and strong they both felt it wrap its cords around them and pull them together in an infrangible grip. They'd shared their blood and the bond that had been made was now as unbreakable as the link between the sun and the moons.

Her resolve fled with the wind and as the first pristine snowflake fell on her icy skin she knew leaving him would be the hardest thing that she'd ever done; but leave she must. It was only a matter of when.

Amun watched the changing emotions wash over her and was about to haul her up to his quarters and show her how much he wanted her, but his visceral response to her was delayed. A large and extremely heavy decorative urn hit his head a glancing blow, sending shards of pottery flying through the frigid night.

As Amun hit the ground he saw the gleaming dagger-like fangs and hulking body of his younger son leaning over him.

"You complete bastard!" Jendal cursed through his bared teeth. The mouth that was normally so quick to smile now curled in a vicious snarl. "You just can't let Elyian have some happiness in his life, can you? No, you took his woman away, right from under his damn nose while he was injured and couldn't fight to keep her!"

Amun's speed defied description. He was off the ground and flying over the edge of the bridge with Jendal in his clutches before Charlotte was able to register what the interloper had said. The two men hit the lake still grasping at each other. They vanished into its depths as Charlotte looked on with her mouth hanging open.

She understood now that this went far beyond a case of male posturing, but that did nothing to ease her discomfort at the situation in which they all found themselves. She grasped the edge of the bridge parapet so hard the granite edge crumbled to dust in her hands.

Everything was her fault. She shook inside with the certain knowledge that if it hadn't been for her, Amun and his sons would not be in this awful place where bitterness and hate seemed to eclipse all else.

Charlotte leaned over the edge, scanning the water that shimmered with the reflected moonlight. As her eyes adjusted she was able to see deep into the water. At the very bottom, two figures moved and she presumed they were still fighting.

Then Amun tilted his head skyward and ascended from the depths, hurtling straight up into the night sky with his arms encircling his son. She saw Amun raise a dripping clenched fist and drive it straight into Jendal's gut; and then in horror she watched him grasp his massive son around the head and twist.

Charlotte gasped as Jendal fell from the sky and dropped like a stone into the lake, his arms and legs flailing loosely like a broken bird around his supine body. Amun stayed in place, hovering over the lake. He raised his head to the stars above and released a gut–wrenching, anguished cry that carried through the chill air and up into the universe above. He stayed there for a several moments, then slowly descended back into the inky depths of the lake.

Charlotte watched the entire thing play out as rivulets of tears streaked her snow-covered face. Amun reappeared carrying the limp body of Jendal in his arms. He strode across the courtyard dripping water and carefully lowered his son onto a stone bench. Snowflakes fell on Jendal's face and formed little drifts in the shelter of his hulking form. Charlotte swung her legs over the edge of the bridge and jumped from the huge height down to Amun's side, landing with all the innate grace that Vampires have in spades.

Amun looked aghast as he stood staring at Jendal's still body, but it was nothing compared to what Charlotte felt. Her entire body was numb with shock. Jendal's body reminded her of Cam's dog Atlas, that had drowned back when she was still human and this bizarre world was something she read about in novels. Jendal's head was twisted round at an entirely unthinkable angle.

"Charlotte, give him your blood. If you're quick he may live through this," Amun pleaded with her.

"He's dead already," she yelled. "You killed him, you killed dear, sweet Jendal! He's your son, how could you do this?"

Amun took her by her shoulders and gave her a gentle shake. "Charlotte, you're wasting time. He has maybe ten more minutes before the lack of oxygen will cause brain damage. Please, hurry. I'll explain why I broke his neck later. Right now you need to heal him."

She looked at him askance. The man was deranged, but she willingly tore her wrist open and forced as much of her life-giving blood into Jendal's mouth as she could, then stroked his throat to get it down and into his body.

The shock of her blood in his system was instantaneous, and his death was so recent that it had immediate effect. His thick neck gave an almighty crack as it reinstated itself into the correct position.

Jendal gave a deep groan then sighed and opened his eyes, blinking away the snow that had settled on his lids. His gaze met the mess that was Charlotte, her face a picture of devastation that transformed to pure joy when she saw him look up at her.

His voice was a little croaky when he spoke. "Apparently you've fixed me again. Thank you, Charlotte. You always seem to be around when I need you. Do me a favor, though, and don't do it again just to make him feel better."

Jendal turned his face away from hers and fixed a glare on his father. "As for you, Father, words fail me." He spat the words out and then, with a look that could turn water into ice, he rose from the bench, wiggled his head a little from side to side as if to settle it more firmly on his broad shoulders, and strode out of the courtyard without a backward glance.

Charlotte touched Amun's arm to redirect his gaze to her. "Amun, you have to tell me why, why did you resort to breaking your son's neck? I know there's animosity between you, but that was going entirely too far. No wonder the stories about Vampires always portray them as vicious, bloodthirsty, inhuman beings. Vlad the Impaler probably did impale, every chance he got!"

"I wanted to teach him a lesson he wouldn't forget in a hurry," Amun replied, "but I also had another motive. I needed one more piece of evidence to take to the Ranic High Court. My winter palace has Leverium2 monitors roaming the grounds constantly. They record everything that happens within the public spaces for security reasons.

"Now we can show them you have this ability and it is indisputable. It was vital to show that your blood is what is different about you." He smiled his seductive smile. "There are many other things about you that are also very special,

I'm sure." He kissed her reverently and when he spoke again his voice was roughened by desire. "I have a suggestion. Let's curtail the talking so I can discover all your hidden secrets."

Every neuron in her brain was firing and screaming at her, willing her to reply, *Yes, take me now. I want to feel your gorgeous naked body next to mine and your lips kissing me in places that will make my toes curl.* She was watching Amun intently as the thoughts rattled around inside her, so she clearly saw the corner of his mouth twitching, as if he was suppressing a laugh.

That's strange. I don't remember saying anything particularly comical.

"I suppose I should be honest with you." Amun grinned at her. "I can hear everything that goes on in that imaginative head of yours. I have a glorious image of your painted toenails curling in as I lick you in places that I have yet to explore."

Her jaw fell open and he went on. "Yes, I admit, the fiction authors of Earth are correct in some respects. A few of us do use our ability to mind read when we wish to, and yours is fascinating place in which to wander. I love your thought patterns. Sometimes they're random, creative and sexy as hell, and other times you show a remarkable clarity of vision with wonderful empathy for the beings around you."

"You ass!" Charlotte was absolutely furious. "How dare you invade my privacy like that? Oh my God, were Elyian and Jendal reading my mind, too? That's just too gross for words. Oh, when I think about them running around in my head while I was with them! It's just sick, but now I know why Elyian drives me crazy. He got it all from you!"

Amun shook his head vehemently. "No, ease up, Charlotte, they haven't read any of your thoughts. There are only a handful of the original Raniculan Vampires left and we're the only ones that can read minds. The rest, my sons included, cannot do that. Our entire race has eyesight many times more acute than a bird of prey. We can, as you know, fly, levitate and far–step. Our hearing is flawless and we're able to heal ourselves to a large degree. We're also many times stronger than humans, although you as a hybrid human come close to our strength.

"However, I'm an entirely different being than most Raniculans. There is one line of our species of which I am the youngest progeny. We were created with the ability to read minds as clearly as if the words had been spoken."

Amun stopped talking as Charlotte's hand flew up to his face with the intent to slap him. He grabbed her hand long before it contacted with his cheek. "Why did you do that?" He seemed honestly confused and startled by her anger at him.

"Why do you think? You jerk. How dare you invade my mind and go exploring inside it at your heart's content! Do you really have no idea how utterly wrong that is?" Charlotte had been delivered the news that swung the pendulum firmly away from Ranic and toward home. "I'm going to see Elyian," she said, her chin quivering as she fought back the new influx of tears that threatened to fall. "He can take me home."

Amun knew her mind was made up though he was trying not to read her; her emotions were flooding the information to him in a tidal wave of pain. He tried again.

"Charlotte, please listen to me. I'm truly sorry. It's such a natural thing for me to do that I rarely even think about it anymore. If you stay I promise I won't ever read you again. Please, don't go." Amun had never begged a woman to stay with him, not once in his nearly eternal life.

But Charlotte was different. The cord that bound them together was pulled tight but wouldn't snap, and every cell in his body was straining in her direction. She stood motionless in the moonlight. The tears she'd been fighting to keep under control now spilled in meandering rivers down her pale, chilled skin. Amun took her face in his hands and gently rubbed the pad of his thumb over her generous mouth. Salty tears had wet her lips and he brushed the moisture away.

"I'll take you back," he said, his voice so quiet she almost missed it. "Is there anything you need to take?"

Her hand went to the ankh hanging on her neck out of sight beneath her clothing. "No. I just need home."

Amun smiled, but the smile didn't reach his eyes which held a world of sadness in them as he drank her in. "Very well, Charlotte, where would you like to be taken on Earth?"

Charlotte thought for a second and realized that the beach house in Sonoma County was the perfect place to lick her wounds and heal from the seemingly constant trauma and heartache that accompanied her whenever she was around the men of Ranic.

"Can you take me to Elyian's place in Sonoma?" she asked him. "Or no, better not; he told me it was mine to use whenever I wanted, but that's probably changed since we're not together anymore." Her brows furrowed while she worked out where she could go.

"If I know my son, and I do know him well, he would want you to keep it. I will speak to him about it, so don't worry."

She moved toward him and his arms closed around her as he tried to ease the hurt they both felt. "Charlotte," the word came out as a plea and a groan.

"No, Amun, I can't do this anymore. I wish I could. Believe me when I say a huge part of me is going to tear apart when I'm there but I have no real choice in this. Your world is so strange to me. Everything is different from the world in which I grew up. The guilt I feel over Elyian and the impact my being here has had on your relationships with your sons is not healthy. I crave you, Amun, but I can't be with you here. I'm sorry. I believe you when you say you wouldn't invade my mind anymore but there are too many other issues I can't ignore. Maybe one day we can be together, and I pray that day will come. However, that day's not today. Please, I beg you, just take me home, Amun."

He pressed her closer so she couldn't see the torture on his face, and as his soul was rent in two he far-stepped them both to Earth. All that was left at the winter palace to show that she was ever there were her footprints in the snow.

Chapter 27

in which the Frey is frozen

Y ET AGAIN, JENDAL and Elyian were drunk as skunks. The pair lay sprawled out on the floor of Elyian's room. An empty cask of fermented Yalon lay on its side, dripping the last few red drops out onto the precious Aubusson rugs Elyian had carried back from Earth sixty years ago. They'd just finished the last of the drink that had been secreted away in the palace larder by the ever-thoughtful Tianala.

Their conversation had drifted away from state matters and meandered back to Elyian's favorite subject. Charlotte.

He was still convinced she was going to be of vital importance to Ranic, and he'd at last convinced Jendal of the fact that he was at peace with his decision to end their relationship and give his blessing to Amun to pursue her instead.

He had yet to talk Jendal into forgiving Amun for breaking his neck. That might take another hundred years or so, which was only to be expected.

"Sooo, Jendal," Elyian slurred. "I need you to come to Earth. Got to get some blod, uh, blood and bring it back here. With almost no Yalon we're going to need a good supply and soon. You coming?"

"Of course," Jendal slurred back. "When? I have some papers to sign first thing in the morning. Vax is being deported so I'll need to do that first, and then we can go."

They agreed on a place to meet and said their goodnights. Elyian was twitchy—booze tended to do that to him—so after Jendal left he decided to take a walk. He far-stepped to the very edge of town and staggered out onto the plain, heading toward the Shoulen Range. He hardly noticed as his legs ate up the miles disappearing under his long stride.

On the other side of the city Havvol Vax rattled the Leverium2 manacles that bound him to the podium. The High Court had just decided on his guilt and it was time for the sentence to be issued. Agen Trace faced him and looked him straight in the eye as he spoke with determination and utter conviction.

"Havvol Vax, you have been found guilty under Ranic law of multiple grievous crimes against both the general populous of this planet and the human companion of His Majesty Elyian Trainor of the third house of Ranic. We, the members of the High Court of Ranic, hereby strip you of all your titles and your position on this court. You are sentenced to spend all the remaining years of your life off world. The planet chosen for your imprisonment is the Blue Planet, known as Earth.

"You will be taken from here to a holding cell. You will then be escorted to a Ranic colony on Earth. How you choose to live out your remaining years there is of your own choosing, with this caveat: should you cause a human to lose their life by your hand or by accidental happening, you will forfeit your own. Your life will also be summarily ended if you leave the confines of Earth. Your movements will be tracked and recorded by orbs. You have the right to speak one sentence before you are removed. Speak now."

Vax's face reddened in frustration and anger as he spoke. "You idiots, I hold the key to the Greyling Frey."

They could have heard a pin drop in the court. They were all too well aware of the problems the Frey had. But the law was the law, and the Raniculans were nothing if not an obstinate bunch. They would have considered their authority to have been dealt a devastating blow if they'd allowed someone to circumvent that law. One sentence was all that was allowed, and one sentence was all Vax got before he was summarily dismissed and led away in chains.

Agen Trace dismissed the court and watched Vax taken under heavy guard to the holding cell. A shiver crawled up his spine.

He left the building deep in thought. It was a frigid evening so he wrapped his coat tighter around his body and leaned into the wind as he made his way home.

To his surprise Esarelle sat bundled up on the stone steps at the entrance to his house. She smiled coyly and stood to greet him. Cradled in her arms was Violette, who was gurgling away, obviously cozy and quite at home in Esarelle's care.

"Hello, Agen," she said in her lovely lilting voice. "I knew you were on your way home so I thought I would save you the trouble of having to go to the palace nursery to pick up Violette. She has been delightful today, as always." Esarelle looked down at the baby and her face softened.

Agen thanked her and was happy she agreed to stay for a late supper. He got lonely, for though he had the baby with him, it wasn't the same as having another adult for company. And he had to admit that Esarelle was wonderful company. They talked late into the night and he was sorry when she at last decided it was time to leave.

On the plains below the Shoulen Mountains a lone Mano trudged wearily through the drifting snow in the direction of the city. On his back rode a female Frey. She was perched on a saddle that was elevated over the spiny back of the beast.

Laila was young, a mere hundred years, and very strong. She had spent her entire life working the fields with her family. Slung on each side of her long legs were two large panniers filled with harvested Yalon, the last ones from their fields. Most of the crop had withered and died while still hanging on the trunks that bore them. Her family relied on the sale of the crop for a good portion of their income and now they were seriously worried.

As farmers they were well used to the vagaries of the Ranic weather. They hadn't seen any changes in the normal temperature patterns, so they were at a loss to explain the devastation that had befallen not just their crop but all the fields for hundreds of miles around. Their friends and neighbors were holding meetings in their barns, trying to find a solution to the problem, but so far nothing had been found.

After much discussion it was decided to send Laila to Ranic, so that she might confer with the court on this matter. So it was that she found herself half-freezing to death in the middle of the night, on the back of a stinking animal. She would have much preferred to be sitting curled up by the fire with her nose buried in a good book.

Laila had been spared the injury at birth that turned so many of their race into Greylings. Her mind was sharp as a whip. She'd read every book available in her village and yearned for more.

She had from an early age wanted to become a healer, but her family insisted on her hunting skills being honed instead. They sent her to the home of a master hunter to further her knowledge, and after half a century under his expert tutelage, she was now as deadly as any man in her village.

Her unusually sharp mind and quick wit had made her the envy of many people. The men were impressed by her dazzling skill on the hunt and the women envied her looks.

She had the grace of a gazelle and a head crowned with a mass of platinum waves, so long that she wore her hair braided to keep it under control. Now thick strands of that braid were coming undone in the ceaseless howling blizzard that had come out of nowhere. It whipped around her legs and froze the breath as it left her body.

She was Frey and the Frey had to breathe, unlike the Raniculans. They also had a beating heart and a single lung that worked efficiently in the summer but struggled in the cold of winter. They could stay outside for a few hours without too many issues, but any longer than that and their breathing became very labored. A Frey would die from asphyxiation if left in the cold for too long.

The freezing temperatures had managed to sober Elyian up. He strode along the riverbank looking at the ice forming on the surface. Soon it would be a frozen road several feet thick and critical as a means to travel during the interminably long, cold winter. In icy conditions the Raniculans used sleds pulled by smaller pack animals than the Manos, since the ice wasn't strong enough to support the great weight of those beasts.

That enabled them to transport large amounts of

merchandise and supplies to and from the cities scattered around this part of the planet. For half the year it was the main form of transport; then every summer when the thaw came, they would revert to using barges to navigate the waterways.

It began to snow heavily and soon the blizzard was in full force, not that it troubled Elyian one jot. His Vampiric body didn't feel the cold.

His preternaturally acute eyesight picked out the form of a Mano which was uncharacteristically sitting on the ground a mile away. The harness and panniers it was sporting told him instantly that it was a domesticated one. Lacking the energy to far-step, he ran the remaining distance after seeing a small form slumped over its neck.

The handler was swaddled in so much clothing he didn't know if it was male or female until the wind changed direction and blew her unmistakably female scent at him.

Elyian climbed onto the Mano's back after breaking a vial of calming herbs under the creature's nose. The vials were always stored in small wooden containers that the animals' wranglers attached to the harnesses of the Manos. The herbs didn't harm them in any way, but were very useful in dampening down their more lethal tendencies.

As Elyian pulled himself up next to her he thought she was dead. Her face was blue as the moons and the hood that covered her hair was stiff with ice and snow. She didn't appear to be breathing. Not a good sign in a Frey. With deft fingers he moved her neck covering away and felt for a pulse. There it was, weak and fluttering but definitely beating under his fingertips.

A Mano would refuse to move without a driver. Sensing she was no longer in control it had simply sat down to take a nap. Elyian gathered the reins and pulled on them until the Mano woke up and lumbered to its feet. As it moved its long body from side to side it nearly unseated Elyian, who also had to tighten his grip on the female so she wouldn't fall. After shaking itself awake it started to move with its undulating sideways gait, lurching them ever closer to Ranic.

At first she thought it was a dream. She was on a boat out on the river and the motion of the water rocked her to and fro. She felt warm, almost too warm. As her body thawed next to Elyian's heat she began to drift back up to the surface.

The realization that she was now awake and on the

back of the Mano didn't cause her any concern, until she felt someone behind her and a vice-like grip around her waist. She sat upright so fast the back of her head connected with Elyian's chest.

"Ahh," he said, "you're awake at last. I was starting to think you'd died. Can I presume that you were on your way to Ranic to sell the Yalon you have here?"

Laila tried to turn around so she could see her rescuer. She'd thought she was done for when her single lung started to seize. Knowing she was nowhere near close enough to Ranic, it was with disgust in her lack of strength that she'd driven herself on until her body gave out. She was delighted to find death hadn't claimed her, but instead she was warm and able to breathe again.

"How did you find me, with the blizzard so bad?" she asked the faceless man who sat so intimately close to her back.

The voice that came back was deep, silky smooth and cultured, something she rarely came across in the villages and towns where she lived. Every word seemed to be delivered with a great deal of forethought.

"I was out enjoying a quiet stroll by the river and I happened to spot your Mano in the distance. Seeing you draped over his back, it occurred to me that you may require some assistance. So here I am."

She snorted. "Nobody in their right mind strolls anywhere in this weather, so that makes you a foolish man of the first degree. Nonetheless, I thank you, sir, for coming to my aid. I surely would have perished out here if you had not found me. My name is Laila. I'm from the village of Danko on the far edge of the plain and yes, you are correct. I'm traveling to Ranic to seek consultation with the high court. How close are we to the city? I've lost track, I'm afraid."

"Not that far, really," Elyian replied. "We'll get there in just a short while." He quite enjoyed the feel of her strong, young body next to his and was inclined to wish the journey would take longer. Although fewer garments would make the entire experience even better.

The brief glance he'd had of her face had shown him she was quite stunning to look at, though it was a little difficult to get the full effect with her hood up and the light covering of snow masking much of her face.

"Hmm," she murmured, her voice getting quiet again.

Sleep seemed to be of the utmost importance and she felt her eyelids getting heavy as the Mano continued its swaying walk towards the city.

Elyian pulled the hood on her cape further over her face, protecting it from the biting wind and driving snow, and turned her inward so that she snuggled comfortably against his chest.

At the palace he had her installed at the guest quarters and visited her there the following day.

She told him of her concerns with the failing crops. It was obvious to Elyian that she was highly intelligent and showed remarkable insight when it came to plant life, so he decided she should accompany Jendal and himself to Earth to seek a cure.

She lit up like a firefly when he mentioned it. To her as a lowly Frey, the chance to travel was a rare and wonderful thing; and to be given the opportunity to leave the planet was unheard of in her circles. The three of them left together, with Laila in the firm embrace of her king as they dematerialized on the little planet in the center of the universe and appeared again in a whirl of cosmic energy at Elyian's beach house on Earth.

Chapter 28

in which the search begins

IT WAS THE dead of night in early fall in Northern California. The heat of the day was tempered by the daily fog that rolled mercilessly in from the Pacific Ocean every afternoon and pulled back each morning to reveal the clear blue skies that were a constant from May through November. Tonight, however, was one of those rare nights when the fog had taken a vacation and stayed just offshore, barely teasing the cliffs with its cold, wet fingers.

The house at the beach was lit up, every light in every window blazing into the night as their bodies reassembled and Amun and Charlotte appeared together, at the front of Elyian's charming beach cottage.

"Someone's here!" Charlotte said, shaking her head to clear her body of the unsettling residual effects of far-stepping. They cautiously walked the remaining few steps up to the front door. With their preternatural hearing they could easily hear the conversation inside. A female's husky, warm voice drifted out to them, shortly followed by the familiar silky, cultured voice of Elyian.

"Yes, of course," she purred, "I'll go with you tomorrow.

For now, can you please explain what this brown grainy stuff is and why you find it compulsory to stick your nose in the bag?"

They heard Elyian laugh and reply, "It's called coffee, and no, you don't eat it. Give me the bag and I'll show you how to make it." She giggled and then they heard the couple move to the back of the property where the kitchen was located.

Charlotte knocked on the door and then with Amun she walked in to a scene of earthly domesticity. Elyian was coming back out of the kitchen, wearing not a lot. Charlotte's eyes widened at the sight of her newly estranged lover in nothing but a pair of ripped and well-faded blue jeans with the button open, the waist slung low on his hips and his bare feet padding forward on the wooden floor. Behind him looking quizzically at them, with her hands cupped around an open bag of coffee beans, was an unknown Frey female.

Charlotte's gaze raked her from the top of her blonde head and stunning face, down to her torso encased in a tight sweater that did nothing to hide her voluptuous curves, and on to her slender, leather-clad legs that ended in a pair of well–worn, sturdy, combat boots. Charlotte wasn't jealous, exactly, but she was taken aback.

That certainly didn't take him long.

It took Elyian no time to asses her reaction to him, causing him to grin in pleasure. He didn't mind one jot that she was more than a little discomfited by his state of near undress. When he saw how she looked at Laila he was even more delighted. He did have the good grace, however, to cover it with a smile and an easy greeting to them both.

"Sire." He nodded a greeting to Amun and then turned to Charlotte. "Charlotte. What brings you both here?"

Charlotte did a bit of spluttering and her mind went inexplicably blank. Luckily, Amun filled the silence, explaining that they didn't know that Elyian would be there. He told Elyian in private a little later how Charlotte wasn't sure she could use the cottage now, and gave him the reasons she'd insisted on returning to Earth. Elyian was sympathetic to his father's feelings and listened gravely as he poured his heart out.

His description of the fight that ended in the watery depths of his lake had Elyian grinning all over again. "You and Jendal really need to get this matter resolved. It's time to end all this fighting. Maybe as king I should command it?"

His father arched one reproving eyebrow and Elyian backed down.

"I'm pleased you're here; it will be most helpful," he told his father. "Jendal is staying in the city tonight. He's trying to track down some large sources of stored blood to take back to Ranic. Maybe it'll help until we can find a solution to the Yalon problem."

The two men stayed outside talking it over. They did a fair bit of skirting around the Charlotte issue. Later they returned inside to find Charlotte and Laila getting acquainted over steaming mugs of fragrant lattes. The two women were laughing so hard one would have thought they'd been friends for decades.

"Hey, guys. Hope you haven't been talking about me out there," Charlotte said ruefully. She knew they had, as a few parts of their conversation had drifted in over her own chatting with Laila.

The evening passed amicably though the tension between Amun and Charlotte was palpable. It didn't get any better as the night drew on and dawn broke over the hills to the east. She could hardly bear to look at him, it caused such pain to ratchet through her.

Amun didn't fare any better. He fought to keep control of his emotions, as he hadn't experienced feelings like this since losing Nefertia hundreds of years previously. When Charlotte left the room for a few minutes, he sucked in air, hoping the act of breathing might help. When she returned he almost lost control. Another half hour passed and just when he thought he couldn't take being in the same room as her for another second, she stood up again.

"It's time for me to go. I ordered a ride a while ago and it'll be here soon. Thank you for being so hospitable, Elyian; and Laila, it was a real pleasure to meet you. I hope you take the time to discover all the delights that my home world has to offer. Don't forget to check out the Valley of the Moon. It's not that far from here, and the views at this time of the year are stunning, with the vineyards in their riotous fall colors."

Elyian rose and hugged Charlotte close to him. He held his lips to her ear and whispered low so the other two couldn't possibly hear. "I truly believe my father has fallen in love with you, Charlotte. Please don't give up on him."

Then he straightened and pressed a key and a piece of paper into her hand. "This is the key and directions to my new house at Lake Tahoe. Use it as long as you need."

With watery eyes Charlotte planted a very warm but platonic kiss on Elyian's cheek, ignoring the possessive growl that emanated from Amun. She thanked Elyian and turned to retrieve the large canvas bag that held her worldly possessions. It was already in Amun's arms and he was striding out of the door with it clutched to him like it was a life raft that could prevent his drowning. She raced to catch up with him.

"Amun, please give me my bag. And go back inside. This is going to be hard enough without you being here to wave goodbye." He held the bag even tighter, his knuckles going white, and kept walking down the pathway toward the beach as if he hadn't heard her. She knew he had.

"Amun, stop!" He stopped on a dime. Undulating waves of energy pulsed off him, arcing with flashes of bright blue from his body down to the ground. When she caught up with him she could see he was shaking all over.

"Amun," she whispered, the word caressing him, soothing his soul if only for an instant. "This is so hard for me. I feel our connection and it's unbreakable, but I'm not ready. I am so, so very sorry, but I have to go."

He handed her the bag, his face showing a man destroyed. His lovely eyes were pools of pain and lines of stress showed around his mouth. A muscle ticked persistently in his jaw and he ground out his last words to her before he turned on his heel and vanished into the stars above. "Until we meet again, my love."

At the cottage Elyian frowned. He hated conflict and he felt his fathers' pain keenly.

Amun returned to the beach house silent and outwardly composed the following morning. It was Amun who took the wheel of the Hummer Elyian had rented the day before as they flew down Highway 101 to San Francisco. His mind spit out pain-fueled venom.

Speed limit be damned. Do these stupid humans really think I'm going to obey any of their stupid damn traffic laws? He pushed the Hummer to its limits, swerving in and out of the traffic easily and competently.

Elyian and Laila were in the back making out like high schoolers on their way to prom, which was doing nothing to improve Amun's foul temper. His carefully wrought outward composure nearly fled entirely when, in the rear view mirror, he saw Laila thread her fingers through Elyian's hair and pull him in toward her for a kiss. Eventually he calmed down and managed to get them safely across the Golden Gate Bridge.

The city was still in shambles after the earthquake but at least the streets were cleared, bridges were functioning and the electricity was now fully restored. Elyian's financial advisor had automatically arranged for huge crews of builders to work around the clock, putting the penthouse back in order. As they pulled into the underground garage they were met by the last of the men leaving the site.

During the journey down the freeway, Laila had been in awe of everything she saw whenever Elyian released her from his embrace long enough to look out the windows. So far she liked Earth. What she'd seen was beautiful. The city, however, was entirely different. It was far noisier and a lot dirtier than her home town and the smells were particularly offensive to her overly sensitive nose.

As for the elevator, that thing terrified her. She clung to Elyian as the gears engaged and her eyes widened in horror as they left the confines of the garage in the rapidly ascending metal box. It suddenly shot out of the dark and into a glass enclosure that ran the entire height of the building. Spread out below them was the city of San Francisco with its masses of humanity running around like little ants busy rebuilding their anthills. She squeezed her eyes shut and prayed it would be over soon.

Jendal was already there. He squeezed the last drop of blood out of the bag he held and let it drip onto his tongue. *Not bad*, he thought, though he preferred O negative blood. The elevator doors opened and he looked appreciatively at the beautiful Frey female clinging to his brother as if her life depended on it.

The four of them sat in the living room all day, trying to decide how best to gather and store all the blood they needed. The more they talked the more implausible the whole idea seemed. By evening they all sat with glum faces as the realization hit home that not only was there no practical way of getting the many hundreds of thousands of units of blood needed to supply Ranic, but the logistical nightmare of transporting it all to the planet was impossible.

With heavy hearts they abandoned that idea and moved on to the issue of the Yalon. Amun knew after his many trips to Earth that some of the greatest minds in the world were to be found at Stanford University. They decided to search there for the answer as to what could be causing the plants to die on Ranic.

It took them a couple of weeks to find just the right person, but when they spoke to him, they knew he was the one who could help. What they did was against Ranic law and it tore at Elyian's conscience, but when the need arose he was quite capable of making a hard choice if it would save his people. They wouldn't die without Yalon but they would get malnourished and very cranky. So on a cold winter's night in the middle of a redwood forest, Amun, Laila, and Jendal watched dispassionately as their ruler sank his fangs into a professor's neck and stopped his heart.

Chapter 29

in which another hybrid is created

Hᴇ ᴡᴀꜱ ʟʏɪɴɢ on a bed, that much he knew. Nothing else made much sense. He couldn't talk; his tongue felt thick and sore and his gums hurt. The sounds were deafening. They roared in his head much like a waterfall hurtling down onto rocks.

Eventually he could filter one voice out of the racket in his head. "Sit up, that's it. There you go. If you need to throw up there's a bucket right here next to you."

His eyes didn't work. A tight wrapping covered them and he tugged at it, trying to pull it loose. He fought the nausea until it overcame him and the contents of his stomach came up to meet the air.

Bucket? he thought. *What damn bucket?*

He heard a curse then, presumably from whomever had been in the way when he vomited.

A cup was put to his mouth and he drank the water down, grateful to get the stinging bile out of his mouth. Two hands pushed his shoulders back down onto the bed and he slept some more.

When he surfaced next he could smell a rich, warm,

spicy scent that curled in his nostrils and made saliva flood his mouth. Another cup was put to his mouth and this time it wasn't water. The rich, thick blood poured down his throat and he gulped at it greedily, relishing the coppery taste.

As it entered his body he felt strength returning to his legs and as his head cleared the noises diminished until they were barely audible. The disembodied voice spoke again, it's timbre high-pitched.

"I'm going to take the bandages off your eyes now. Please keep them shut until I tell you to open them. Your pupils will need time to adjust." He felt fingers then, tugging at the back of his head and then blessedly the wrapping was gone and he could feel light passing through the thin skin of his eyelids.

"All right, good," the voice said. "You can open them now, but slowly, please."

He cracked open one eye and then the other, then squeezed them shut again in disbelief.

Shit, I didn't really see that, did I? Ever so slowly he tried again, first one and then the second eye opened and he found himself looking at a woman. Or at least, some sort of female. It was a little unclear.

She had skin so white it was almost transparent. He could clearly see a network of blue veins crisscrossing the face. A veil covered her face but it was so thin it did nothing to conceal her features. If anything it enhanced them as the fabric shifted color as she moved in an every changing rainbow.

Her eyes shone out from under the veil, a startling electric pink, much like a rabbit, he thought. Her little ears were delicate and almost came to a point, and from the lobes hung delicate silver strands that swayed with her every movement.

She bobbed her head up and down in pleasure when she saw him watching her. "Good, good," she said, and then she tore out of the room as fast as her little feet could take her. He blinked rapidly to clear the purple haze from his vision.

The little Frey jumped up and down like an animated rabbit in front of Elyian. "Your Majesty, he's awake!" she squeaked, hardly able to conceal her joy.

"Ah, that is good news. I'll be there to see him shortly. Thank you for your care of him, Irina." Elyian dismissed the servant, closed the book he was reading and hurried out of the room. He stopped at Jendal's door on the way and hammered on it until his brother stepped out, rubbing his hands over his stubble-covered face in an attempt to wake up.

"Good morning, brother," Elyian greeted his sleepy sibling. "Can you send a message to Amun to meet us? It's time to talk to our new friend."

Elyian then crossed over to the guest quarters where he found Laila. She was in the gardens outside her room and it looked to Elyian as if she'd spent her entire morning rolling around in the dirt. Her hair was a tangled mess and streaks of red soil covered her arms and face.

She was so intent on her gardening that she didn't see Elyian at first. He stood unnoticed, taking in the sight of her well-toned body as she stretched and bent over the plants she was tending. Dirty she may have been, but that didn't make her any less enticing to Elyian. His shadow fell across the ground in front of her and she looked up at the elegant man looming over her.

He was dressed as he usually did when at the palace, in black leather pants. His lean but muscular frame was further enhanced by a form-fitting shirt of a blue so pale it was almost white. With the morning sky behind him, he was the most beautiful being she'd ever seen. Her power of speech was momentarily halted by his sheer physical presence, so he filled in the silence.

"Laila, how are you? I wanted to let you know our guest awoke this morning. Would you like to come greet Ranic's newest citizen?"

She smiled up at him and brushed her hands over her hair in a misguided and futile attempt to tame the unruly mess. "Sire, please excuse me. I am not in a fit state to greet anyone. Least of all yourself!"

He laughed at her obvious embarrassment. "Nonsense, Laila, you merely need a few minutes. Why don't you go clean up? I'll wait here for you."

She thanked him and ran inside.

Elyian was examining the plants she'd been tending when she reappeared, looking much improved. She'd changed into an extremely flattering long dress that hugged her body in all the right places, and a quick brush of her hair had turned it back into the mass of golden waves that now formed a halo around her face.

She would have been the picture of femininity had it not been for the lethal curved dagger she wore at her hip and the sturdy combat boots that peeked from under the dress.

He lifted his eyebrow quizzically. "Are you intending to fight our friend or merely preemptively cut his throat?"

"Just being careful. I was taught to never be unprepared for any situation."

"There'll be at least three or four of us with you, and we're all hunters. The human is no threat to us."

"Ah, but he's not really human any more, is he?"

"True." He smiled that lovely, open, warm smile and her cheeks warmed. "Are you ready?"

"Quite ready." She looked up at him in surprise when he took her hand and led her back into the palace.

In the small bedroom at the rear of the palace, the man pulled on the heavy iron latch that kept the door closed. With a grating sound it lifted and he easily pushed it open. He could just make out a passageway and a short flight of steps that ended in a light-filled courtyard. He was about to step into the passage when someone filled the empty space before the stairs.

The shape was a huge and looming presence that seemed oddly familiar to him. His mind still fuzzy, he was unable to form a complete coherent thought and had no idea where he was or how he got here. The last thing he remembered was working in his lab at Stanford.

Alone?

No.

It was coming back now. His knees started shaking so he slid down the wall and rested his head on his knees, trying to attain clarity. There'd been people in the lab, but why?

Not sure. God this was hard. *Try again.* Four people, three males and a female dressed like a sexy ninja. The men were massive, young and had the palest skin he'd ever seen. They talked to him for hours about plants and disease and genetics. That's right…it was fascinating, what they discussed.

Then he left with them and went somewhere in a car, a journey of maybe an hour or so through vineyards and trees. Yes, that's right—redwood trees!

He grasped onto the pieces of the puzzle that were slowly and inexorably slotting into place. Plants placed in his hands, strange red bulbous things that had green and yellow stuff growing down in the folds of the fruit. They were moldy and smelled really bad, like dried, stale blood.

Then the tallest one, the one they called Eliean or something like that, he had knelt down next to him and apologized for something. Yes, that's right. He said, "I'm so sorry for taking this life away from you, but it's for the good of Ranic."

Then he smiled and opened his mouth—good lord, that's right—he had fangs! Then the pain. Excruciating, mind-numbing pain had spread throughout his body.

Then nothing, until he woke up in the midst of throwing his guts up, here.

Wherever here *is.*

"What the hell happened to me?" he mumbled out loud through a mouth that felt odd. His tongue was swollen and sore. He tried to feel his teeth but a sharp pain stopped him. His teeth felt weird; they were long, much too long!

The large shape at the end of the passageway was joined by three others. Together they walked toward him. As everything came flooding back with increasing clarity, he pushed his body back against the security of the great wooden door, trying to put as much distance as possible between himself and the four beings moving in unison toward him.

"Cameron Grant, it's good to see you almost recovered."

The biggest one sort of growled at him. The tall, slender one put his hand on the big one's shoulder and moved to stand beside Cam cowering by the door.

"Let me help you." He offered Cameron his hand and pulled him to his feet. The woman and the other man hung back a little, saying nothing.

Elyian planted his feet in a wide, firm stance and folded his arms over his chest. "You have questions and we're here to give you the answers. We will give you anything you desire to make you more comfortable. Let's start with some food and go from there, shall we?"

In the weeks and months that followed his abduction, Cameron came to understand that he'd been turned into a human/Raniculan hybrid, known on Earth as a Vampire. The first weeks were torture as his adaptation didn't go well.

Among other things, he tried to drink from the poor little Frey who'd been such a good nurse while he was recovering from the passage here. His body hadn't taken well to being disassembled and flung through space. He vomited a lot and developed a fever that took weeks to break. His fangs shredded his tongue and his body had to heal the wounds on a daily basis. Eventually, his body and his mind learned to accept the chaotic changes.

The others explained to him again about the shortage of Yalon, and he thought about how to help them. His anger toward the one that changed him had morphed into a fascination with the species. He didn't miss his old life, mostly because the new one was so different and strange there wasn't time to think about what he'd lost.

He had rooms at the palace and access to all the scientific equipment he'd need to help them. There were only two things he did miss dearly: his friend and former assistant Charlotte, and the regular thump of his own heartbeat.

He longed to talk to Charlotte again, just to sit and chat about art and music and all the things that made life worth living. Although she'd been his assistant she was also a dear friend, and on Earth he'd felt the lack of her presence since she went missing.

The months on Ranic rolled by and Cam fell into an easy routine. He'd taken on Laila as his lab assistant and found her to be sharp as a whip and eager to learn everything she could about botany. She was like a sponge so he taught her everything he knew about the fauna and flora of Earth. He only had to tell her something once for her to lock it away safely in her mind, ready to be used when needed.

He was close to finding the solution to the problem of the dying Yalon plants. With carefully controlled experiments he'd narrowed down the possibilities. It had taken a long time to get used to a different way of conducting experiments here. Liquids boiled at far higher temperatures due to the lower air pressure; and unused to his new strength he kept breaking the precious glass test tubes Elyian's hunters brought him from Earth.

At first he assumed a local species of lichen caused the problem, and spent many fruitless months trekking all over the countryside trying to find other examples, but without success. He'd lately come to the conclusion that *Caloplaca marina* and *Xanthoria candelaria*, yellow and green lichens seen mostly on the rocks that line the shoreline of the central coast of California, had infested the Yalon fields.

Now he had to find a method of killing the lichen without hurting the underlying plant. As to why two lichens that normally liked moist environments had taken a foothold in the hot Yalon fields of Ranic and how the hell they had gotten there, that might never be known for sure. It had probably been introduced when a hunter brought back some Abalone and a stray lichen-covered rock found its way into the bag they used to transport the shells.

As Cam endlessly turned the problem over in his mind Laila watched, learned and listened. Each night she went back to the palace and reported to Elyian on the progress or lack of it that had been made that day.

The populous were getting increasingly desperate. Supplies had dwindled to next to nothing and both Raniculans and the Frey were now suffering the effects of severe malnutrition. Elyian's hunters ate well, delighted that they were given so many opportunities to travel to Earth as they were then able to feed and regain their strength; but for everyone else, the situation had become critical.

Chapter 30

in which she mixes purple

SHE CRANKED THE music ever higher until the sounds of heavy rock filled the car with booming bass and earsplitting guitar riffs. That way it filled her head so she couldn't think.

She stopped for a brief while in Sacramento, where she picked up a veritable arsenal of art supplies, including a fine French easel, oil paints, brushes, canvas and wooden stretcher bars. Another stop filled the car with a good supply of very warm winter clothing and a few other essentials to get her started at the lake house.

Who knew how far from town his place would be. So, with admirable forethought, coffee, chocolate, toothpaste and a few other essentials were added to the trunk.

She plugged her new smart phone into the car charger and hit the gas. In her pocket was a large bag of assorted precious gems that she'd picked up off the streets in Ranic before she left—diamonds, rubies, and the finest emeralds. If she needed cash, any one of them would provide her with plenty of extra funds.

Feeling more composed now that she'd organized her immediate needs, Charlotte turned her attention to the long, winding, and often, in winter, treacherous haul through the foothills that preceded the Sierras. Lake Tahoe, her destination, was eighty miles ahead and she was making good time. She reckoned she'd get there well before dark unless she hit rush hour traffic.

Which was a good thing, because finding an unknown house in the dark and in snow was challenging, even with a GPS to help. Charlotte knew the difficulty of finding a house number from trips with college friends to go skiing for the weekend when there were drifts five feet deep at the curbside. She had many happy memories of that time and had shared those with Elyian. He'd neglected to tell her about the house he owned there, which was strange; but then, so many things about those darn Raniculans were strange.

Charlotte berated herself—she was trying not to think about anything to do with Ranic. To make matters worse, she hadn't thought to buy food for the journey and she was now ravenous because when she thought about Ranic, blood came to mind. Her fangs snicked down and her stomach rumbled, a physical and visceral reminder that although she was running from reality it was still right there waiting to punch her in the gut.

The dulcet female voice on her guidance system told her she was nearing the house. She slowed to navigate the driveway and was startled to see the familiar symbol of an ankh etched onto a piece of stone that marked the entrance. Charlotte put her hand up to her throat and felt for her mother's gold ankh that she kept around her neck, its weight familiar and comforting.

Ahead of her lay the house. It spread out over the rocky promontory, a modern marvel of glass and stone. Its form was low, echoing the lay of the land. For such a large structure it blended in remarkably well with the landscape on which it stood.

Nobody had known she was coming so it was mostly dark. Only a few lights marked the edges of the driveway and they were half hidden under the light snowfall, the first of the season. As she approached the house it blazed into life. Lights shone through every window when the automatic system sensed her keys turning the lock.

Charlotte smiled. How like Elyian to have embraced Earth technology like this.

She walked into a massive great room where the remote-controlled fire had roared to life in the stone fireplace. It was flanked by a matching pair of deep, down-filled sofas that invited curling up with a great book and cup of hot cocoa. She tossed the first of her packages down on the nearest chair and went off to explore her new digs.

The first morning her emotions were still raw but she was so busy settling in that she didn't have time to miss Amun. Not much, anyway. A good night's sleep in a bed that was so huge she felt lost in its cozy depths had gone a long way to making her feel better.

She flung open the heavy drapes that covered the wall of windows and gasped in pleasure at the vista it revealed. She looked out over a spectacular winter wonderland where banks of twinkling, pristine white snow half covered massive granite boulders and the branches of nearby pines dipped with the weight of their icy mantle.

The rear of the house stood on the edge of a rocky outcrop over a drop that went straight down until it met the azure, icy waters of Lake Tahoe a few hundred feet below. She could see clear across the lake to the scattered little towns that fringed the North shore.

Here, she thought as she gazed out the window, *here I can heal and regain some equilibrium in my life.* She smiled as a little ground squirrel sped up the trunk of a nearby pine tree.

The next day Charlotte passed the morning on snowshoes exploring the immediate area. After lunch, she requisitioned the finished attic room as her studio and set up her new easel at the huge picture window that faced north with sweeping views of the lake. She spent the rest of the day stretching her first canvas and beginning the underpainting. It wasn't until she was so tired she could barely stand that she eventually fell into bed that night. She wanted to sleep for a very long time.

She dreamed of Ranic and lovely, long-legged, green-eyed men who swept her up in the storm of emotions that were their constant companions, and when she woke to find that cavernous empty space in her soul, she wept for the life that was and the loneliness of the life she now had.

Every day was spent in much the same way and the repetition was a balm, a steadying constant in her world where nothing had remained the same. It would take a long time, but eventually the pieces of her broken spirit would knit together like the broken bones she alone could heal. Maybe then she'd be able to look back on the past with peace and toward the future with hope. For now she was a shell, a shattered remnant of the person she'd once been.

Amun's face drifted in and out of her mind when she least expected to see it. She would be focused on mixing just the right shade of cerulean blue or dabbing a tiny highlight of white on a drift of lilac-shadowed snow when his face would come unbidden to mind and her cold, dead heart would give a virtual thump behind her ribs.

The first time it happened she was so shocked she ran out of the house barefoot, hardly noticing the freezing cold until she looked down after running a few miles and saw that the skin on her feet had shredded.

The next time, she opened the studio window and plunged out, doing a perfect swan dive into the icy lake. She was baking cookies one day to share with the squirrels when the thump caused her to add her own spicy blood to the mix when she bit her lip clean through while leaning over the mixing bowl. Amun's soul was imbedded in her veins and it was not giving up its place without a fight.

Winter passed in an almost seamless passage of time. She invited the occasional visitor to help relieve the loneliness of her days. A few girls that lived down the road in a shared house invited her for a glass of wine one evening after they met her in a local liquor store stocking up on her favorite vodka. They were easy to hang out with and asked no difficult questions. She told them she was divorced and a painter and that seemed to be enough for them.

Every now and again she would buy salsa and chips, chill some wine, order pizza and have a "girl's night" where the main topic of conversation was inevitably the best movie or the cutest Jimmy Choo knock-offs that one of them was saving her hard-earned supermarket salary to buy.

Charlotte was scrupulously careful to never invite them over unless she fed before they arrived. She was terrified that one day she'd let her fangs slip and dreaded the thought of that scenario.

Christmas came and went and Charlotte barely noticed. The early spring thaw brought tiny buds poking through the melting patches of snow. Mule deer came right up under the windows to graze on the succulent plantings that surrounded the house.

It was March when the stranger came up the driveway. She'd sent digital images of her completed artwork to a gallery in San Francisco, and the director had quickly replied that he was extremely interested in them and would come up to the Sierras to view the finished pieces. They could discuss the possibility of his gallery carrying her art, starting with a one-woman show in a few months.

Eric Vanlen spent several hours talking to Charlotte and examining her body of work. He loved all the paintings, and they decided he'd take most of the pieces away with him. She would finish the last one and bring it with her in time for her show. He accepted that one sight unseen, having confidence in it based on her other work.

One night several months into her stay at Tahoe, something disturbed Charlotte from a sound sleep. The hairs on the back of her neck prickled from a rush of adrenaline and she felt the air moving in the room.

When she opened her eyes, she could have sworn she'd seen a shadow move out of her room, faster than she could track. She got up and switched on all the lights upstairs but nothing was out of place.

Putting it down to her over-active imagination was easy these days. After what she'd been through, who knew what else was possible.

The next morning she sat in her now almost empty studio and wondered at the curves in the road that life seemed to constantly throw her way. She was enjoying a rare freedom that allowed her to express herself and enjoy her creative side, which she'd always longed to let out. A blank canvas allowed her mind to roam and then settle on a direction of her own choosing. She loved the way she could manipulate the paint, how the seemingly innocuous addition of magenta to cyan could make a rich purple, and how adding white turned it paler and paler until it became the exact shade of the Ranic sky. She painted rivers and lakes, mountains and moons.

One day she painted Amun. She didn't mean to, but her brushes had taken on a life of their own. Hour after hour she stroked the rich, creamy oils onto the canvas, willing the brushstrokes to blend and highlight until his face emerged from the background. She completed his strong jaw with its shadow of a beard and was starting on his neck when the thought slammed into her like a freight train.

Of course! How could she have been so blind? Amun

wore a pendant. She'd only seen it one time, for a few seconds that morning she'd woken up next to him in the circle of trees at his summer home. She wore the same symbol, and an exact copy was carved into the stone at the entrance to this house. A golden ankh.

The memories of her all-too-brief time with Amun came hurtling back with such force that her head ached with all the images that flooded in. Amun asleep in the circle of trees, and the devastated look on his face when she told him she was going back home.

She longed to see him again, to touch his body and have him hold her in his arms. The solitude that had been such a comfort to her when she first arrived here was beginning to feel like a life sentence. She clasped her hand to her chest to feel the familiar smooth surface of her pendant and was shocked to realize it wasn't there.

It must have come off during the night or while she was out in the snow, or maybe she'd put it down in the house somewhere. She turned the place upside down and searched for hours outside the house and on the paths she regularly took, but much to her distress she never found it.

Later, Charlotte stood in the shower letting the steamy hot water cascade over her and watching it run in rivulets over her unadorned chest. Her fangs snicked down and she cried, hot tears that mixed with the shower water until they vanished down the drain at her feet. That ankh was her last link with her mother and the very last thing that connected her to Amun.

Her hands clenched into fists and she slammed them repeatedly into the marble surround until a spider's web of cracks covered the surface. Still her tears came, unstoppable.

She never framed his portrait. It was too hard to look at his face every day and never be able to talk to him. Instead she removed it from the stretchers, carefully rolled it and tucked it away in her portfolio for safe keeping.

When the time came to go to the city for her opening show, she was less than enthusiastic at the knowledge that she had to dress up, drive down to the Bay Area and talk to complete strangers for hours on end about her work.

Maybe I can call the gallery and cancel.

No, that would be unprofessional. There was no way around it. She'd signed a contract and had to follow through. So it was with grit and resignation that she drove into town, bought an edgy and shatteringly expensive new dress at a trendy, upscale little boutique, and set off on a lovely warm day on the four-hour drive into San Francisco.

She checked into the Four Seasons and luxuriated in their spa. Then with trepidation she got ready for the opening of her show.

Not too shabby, she thought as she did a twirl in front of the bathroom mirror. Her toned legs were a pale gold, tanned from the many hours of hiking she'd had done in the last few weeks. It was warm enough for shorts and she'd taken full advantage of the weather to get out and soak up the glorious California sun. Her pale skin was extra sensitive to the rays now that she'd been turned, but a healthy dose of sunscreen helped enormously.

She felt better once she was ready to face the critics. *Amazing what a swipe of lipstick and new shoes can do for your bravado*, she thought as she grabbed her portfolio, picked up her clutch, threw in her phone and gave her face a quick once-over before leaving her suite.

San Francisco, on a warm Friday evening in early May, was the happy, vibrant place she'd loved. The streets were free of debris and all the earthquake damage had been rectified.

People bustled to and fro, on their way to the theater or dinner dates with friends. Cable cars continued to jangle up and down streets so steep that cars were required to curb their tires to avoid runaway disasters from emergency brakes not being properly engaged. Seagulls circled overhead, wheeling and crying into the wind and Union Square was, as usual, packed with tourists, local shoppers and pickpockets. Life was back to normal.

Charlotte walked the couple of blocks to Schoggi, the Swiss Chocolatier, to pick up a small bag of her favorite truffles, The Thai Princess, an amazing confection of Kirsch and dark chocolate topped with a pinnacle of gold leaf. She munched on them happily as she continued the ten blocks to the gallery.

Soon her feet hurt. The mile-high stilettos she'd been talked into buying by the boutique owner were a life-threatening hazard, even for her. So she called a cab and arrived at the gallery with ankles intact, well before her show was due to open.

Eric greeted Charlotte warmly. He couldn't have been more pleased at her appearance. The change from when he'd seen her in Tahoe was remarkable. The woman he'd met that day had been unkempt and flustered and had shown little interest in really selling her work. She'd been constantly distracted and looked as if she'd been crying.

The female that stood in the foyer now didn't act or dress like the same woman at all. Her entire persona was different.

Caterers scuttled around, carrying boxes of wine glasses and huge platters of elegant and tasty hors d'oeuvres that they stashed away, ready to bring out when the guests arrived.

The director flicked on the main switches that flooded the space with light, beautifully illuminating her works as they hung on pristine walls that had been painted a soft, creamy white that held just a hint of lilac. Together they walked up and down the exhibit, making sure everything was in order. She gasped as the images came to life.

There, hung on every wall, was the world of Ranic, featuring images of everyday life. The inhabitants, as they swept the steps outside their homes or rode on wagons pulled by Manos. The opulent palace of Elyian, and the gorgeous, dreamy winter palace that was Amun's home.

She'd captured every place she'd seen on huge canvases, in glorious, riotous, saturated color that captured each nuance of the light as it changed throughout the day. The deep, dusky purple of night with the two huge blue moons, and the pale, hazy lilac of the morning which deepened to a vibrant purple as the day wore on. It was all there, laid out in detail for this world to see.

The gallery visitors would enjoy a vivid world of artistic creativity with a healthy dose of imagination, but for Charlotte it was a cathartic release of all she'd begun to hold so dear and then had to leave behind.

There were no intimate portraits, nothing that showed the people unless at a distance, involved in some task or other. In one scene by a riverbank, a slender but well-muscled man crouched down skinning an animal, obviously about to cook it on the nearby fire. His legs were encased in skin-tight leather but he was bare from the waist up. Hanging from his neck on a silvery cord was a golden pendant. It would have taken a magnifying glass to see the shape of the pendant.

Charlotte stood a long time looking at the scene, then touched his face and turned away. It was enough, for now.

A man stood outside the gallery, biding his time for the proper time to enter. A massive poster spread across the window declared in bold black typeface on a soft lilac-grey background:

Threads of Ranic
a collection of original work by
CHARLOTTE HAYDEN

Eric Vanlen paced the polished concrete floor of the cavernous gallery, waiting for the appointed time to unlock the doors. He was blown away by her work and couldn't wait to share it with the rest of the illustrious art world in which he lived.

One buyer in particular, to whom Eric had been selling high-end pieces for years, had requested photographs of the work of this unknown artist, and he was coming, along with at least three other people Eric knew to be avid collectors of fantasy art.

Ten minutes remained before they would arrive so he went to find Charlotte. She stood in a secluded corner, her head bent over a square of painted canvas. She heard him approach and tried to secret it behind her back. Eric frowned, puzzled at her reaction.

"Charlotte, whatever do you have there? Come on, don't be embarrassed. I'd love to see it."

She looked up, maddened by her poor attempt at subterfuge. "Oh, it's nothing," she said, trying to look nonchalant and failing miserably. "Just the start of a portrait I didn't finish. I guess I can show you, it doesn't really matter."

Charlotte held up the canvas and he found himself looking at a face that would haunt his dreams for years to come. Being gay, he truly appreciated the beauty of the person depicted in the work, and he reached to hold it in his hands.

The man portrayed was staggeringly handsome. High cheekbones and pale, luminous, perfect skin framed by hair that was almost black but not quite. She'd captured glints of copper and gold threading their way through his long locks. His eyes were the most brilliant emerald green he'd ever seen and they peered out with a savage intensity from under long, black lashes. A wide, generous mouth was quirked up at one corner in the start of a smile. A trace of shadow gave a rugged look to his square jawline and there was a small dent in the center of his chin. He was bare, apart from a single piece of jewelry that rested on his broad chest.

Eric felt the sweat break out on his palms. He experienced a visceral sexual reaction to the image of the man, and quickly handed the canvas back to Charlotte. She thought he didn't like it.

"Yes, well, like I said, it's not finished." She couldn't deny being hurt by his reaction.

Eric gaped at her. "It's truly wonderful. We must show this tonight, finished or not. This is masterful!"

"Really? I didn't think you liked it. And it's not framed. Besides, I don't want to sell this one."

Eric floundered around for a minute and then with relief found an answer. "No problem. We can pin it to the wall and put a note under it. We'll say it's your muse, and muses can't be bought for any price! Now, we have some other fine art to sell, so let's get this hung, yes?"

At last it was time.

Soon the gallery was packed. The art community had come out in droves, as the buzz around this opening had been building for weeks. Elegant women dressed in Posen and Schouler vied for attention with a plethora of men in Armani and Jacobs. It was a sea of bright dresses, dark jackets and high end shoes with purses that cost more than most people make in several months.

They mingled around the gallery with crystal champagne flutes clutched in their perfectly manicured hands. Small groups stood talking in front of each piece of work that lined both the outside and dividing walls in the modern space.

Charlotte found herself trapped at the back of the room, crushed between Eric and a balding man gesticulating toward a painting, his wrist sporting a diamond Rolex watch. Charlotte's attention was caught by a large group of women ogling the 'pinup' that had pride of place on the center of the wall.

Charlotte's Vampiric hearing kicked into overdrive.

"My word!" she heard an exceptionally tall woman wearing a skintight red dress exclaim in a very cultured English accent. "I wouldn't mind a bit of that on a Saturday night—or any night at all, come to that!"

Charlotte's fangs pushed on her gums and she turned her head away, willing them not to drop. She lost the battle as jealousy threw out a long lasso and reeled her in. Giving her excuses to Eric and the potential buyer, she made her way through the crowd.

A few groups stopped her passage, unanimous and voluble in their praise of her work. By the time she got to the painting of Amun, the group of women had moved on, their place taken by a lone male in a black suit and a hat pulled down over his face, who stood motionless in front of the piece.

Eric suddenly appeared again and pulled on her arm excitedly. "Charlotte, look," he said, pointing at the back wall where every piece of art had a red sold dot next to the price.

She smiled and nodded her approval. "That's nice."

"Nice! What do you mean, nice? You just sold more in the first half an hour of a show than I've ever seen, and I've been in this business a long time. That's not nice, it's damn amazing, that's what!"

She wasn't really listening as he prattled on about "genius" and "fortune" and something else she didn't hear. She pulled away from him and pushed through the crowd. That man at the painting, there was something about the set of his shoulders, the height...

By the time she got there he was gone.

The rest of the evening wore on endlessly. Her skin prickled, the new shoes pinched her feet, and her head felt as if it would explode from the inexplicable tension in the room. She popped her last piece of chocolate in her mouth. At least one part of her anatomy now felt good. Everyone had gone home and she was about to find Eric to say goodbye when she saw the man again. It had to be him, just the height alone... He stood stock still, gazing at the portrait.

He felt her approach from behind and every cell in his body came alive as silvery threads fought to bridge the gap between them. The rent in his soul began to close and he shivered at the thought of talking to her again. He tried to will his feet to move but they remained firmly planted in place. Terror at the thought she would reject him kept him turned away from her.

Charlotte's breath moved around him. "Hello," she said, trying to remain calm and collected. Suppose it wasn't him? She'd feel like a right idiot if she'd gone and flung herself at a ridiculously tall, complete stranger.

He made a decision and swiveled around, so inexorably slowly it felt like time had stopped and he was the only moving thing in the universe. At that moment, the stars realigned and thrust the two of them back into the same plane of existence.

Amun's head was lowered, just in case he saw rejection in her eyes. Eventually he raised his head a few inches and saw her gold-painted toenails as they peeked out from under a long, emerald-green gown of luxurious silk velvet. Unable to resist, his eyes followed the curve of the dress as it hugged her hips and then folded in elegant soft drapes over her breasts which moved in time to her breathing. As their eyes locked, he sank into the depths of her and his world stopped.

He knew that no matter what she said or did in the next five minutes, he was not going to leave Earth without her. She looked drop-dead gorgeous in her form-fitting gown with her face surrounded by those magnificent red waves that cascaded down her bare back. Long strands of silver threads moved out from her body, unseen by any human. The threads steadily spun out toward him until his touched hers and they coiled together like the spiraling tendrils of a wayward vine.

She drank him in, her unneeded breath coming in hitches. Charlotte's hands shook as she gazed at the man whose portrait was pinned to the wall just a few feet behind him. His lovely face was tortured and etched with lines that had not been there when she left him. Behind the mask of pain drawn on his face lay her beloved Amun, the one male that sent all other men into the history books, including his own son who'd once lit up her libido like a bonfire.

His emerald eyes flashed as they locked with hers. His fangs crashed out of his mouth in unison with hers and they came together before either of them could register the thought. As they collided, they fell backwards into the gallery dividing wall. The wallboard buckled, then shattered under their combined force. The portrait wrapped itself around the back of Amun's shoulders as they fell through the divider wrapped in each other's arms.

Eric's first thought was that yet another earthquake hit; his second, before he entered the main room of the gallery, was that a car must have crashed into the front of the building. The third thought brought him to his knees. Charlotte's painting, which had been etched into his frontal lobe since the moment he first saw it, had come to life.

He stood watching them, transfixed by the scene before him. They rolled around on the concrete floor, oblivious to the chunks of wallboard that had exploded around them in massive shards. Amun's hands clutched her hair, tangling into its depths. The passion with which they clung to each other made Eric moan aloud. They didn't register the sound—and even if they had, it wouldn't have torn them away from each other. It wasn't until he saw blood that Eric moved forward and cried out to them.

"Get up, Charlotte, you're bleeding!" The room went so quiet that Eric could hear the drip of a faucet that a caterer had left on in the kitchen.

They both turned and faced him, fangs dripping blood.

Eric checked out.

"Shit." Amun rarely cursed but letting a human see his fangs could have catastrophic implications. "Charlotte, we have to get out of here, right now."

"Yes, of course.'" She hurriedly clambered out of the mess they'd created. She retrieved the canvas portrait, dusted off the layer of plaster dust, rolled it up, and left Amun's side to fetch her purse.

By the gods, Amun thought, *why let a good meal go to waste?* He might look like a god himself but he definitely wasn't perfect. Amun knelt over Eric and smiled somewhat lasciviously as he sank his fangs into the human and had his first drink of human blood in five hundred years. He made sure not to inject any venom; he didn't want to turn the man into a hybrid. And he left a sufficient quantity of blood in Eric's system to ensure his survival.

Charlotte wasn't back so didn't see him drain the human, which was just as well; he didn't want to give her yet another reason to leave him. When Eric woke up he'd feel very tired and the authorities would assume there'd been a fight after the show closed. The cleanup crews would take care of any stray evidence, ensuring that Eric's story could never be believed.

Charlotte and Amun left the gallery clinging to each other like limpets on rocks. She collected her belongings from the hotel, then they far-stepped to the house at Tahoe.

On the balcony that night they stood under the canopy of stars over their heads. He held her tightly in his arms and kissed her with all the passion of a drowning man.

"Charlotte," he said, his voice deep and grating as he forced the words into her open mouth. He pressed his hard length up to her and she groaned as the man she couldn't live without scooped her up and had them both horizontal on the huge bed before she could blink. All Charlotte could hear was his voice, and all she could feel were his hands as they restlessly roamed over her heated body.

That night as the rest of planet Earth plodded quietly along on its path to Vampiric enlightenment, the pair of beings that now belonged to a world so far away took each other on a trip across the universe.

Chapter 31

in which Earth shudders

"MR. PRESIDENT, YOU need to see this." A piece of carefully folded paper advertising a feed store in downtown Truckee was shoved unceremoniously onto the desk in front of him, its edges torn and dirty as if it had spent the last five years being carted around in the pocket of a homeless person.

The president unwrapped it carefully, not knowing what was secreted within its grimy folds. As he opened the last side, he found lying at the very center a scratched and dented golden pendant in the shape of an ankh, with a small piece of mother-of-pearl imbedded in the center loop. He picked it up and turned it over in his hand, revealing a hieroglyph etched deep into the gold.

"Please don't waste my very valuable time, Senator Vax," he said with a just a hint of annoyance coloring his normally smooth delivery. "Just tell me what this is, and why it's deemed to be of such vital importance that you've interrupted my meeting with the heads of S.E.T.I."

Vax answered, his voice so low and menacing that the president pushed a little further back in his leather armchair and the pair of Secret Service agents standing guard in the

Oval Office tightened their grips on their sidearms.

"Although to you this Egyptian ankh may seem like an innocuous piece of jewelry, it has been thoroughly examined by various experts, including myself. We unanimously agree that it was made before or during the reign of the Pharaoh Akhenaten and his Queen Nefertiti, in 1350 B.C.

"There's no definitive evidence of what happened to Queen Nefertiti, other than that she gave birth to six sons and later six daughters. One of those daughters was named Nefertia. Nefertia's image always showed her wearing an ankh just like this. She is depicted on the walls of a tomb in the Valley of the Kings with this around her neck, and at her side a very tall and handsome young man.

"His name is Amun. His half-sister Nefertia became his wife, and this," he flipped the ankh over in his hand, "is his glyph. The world didn't know the sons existed, and they were kept in seclusion until each one was old enough to leave for his own planet with the hope that they would seed that planet with their very unique progeny. My younger brother Amun was given Ranic, the planet that I, as the eldest son, should have been granted."

Havvol Vax stopped talking and waited for the meaning of what he told the president to truly sink in. He watched as the faces of the Secret Service men and the president paled with the knowledge that the man who stood before them was an ancient being.

"Amun and his half-sister vanished together from Earth in the sixteenth year after his birth." Vax paused a beat to give his words extra weight, then added, "He is known as a Vampire to you humans, and he is coming to rule over all humanity, Mr. President."

The night before Vax delivered his little piece of revenge to the president, an elegantly dressed woman sat at her dressing table, in a quiet upscale home on an avenue that bordered Golden Gate Park. She slipped pearl earrings onto her lobes. She detested the clips but had no other option, as she was unable to wear pierced earrings. As a Vampire the holes would heal instantly. She'd tried dozens of times, but they always closed before she got the post anywhere near her ear.

She pulled her hair back into an elegant chignon and slipped her feet into a pair of black suede Louboutin heels. They didn't come cheap but money didn't enter the equation for her new spouse. Her lipstick-red, Herve Leger bandage dress screamed "Look at me!" but tonight wasn't about blending in.

She was so sick of hiding, of pretending to be human. Tonight was her coming-out party, but first she had that stupid art opening to attend. Her husband tugged the pristine white cuffs lower under his custom silk dinner jacket and straightened the mother-of-pearl and platinum cufflinks. He cleared his throat to alert his wife to the fact that he was down in the hall waiting for her. She moved like lightening down the curved staircase and huffed in irritation.

"All right, I'm ready. Why do we have to go to this event again? It's not like she's known. I suppose at least Kendra will be there, so I'll have somebody interesting to talk to while you're networking."

He took her arm and led her out to the waiting Lincoln. The engine purred into life and as they sped off in the direction of the gallery he at last deigned to give her an answer.

"I realize we haven't known each other very long, Suriana, but you should have learned by now that I never do anything without a reason that will ultimately benefit us both."

She turned her perfect profile to face him and grinned. "Havvol! I should have known you had something up your sleeve other than those cufflinks. Would you care to elaborate?"

Havvol Vax nodded. "The artist showing tonight is a female with whom I have...well, let us just say, there's no love lost between us. Do not indicate in any way that you know of her connection to me. Do not engage her in conversation. Your only job is to acquire as many pieces as you are able, without garnering too much attention. Are we quite clear?" The look he delivered was enough to render her silent for the remainder of the short journey.

As they left the car with the valet, Vax added a pair of dark glasses to his airbrushed suntan. "The bronzed, undercover look suits you, my dear," his wife said sarcastically. Vax shot her a look that could and most probably would kill her, and within the next couple of hours if she didn't learn to keep her mouth shut.

Chapter 32

in which H is for hemoglobin

CHARLOTTE'S FINGERS STROKED the smooth, firm skin of Amun's rock-hard pecs. Nestled in the very center of his breastbone, glinting as the morning sun sent shafts of mountain light through the window, lay his pendant, worn thin and smooth as silk from the hundreds of years it had spent against his body. She swept her fingers gently over the warm surface, then clutched it in her hand.

"Mine is gone," she said through a throat so tight she could hardly force the words out. "It's missing."

Amun sighed. "I know, Charlotte. That was the first thing I noticed once I was capable of seeing anything but your face last night."

She told him about the morning she'd realized it was missing as she showered, and how the night before that had been so strange. He made her go over the details two more times and then a strange look crossed his face.

"What's wrong?" she asked when his features darkened. A deep and feral growl rose up from the hellish depths where he normally kept that emotion firmly locked up in chains.

"This house," he said, "doesn't belong to Elyian as you

were led to believe." Charlotte raised one curved eyebrow but refrained from commenting as he went on.

"It's mine."

She smiled. "I kind of figured that out when I remembered seeing you wearing the pendant. You have the same symbol etched on a stone at the entrance. Besides, the pants in the closet are a size larger than Elyian wears. But why the subterfuge, and what does that have to do with my missing pendant and you growling at me?"

Amun got up, pulled on a pair of faded blue jeans and strode to the window, flinging it open before he answered. "I thought you'd turn down the offer if you knew it was mine. I had someone come before you arrived to remove anything with my name on it and some personal effects, but I forgot to tell him to obliterate the etched ankh at the entrance."

He grinned. "I guess subconsciously I was hoping the wrong jeans would be a clue. As for why your pendant is missing..." His expression changed instantly, becoming dark and broody. He lifted his head and faced the open vista, his profile silhouetted against the morning light. "The one to blame for that is Havvol Vax."

In the silence that filled the space between them, the bitter Arctic wind that howled through the Tahoe basin until summer's heat truly arrived found the open window and blasted into the bedroom, chilling the air. Just the mention of that name made Charlotte want to throw up. Her gut clenched into a fist and bile rose in her throat, burning on the way up her gullet. She forced it back down with sheer will.

"No, not him. Do you mean to say he was here in my room? That disgusting piece of shit! Oh God..."

She darted off the bed and flew into the bathroom where she promptly emptied her stomach of its contents. As she clutched the porcelain her entire body shook and beads of sweat rolled off her.

She felt his arms come around her waist and gently pull her up, steadying her as she stood. "I should have broken that news to you in a different way. I'm sorry it was such a shock."

Charlotte shook her head. "No, I needed to know what was going on. How do you know it was Vax and what are we going to do about it?"

Amun handed her a glass of water, smiling. She'd already bounced back and was ready to tackle the problem head on.

That was part of what he loved about her. No matter what she was dealt, she always came back for more. She may have a weak stomach but her heart was like a lion's.

"I know it was Vax because I smelled his scent when we first arrived. I told myself it wasn't possible, put it down to my paranoia over your safety. But this solidifies my suspicion. Vax can become almost transparent, like smoke. He can halt the process of far–stepping, and just before he disappears he takes on a wispy form and moves soundlessly."

He paused, glanced at her then away. "There's something else you need to know, Charlotte."

She braced herself for whatever was going to come out of his mouth next.

He looked embarrassed as he admitted, "Vax is my eldest brother. There are six living male siblings. Our human ancestor was Queen Nefertiti. We were all born on Earth but our sire Cyrus was from somewhere else in the galaxy—none of us know where. He used Nefertiti merely as a vessel. Her beauty was legendary and he wanted to mix human blood with the other races.

"Every son of every generation since then has been allocated a planet on which to live, so he could add his DNA to the mix on that planet. I was given Ranic, and Vax got Earth. He detests the planet, so he's always lived on Ranic. He's been trying to get Ranic away from me and then from Elyian for centuries. He'll stop at nothing to get what he wants.

"That's why I abdicated the throne. I never had any real desire to rule Ranic; Elyian is a far more effective leader than I could ever be. I wanted to live a simpler life working alongside my people, not ruling over them."

Amun stopped then and tried to gauge Charlotte's reaction, but she was doing a sterling job keeping her composure. "Keep going, Amun. Why my ankh? Where do I fit into all this?"

He sighed and tried to rub the stress from his temples. "I can only presume he has some way of using that piece of gold to help him achieve his goal. As for why you have it, one was given to each female that carried the mark of Creck, and they passed their ankhs down through the centuries. The Ranic Creck bird is a genetic marker. I believe that if your blood mixes with that of one of our direct line, and a child was born, it would have some meaning, although I cannot begin to imagine what."

Charlotte was mulling that over when she remembered something else that made her different, other than the fact that she owned a beautiful matched set of shiny white fangs. Not unique, but certainly unusual. Her blood type.

She was type HH, the single rarest blood type on Earth. Only four in one million people were type HH, universal donors with no antigens in their blood. Charlotte wondered if Esarelle was HH, too.

When she told Amun he was astonished. "Is there no end to your unique qualities, Charlotte? But enough of all this for now. If we don't take a break, our minds may well explode, and there's no HH blood to give you." He laughed. "Come here, my little vamp."

Amun grabbed her shoulders and pulled her close. As her hair tumbled over his chest he turned her head and gently licked the outside of her ear, then whispered, "Our problems can wait another day. Right now I need your undivided attention. It's been too long, Charlotte, and last night wasn't nearly long enough."

"Stop talking, Amun," Charlotte said, her voice raw and full of pent-up emotion. She pulled back and held his gaze as her hand dropped to his groin where the very obvious manifestation of his lust was straining at the fly of his jeans. Her pupils dilated and she dropped to her knees. She wanted every part of him and she wanted him every way possible.

Amun lasted just long enough to realize that no amount of time with her was going to be long enough. They made love the rest of the day, until hunger drove them from the bed as the sun sank again over the Sierras.

Charlotte left him lying in all his resplendent naked glory on the destroyed bed. He watched avidly as her naked behind disappeared downstairs. In the kitchen she threw food on a plate and headed back, entering the bedroom munching on a chunk of raw steak that had looked oddly appetizing. She found Amun sitting bolt upright. He'd turned on the television and his eyes never left the screen as she walked in.

"You made the news," he said with a grin. "They just said there was a report coming on about your show. Hurry, the segment's about to start." He patted the mattress and she dropped the plate on the bed and scooted next to him. He wrapped his arm around her and together they watched the volcano erupt.

The reporter stood outside the gallery in San Francisco,

his collar turned up against the wind. "Last night this gallery in downtown San Francisco was the venue for an opening that will go down in the annals of the art world as the opening to end all openings. A previously unknown painter, Charlotte Hayden, wowed the critics with her imaginative renditions of surreal worlds. Her scenes of everyday life on a planet she calls Ranic are intense, detailed, and vibrant, showing a complete mastery of composition and light.

"She sold virtually every piece in the gallery within the first half hour to a buyer who wished to remain anonymous. Her sales were well over two million dollars, which by any standard is sensational, but especially for a young woman who, until a few months ago, had not sold a single piece. The remaining pieces were snapped up by various buyers, except for a single unframed portrait, a dramatic and intensely moody rendering of a pale and handsome man, that by all accounts she refused to sell.

"As if that wasn't enough drama for one evening, Mr. Eric Vanlen, the gallery director, had a nasty accident after the show closed when a central pillar collapsed inside the building. Although he suffered a bad neck wound, Mr. Vanlen is recovering at UCSF hospital, where he is said to be in stable condition. The hospital declined to answer any other questions due to patient confidentiality. We've tried to reach Miss Hayden to get her comments but are not able to locate her at this time. This is Miles Grant—"

Amun clicked off the TV and turned to Charlotte.

"Wow, looks like your fifteen minutes of fame have started." He flashed that smile and the warmth in his eyes was matched only by the look she returned to him.

"Yes, I was thrilled my art sold so well, but I don't need the money. The gems I collected before I left Ranic would keep me in opulent luxury here for the rest of my life. That's assuming I still want to stay here. Earth is the last place I want to be if you're not with me."

He felt and heard the passage of the ages as they sat together, still as stone on the bed. A clock ticked, keeping perfect even time on the bedside table, and a woodpecker hammered on a nearby tree, its beak marking a steady musical thrumming on the trunk of a pine. In his entire long life, he'd only told one woman that he loved her, and that woman had been dead now for many centuries.

He wanted to say them now, but the words stuck in his

throat. Years of solitude had done nothing to make him more voluble. After what felt to Charlotte like a century of silence, he held her face in his hands and spoke the words she'd been craving.

"My life has been cavernously empty, without focus or purpose for so long. The moment you slammed into my body outside of Esarelle's home and I looked into your beautiful distraught face, my world changed. My entire being shifted in your direction. There's no going back, no thought of taking another road, and as much as I hated to hurt Elyian, I knew you were not his to have.

"You and I were meant to be together. Fate has its reasons for sending us on paths that are not immediately obvious to us. I knew I loved you, Charlotte, on that first morning we woke up together, even though you were mad as hell at me. You are my reason for being and my mate. I'm never letting you go again. I love you."

His declaration of love hit her like a freight train hurtling down a steep grade with no driver and definitely no brakes. "Oh, Amun, I love you, too." She wiped away the tears that had fallen, leaving salty raindrops on the snowy linen sheets.

He claimed the mouth of the woman that had captured his soul. She didn't have the time to say more, and her lips were busy anyway.

Chapter 33

in which the trail is followed

AGEN AND CAM shared a laugh at the sight of the voluptuous bartender, a female Aborinth with a long, leonine tail. She was perched on the bar whisking it seductively over the supine form of a drunken Frey, then dipping the furry end in his drink and seductively sucking it dry.

They were holed up inside The Midnight Pearl, a night club on the outskirts of town, lounging on a curved seat at one end, eyeing a constant parade of young, unmated Raniculans strutting around in a blatant show of female sexuality. The few off-duty palace Frey who were there gathered at one end of the bar, trading back thumps. One of them had collapsed in an unconscious heap next to a table where he was repeatedly stepped on by the passing females.

Two dozen tiny orbs spun around the ceiling of the room, offering the only illumination in the darkness. Cam handed Agen another shot of Macallan Single Malt, hauled back from Earth by the bar owner's hunter son and so precious it cost a fortune on Ranic. He chucked it to the back of his throat with a single swallow.

Talking was impossible as the music hammered away

in an incessant, ear-splitting drone. A posse of dancers undulated in time to the beat, wearing skimpy, body-hugging scraps of fabric held together by chains so fine they were nearly invisible, the garments shifting colors as the dancers moved in time to the music.

A group of hunters, armed to the teeth and dressed in black from head to foot, were hard to spot in the low light.

Agen didn't get out very much at night. His duties as a single father to an energetic toddler ruled out much socializing. Tonight, however, he'd been dragged from the house by Cam, who arrived at his door with Irina, the very same Frey that had taken care of Cam when he'd first arrived on Ranic.

Irina had immediately swooped on Violette and had her giggling away within seconds. She'd been delighted to look after the child and had quickly dispatched the two men out the door for the evening.

Friendship had blossomed quickly between the hybrid and the Raniculan. Cam had grown to love this world and blossomed in its charged atmosphere. Always up for a challenge, he relished the opportunity that he'd been given to immerse himself in this, his new and wonderful life.

He looked up as two newcomers entered the dimly lit space. They stood so close together that virtually no light passed between their bodies, and where they didn't touch little sparks of energy arced across the gaps. The man was quite possibly the single most splendid example of blatant maleness Cam had ever seen.

Cam was not attracted to other males—his feet were firmly planted on the other side of that fence—but there was no denying the sheer physical beauty the guy had in spades. Every last being in the club stopped and bowed their heads in greeting. Recognition stepped in.

Cam had only seen the man from a distance a few times since his abduction and that part was still a little hazy, but there was no doubt in his mind.

This was the infamous Amun, Elyian's father, who'd traded in the constant headaches of being monarch for a life of quiet solitude. It wasn't until Agen shouted a greeting to Amun that Cam turned his attention to the female Amun escorted.

Charlotte saw him first and disbelief caused her head to whirl. Was she dreaming? No, she was definitely here at the club with Amun and sitting right across from her was her old boss and friend Cameron Grant!

Cam saw her standing slack jawed. Shock was written all over her face, and his face mirrored hers.

"What are you doing here?" Exactly the same words came out of both their mouths, at almost exactly the same time.

Cam stumbled to his feet, his alcohol-saturated body not responding very well to the sudden, urgent need to move her direction. She let go of Amun's hand and closed the distance between them. His arms came around her and in that moment he knew that fate or serendipity or whatever it was, had been hard at work.

He would have stayed there breathing in her familiar scent had it not been for the pair of iron-clad fists that slammed into the side of his head. Amun lifted him straight up off the ground by his shoulders until they were eye to eye. Through a haze of searing pain and booze he heard Amun growl.

"We still need you to fix the Yalon, otherwise you would be a dead man right now. I might just rip off a leg or two anyway, to make my point. Never touch my mate again without my permission. Are we very clear on this point, human?"

Cam managed a weak nod of his head and answered, "Crystal clear."

Charlotte pulled on Amun's arm and begged him to stop, but the instinct in Raniculan Vampires to protect their mate was so powerful she had little effect. It was Agen who eventually talked Amun out of ripping off Cam's limbs or tearing out his throat, and he got the four of them seated in a discreet corner where they waited for the attention to die down.

Charlotte was thrilled to see her friend. She wanted to speak alone with him but that was impossible tonight. Time was needed for tempers to cool and explanations to be made. She did learn why he was there, and was delighted to hear he, too, was now a hybrid, so she had at least one other person on this planet who knew exactly how it felt to have everything you know, and everything you love, changed in an instant.

The Aborinth female prowled over, bringing a large pitcher to the table, and bowed to Amun.

"Sssire," she purred at him, her irises elongating into black slits in her orange eyes as she flicked up her tail and suggestively stroked it up between her legs. "We had this hidden in the cellar and kept it for you. It could be the last

Yalon we get for a long, long time."

This time it was Charlotte who felt the sting of jealousy. She snarled at the bartender, who looked back at her with a sneer before skulking back to her other conquest. Charlotte snicked her fangs back in and snuggled closer to Amun.

Cam had the situation figured out now. Charlotte belonged to Amun. End of story.

Not that it mattered to him on a personal level. He'd been dating Irina, the little Frey who nursed him when he first arrived. He hadn't had a clue just how fertile the female Freys were until he noticed within weeks of first sleeping together that her shape had changed. Dramatically.

Now he was besotted with Irina and thrilled at the prospect of becoming a father. Not exactly in the way he thought it would happen, but what the hell, nothing about his life was normal any more.

Later that night Cam was heading back towards the palace with Agen when he noticed a small snail clinging tenaciously to his pant leg. He bent down, intending to flick it onto the ground.

Agen saw it and snorted. "Yech, what is that?"

"Just a snail," Cam said, pinching the shell gently in his fingers and depositing it in his open palm. Agen bent down and took a closer look.

"That's a really odd-looking thing! Where'd it come from?"

When Cam realized there was no such creature on this planet, they quickly surmised that the snail must have been carried back to Ranic hitching a ride on Amun or Charlotte's clothing. It must have crawled onto Cam's leg while they were all at the bar.

Agen asked him a few questions about snails and as Cam answered, the lightning bolt hit.

"That's it, Agen! By the gods above, that's the answer we've been looking for!"

Cam forgot all about sleep that night, and was still hunched over his lab table sporting dark circles under his eyes the next morning when Laila arrived to start her work for the day.

"Look, Laila," he cried. He held up a Yalon fruit for her to inspect. They both stared at the snail as it perched precariously on top of the fruit, leaving a sticky, silvery trail as it moved over the gently undulating surface. As it crawled forward it munched a clean pathway through the lichen, leaving the underlying fruit pristine. "Run and fetch Elyian."

Elyian was ecstatic at the breakthrough and instantly ordered his hunters back to Earth. He couldn't accompany them, as enough time hadn't elapsed for him to recharge his internal batteries since his last visit. But they didn't need him to catch snails. Besides, if he was honest with himself, he was far more interested in spending the next few days pursuing the ever-elusive and fascinating Laila.

On Earth, the hunters gathered hundreds of thousands of snails, from every park, garden and woodland—anywhere they could gather them unseen by humans—and brought them back to Ranic in massive sacks.

Teams of wagons pulled by Manos took farmers and civilians alike out to the fields and way past the mountain ranges to other outlying parts of the planet. They distributed the snails, scattering them among the plants. Within weeks the snails had totally destroyed the infestation.

And now, Cam thought as he surveyed the thriving fields of Yalon the following month, *how the hell do we get rid of the snails before they endanger the balance of life here?*

He grunted, flashed the whip over the back of the nearest Mano and turned it in the direction of Ranic.

"Another problem for another day," he sighed. For the time being, he'd saved the Yalon crop. Smiling at the accomplishment, he began his journey back to the city.

By the time he got back he was hot, tired and cranky. The Mano had moved at a pace not much faster than the snails in the fields. Every so often it turned and hissed at him, dripping that disgusting goo from its fangs. Cam liked just about everything about this planet, with the notable exception of those hideous creatures. There was nothing appealing about them at all, and he couldn't wait to leave this one behind as he passed it to a group of handlers at the palace gate. He flung the reins at them and jumped down from the rickety wagon.

I really need to spend some time teaching these Raniculans how to embrace the idea of decent vehicles, he thought as he dusted the day's grime from his clothing and wiped his face on his now-filthy sleeve. *Quite astounding how these idiots, who claim to be super intelligent, can travel back and forth to Earth over a thousand years and still prefer to travel by Mano-drawn wagons instead of coming up with a fuel-driven vehicle.*

"Freaking weird if you ask me."

He didn't realize he'd spoken that last sentence aloud until a voice in his ear rumbled, "Nobody's asking you, human!"

Cam jumped at the voice, then grinned when he attached it to the familiar face of Agen. "Agen, good to see you! Anything interesting happen while I was gone?"

Agen's eyes dimmed with the knowledge that what he was about to say could put his friend into a complete tailspin. "Nothing, really, unless you count the screams coming from your rooms as interesting."

Cam paled considerably and clutched at Agen. "What do you mean?" But even as the words came out he knew. "Irina? It's Irina isn't it?"

Agen nodded. "Yes, she's been in labor for the past day. Her mother is there with her so try not to worry."

Cam didn't hear the last part, as he was already running full tilt to his quarters. Agen planted his feet at the base of the stone wall and slid down its surface. His remembered torture at the loss of Chimara and her agony in childbirth tore into him with such force that he choked as the sobs heaved up from his chest.

He prayed that Cameron would not have to endure the same loss.

Chapter 34

in which the link is found

ESARELLE FOUND HIM there a short while later, crouched on the ground a mere shadow of his former self. She'd watched Agen from a distance for far too long. Now it was time to step up.

She knelt by his side, sensing what had caused his breakdown. She'd admired Chimara. It had been Chimara who guided her through the maze of palace rules, and had helped her land the job in the children's care center. The loss of the Frey had been keenly felt by many Raniculans, including Esarelle.

Her voice was gentle and coaxing as she lowered herself down to sit next to him. "Hello, Agen" she said, casually slipping her arm over his shoulders. His muscles quivered under her touch. "Sorry, I just thought..." her voice trailed off as she removed her arm.

"No, it's not you." Agen's eyes were two huge pools of pain. "I'm fine, really. It's just that when I had to tell Cam about Irina—well, I just pray he won't have to go through what I did, that's all." He shook himself as if to free his body of the lingering memory and stood up, pulling her up with him.

"Thirsty?" When she grinned at him and nodded, he took her hand and led her through the market, which was closing down for the day. A small piece of fruit rolled out from under a vendor's stall. Esarelle stumbled on it, momentarily losing her footing. Agen grasped her arm to aid her balance. Once he had hold of her, he was disinclined to let her go, so he slipped his arm around her waist, hoping she didn't object. Had he been able to read her mind he'd have seen hope flaring.

She felt the heat rising in her body as they moved together through the quieting streets. Their bodies moved in perfect time with his stride shortened to match hers. By the time they reached The Midnight Pearl she was virtually panting. She couldn't remember a time she'd reacted with such immediate, unbridled lust to the feeling of a male simply standing next to her.

We're not even doing anything, she thought as she took a quick, secretive look at his familiar profile.

Agen passed the Frey bouncer a few pieces of mother-of-pearl, then pushed open the door. Tonight it was fairly quiet in the dimly lit room. A faint smell of fermented Yalon hung in the air, coppery and rich, enough of a temptation to the senses to make his fangs drop.

A lone Ireculian singer stood in a pool of blue light crooning a love song. Her exceptionally long, slender neck curved in twin loops before ending in a petite and delicate head. She was the color of the twin moons, the palest of blues, with a sprinkling of silver freckles over her upturned nose. Her voice rose and fell in perfect pitch, her long neck providing her with extended vocal cords capable of producing sounds far out of the range of possibilities for either a human or Raniculan voice. Her song caressed the air and filled the room with superlative sound. Agen and Esarelle stood bewitched by her song, the heat between them rising like an active volcano.

Charlotte was on her way to see how Irina was faring when she saw Agen and Esarelle enter the bar. She smiled to herself as she watched them pass through the doorway hand in hand. She wanted to see Agen find a mate. He was a good man and so deserving of some happiness.

At the palace she summoned Arun, who gave her a quick update on Irina's condition, and then went to see if she could help.

When she entered the Frey's room Cameron was feeding her little sips of water. He'd defied the local custom to turn a delivery room into as dark and hot a place as possible, instead flinging open the windows to let in the cooling evening air.

Irina's mother was appalled at this brazenness. She had left, hoping the midwife would be able to do what should be done. But the midwife napped in a far corner. She had nothing else to do since Cam insisted on caring for his lover. He had a fair amount of medical knowledge as he'd had completed several years of medical school before changing tack and entering the field of botany. He kept Irina as cool and comfortable as her condition allowed, which, judging by her groans, wasn't comfortable at all.

When Irina dozed off a little later, Charlotte and Cam spent a few hours chatting about their past, Earth, and all the things they missed. They cared for Irina each time she awoke, and resumed their discussion when she dozed again. They decided a proper hospital with trained doctors and nurses was desperately needed here. Even though the Raniculans and the Frey healed very well from most things, there was still a real need for skilled maternity care and broken bone care.

Charlotte told Cam about the way her blood had healed Elyian and Jendal. He was fascinated to hear the details, his professor's keen mind coming to the fore. They talked all through the night.

By morning it was nearly over. Irina pushed one last time and as the sun peaked up over the Shoulen Mountains, their son entered the world. Irina looked at Cam, who held the new infant in his shaking arms. The gray-skinned baby shivered even after he'd been warmly wrapped.

The midwife merely shook her head despondently. "Nothing we can do," she said. She took the infant from Cam, wiped the newborn's face with a cloth, and handed him to Irina. "He will survive, as all Frey babies do that suffer like this, but he will not be a clever one like your friend Agen's child."

Cam shook his head, angry at her seeming lack of concern. "No," he yelled. "This isn't right. There has to be something we can do. Charlotte, what can we do?"

Charlotte looked at the precious little boy suckling half-heartedly at his mother's breast. With his father's blue eyes and a smattering of red curly hair, he looked for all the world like the progeny of a Scottish Highlander. His pallor didn't improve and Charlotte knew that if anything was going to change the baby's prospects, it had to be done fast.

She turned to Cam. "I'm not sure, but maybe my blood can help."

He shook his head vehemently. "No. No child of mine is going to have his first meal be blood. They may have turned me but my son is part human and part Frey. He doesn't have fangs. Besides, do you even know what blood type you are?"

"We probably only have a couple of minutes at best before the damage will be irreversible." Charlotte's voice was urgent. "My blood won't hurt him and it might just help. I'm type HH, the best universal donor there is; and when you add in the fact that I'm a hybrid Vampire, there's no telling how much good it will do."

Cam went very quiet as the analytical part of his mind went into overdrive, kicking various scenarios around. At last he spoke. "Do it."

Irina, who was far more used to seeing fangs and blood than Cam was, seemed a lot happier with that decision. "Yes, thank you, Cam. I want him to at least have a chance." She handed the baby up to Charlotte.

Charlotte didn't waste a second. With the baby securely tucked in the crook of her right arm, she turned her wrist to her mouth and tore into the flesh. Her blood welled up and she held her severed vein to the baby's puckered mouth. He whimpered and screwed up his tiny face in a show of disgust. Then, as the first drops made their way past his lips and down his throat, his entire demeanor changed.

First his face relaxed, a look of contentment passing over him as the rich fluid was quickly absorbed into his system. Color washed into his face, the grey receding and swiftly replaced by the healthy, luminescent pale skin of the Frey with just a slight flush of human pink. His cheeks became rosy, and they were even more astonished when a mark began to appear just behind his ear. There for all the world to see was a tiny, perfect, blue Creek bird.

The room exploded with excitement. It was like the Fourth of July, Hanukkah, The Festival of Arn, and Halloween all rolled into one huge holiday. As the noise abated Cam burst into tears, as did Irina and Charlotte. The midwife ran to fetch the king. An event of this magnitude merited royal attention.

When Elyian entered the room, all of them lowered their

heads respectfully. "Please, no," he said. "We're all friends here. Where is this miracle child then?"

Irina held up the infant for him to see and his eyes widened as he gazed upon the mark on the baby's skin.

"So," he said, rubbing his hand over his eyes as if to make them see more clearly, "let me see if I have this correct. What I've been told by the midwife is that this baby was a Greyling at birth, but that Charlotte's blood cured him and added the mark of the Creck upon him. Is that right?"

When everyone in the room affirmed this, a huge smile broke out on Elyian's face.

"Well, come on, then," he said. "Today started off badly but this has turned it around. Why are you all standing about? I'm sure Irina could use some rest, and I'm equally certain we need to do some celebrating. It's not every day a cure is found for a problem that's been the scourge of our planet for millennia. And now that Cameron has also found the answer to the Yalon issue, we can all rest easier tonight. The drinks are on me!"

It was a festive group indeed that made their way across the city that night. Elyian, Cam and Charlotte were joined by Jendal, who was as delighted with the news as everyone else.

But Cam had a worried look on his face. By the time they reached the bar, the worry had turned to a full-blown panic attack, which his extreme fatigue did nothing to help. He didn't know how long the effect of the donated blood would last in his son, or how they could synthesize Charlotte's blood so that it could be distributed to others who needed it.

What he needed was his human laboratory, or any lab that contained something more sophisticated than the vials and potions found at the apothecary's home—the apothecary whose body had never been found. Everyone assumed he'd perished somewhere in the outlands, and with him had died the last of the old healers. It was time for change.

While they downed the first drinks they discussed the logistics of bringing the necessary technology from Earth. It could be done, it was just going to take some time. Cam calmed himself with the knowledge that the worst was over and soon they'd have all the answers.

The mark of Creck had been passed, and every being that carried it could heal both Raniculans and Frey with their blood. Now that the link had been found they could work with it to find a way to make it accessible to every being that needed healing.

As they sat and turned every possibility over and over, Charlotte kept her head turned toward the door. She hadn't seen Amun since Irina had gone into labor, and her nerve endings were getting twitchy without him nearby. They'd sent an orb to let him know where they were but he hadn't shown up. Elyian saw the concern on her face.

He also noted the change in her when his sire suddenly appeared at her side, having far-stepped right into the club. When he became corporeal her face lit up and Amun stepped right into her waiting arms. They kissed like they hadn't seen each other in years, neither one wanting to break contact with the other.

Elyian cleared his throat to attract their attention and Jendal dug into his ribs. "Subtle, E."

Neither Charlotte or Amun looked away from the other. Elyian turned to his brother, his face registering serious concern. "It appears we're excess baggage. Come on, Jendal. There's something I have to show you." They moved to the privacy of a quiet corner and Elyian pulled something out of his pocket. "I received this message just before coming here tonight."

The Leverium2 orb spun and played a scene. It showed the interior of a large office on Earth which Jendal immediately recognized as the Oval Office at the White House. The expired body of the president was draped over his desk, lying on his back with his feet on the floor. His eyes were open, pupils fixed and dilated, and there was nothing left of his throat. His entire neck had been ripped open. Pools of blood ran over the surface of the leather-topped table and trickled in a slowing stream down into the ever-growing stain on the rug below.

Jendal cursed. "That's a problem. What happened over there?"

Elyian groaned. "Keep watching, brother." As they watched, a familiar form appeared on screen. The man walked to the desk and with a careless shove pushed the president's body so it slid unceremoniously off the desk and down onto the carpet, landing in an untidy heap.

The man sat down at the desk and pushed a button under the drawer front. A large part of one wall slid silently to the left, revealing another wall directly behind it. There, hanging in the glare of individual halogen lights, were six large paintings. Scenes of Ranic.

Jendal's mouth went dry. He growled and his fangs dropped as he watched their uncle and mortal enemy relax back in the chair and sling his feet carelessly onto the previously unmarked leather top.

"Vax." Jendal hardly dared say the name that left such bitterness on his tongue. Elyian was grim as he shut off the image and replaced the orb in the pouch.

"Have you told our father about this yet?"

"Yes," Elyian replied sadly. "He's leaving for Earth tonight, but wanted to see Charlotte first."

They both looked over at the lovely human who'd captured all their hearts. She was gazing at Amun like he was her only reason for existing. Amun was talking to her quietly and discretely, though discretion wasn't necessary as Cam was now slumped over his folded arms, fast asleep at the table. They saw her gasp and shake her head then grab at his arm as he tried to stand. Jendal and Elyian didn't need to hear to know what was passing between them.

They were unsure how much was known on Earth of the existence of the Ranic Vampires. Had Vax broadcast this around the world, or was it meant for their eyes only?

They hoped for the latter but mentally prepared for the firestorm that would accompany the former. Of one thing Elyian was certain: Amun was going to kill his own brother. They shared a look, then left the bar without a second glance and headed for the home of Agen Trace.

"Oh, Agen, do that again! It feels divine." Esarelle dug her nails into the soft cushion where she lay naked under his rock-hard abs. He complied, delighted with her reaction, rocking over her and relishing the feel of her soft, pliant body encasing him. He groaned and drew his fangs gently down her breast, careful not to nick the tender flesh.

They both shot upright at the deafening hammering on the door. Agen cursed, got up and hastily threw on his pants. He didn't even have time to open the door as the next second Elyian burst in with Jendal right behind him.

Esarelle looked around, trying to find something, anything, she could use to cover her body. Her clothing lay scattered around the room, none of it within grasp. She quickly decided that since they'd rudely burst in, she wasn't going to worry about it, so she stood up, naked as the day that she was born, much to the astonishment of her king.

Elyian tried to look anywhere except at Esarelle. Jendal

stared at her appreciatively and Agen, ever the gentleman, tried to put everyone at ease.

"Elyian, what brings you here tonight, and in such a hurry?"

Elyian filled him in on the message from the orb and watched as Agen's face changed to reflect his thunderous rage. He never lost his temper, always retaining his cool, but now he showed every emotion he'd ever locked away.

The men helped Agen gather his weapons and pack a few personal items. He'd never gone to Earth, lacking both the need and the desire, so he had none of the things that the other men considered essential.

At the palace they packed Yalon, orbs and some gemstones. These were for Agen, since Amun and his sons already had plenty of resources on Earth that they could tap. If they were separated Agen would need to be self-sufficient. Once he was ready, they left in a blur to shut down the poison that was Havvol Vax.

Chapter 35

in which the hunt begins

THE FOUR RANICULAN Vampires stood on the roof of the White House. There was a single metallic clink as the hilt of Agen's sword knocked gently on the dagger secured at Elyian's hip.

"Quiet," Amun hissed at them. As the patriarch, his was the voice of authority when they were off Ranic. His word was taken over Elyian's while they were away hunting, and this particular Earth trip most definitely counted as a hunt.

"Damn, Amun," Agen spluttered, "you couldn't have arranged for us to land somewhere a little less visible?"

"Do be quiet, Agen," Amun retorted. "It's fine. They can't see us up here. I had one of our internal crew handle the security system. It's going to be out of commission for at least the next hour. They'll put extra boots on the ground but we can neutralize them easily enough. Talking of which, here comes a pair now."

The two security guys in question were performing a sweep of the house perimeter. They were thorough in checking the landscaping that surrounded the building. They did not, however, look up, and Elyian and Amun landed on the ground behind them without a sound.

The sounds of the guards' vertebrae cracking under the twisting wrench delivered to their necks were like the retorts from a pair of guns in the night air. The hunters rolled the guards over to inspect their faces.

"Yep," said Elyian with a slight snarl, "just as we thought. These guys were sent here by the high court a couple of decades ago. I recognize this one. I thought then that it was strange to sentence them to Earth. Vax must have been planning this for a long time. We have to take him out tonight."

They beckoned to Jendal and Agen, who silently joined them on the path, then all four quickly disappeared through a side door. Finding their way to the inner sanctum was easy, thanks to the help of the female Raniculan who'd been working there under cover for the past few years. Her job as a press assistant gave her a great cover and as such she was able to intercept any news stories that could be potentially dangerous for the Raniculans.

Dressed in a dark suit with modest pumps, light perfect makeup, immaculate hair and lightly tinted eyeglasses, she was the very model of professionalism. Only an extremely attentive person would have noticed her very unusual eye color, and then would have put it down to turquoise contact lenses. She was the one who'd discovered the murder of the president and sent the orb to Elyian.

Coming in through the Rose Garden entrance would have been too visible so she lead them through a maze of rooms, offices and endless corridors, returning at last to the Northeast door that led directly into the Oval Office. They burst through the door, swords raised, expecting to find Vax and various minions armed to the teeth on the other side.

Instead all they found was an empty room.

The carpet of the Oval Office bore the seal of the president in front of the huge Resolute Desk. Or it had, until this day.

Now the huge circular motif had been neatly removed and in its place lay a map created with a stunning mosaic of stone. Inlaid into its surface a rainbow of precious stones, marbles, and granites all came together in one perfect art form. It depicted Ranic, the side of the planet that always faced the moons. The city buildings gleamed with shards of crystal and the mountain ranges were depicted with bloodstone. Rose quartz rivers and lakes of *Lapis lazuli* dotted the surface. It was their world and it was front and center.

The men looked at each other. "Now what?" Agen asked, his eyes still roaming the picture of his home world. A detail not in keeping with the rest of the mosaic suddenly grabbed his attention. "What's that ankh doing there?" He pointed at the gold form that rested in the center of a circle of fine gems.

Amun pushed Agen away so he could get a closer look and the cry of anguish he let out would have been heard all across the city if it hadn't been for the superlative soundproofing the room possessed.

"That ankh belongs to Charlotte," Amun roared. "Vax stole it from her while she was at Tahoe." He raised his sword and brought it down in the center of the circle, shattering every piece of stone into a thousand fragments. The ankh fell free and Amun bent to retrieve it.

The realization hit him suddenly.

"No!" he cried as the full implication hit him. He clutched the precious ankh in his fist. "Vax has tricked us into coming here... and he has Charlotte!"

They left the White House by running out the Rose Garden door, and every Raniculan traitor agent that tried to apprehend them was cut down so fast he didn't see the sword fall.

The USA had no President, but the country didn't yet know it. The official story was that the president was away on vacation, skiing in some remote area of the Swiss Alps.

The heads of state in the rest of the world waited with bated breath to see where the chips would fall. The Vice President was holed up in a bunker somewhere with the members of the cabinet, as they had been for days.

Neither Agen, Elyian or Jendal could far-step back to Ranic alone; they didn't have enough power left. But Amun was an original. At his age he was more powerful than the three others combined. He slung a Leverium2 rope around them all, binding the four men into a single entity. Then with single-minded determination he threw an orb high into the sky over Washington and vanished them into its wake.

They landed a good hundred miles from their intended destination in an untidy heap of tangled rope and muscular legs. The slender but razor-sharp sword of Jendal's that had stabbed Amun in his torso during the reformation of their DNA did nothing to improve his temper and the loss of blood was making him dizzy. It had neatly pierced his lower left side, skewering a kidney like a kabob.

He grunted as Elyian helped pull it free. "By the gods, Jendal, are you still trying to kill me?"

Jendal grinned at his father for the first time in a hundred years. "Not anymore. I think it's time to let that go, Daddy."

Amun raised a cynical eyebrow. "That's fine with me, but trust me when I say that if you come anywhere near me again today I will skewer you back. Kiddo!"

The exchange broke the tension and they all relaxed a little. Elyian gave his father some blood to help the healing along and they all rested a bit before trekking up to the summer home. Landing in the correct place was easy for one man alone or with a small female, but to transport four fully grown and massive men across the universe and landing within spitting distance of your goal was next to impossible.

At least, Amun thought as he fell into a restless sleep, *I'm back on the same planet as Charlotte.*

Chapter 36

in which evil lurks

KNOWING AMUN HAD gone to confront Vax was tearing Charlotte to pieces. She shook Cam awake and shakily told him what had happened. He did his best to console her, but nothing could change how she felt.

He walked her back to the Winter Palace and left her at the gate. The guards bowed as she walked through the ornate iron entrance. The pair of doors that flanked her were thirty feet high with coiling spirals and hand-wrought leaves, and although beautiful to look at they were nonetheless topped with rows of lethal-looking spikes. They opened onto a crushed-stone path that glittered in the light and led in a circuitous route past gargoyle-guarded walls to the secluded inner gardens.

The sun was now high in the sky and the lake shone with a deep purple glow, reflecting the sky above. A pair of birds glided together like swans on the surface, diving occasionally under the water to fish for the small creatures that inhabited its depths. The birds had scaly, mottled white and grey skin with huge feathery wings that they kept folded over their bodies. Their beaks were curved up in arcs ending in a single spike, which they used to spear the fish they ate.

Amun had told her that they mated for life and she could believe it. The pair were like aquatic dancers, moving in unearthly synchronicity across the surface of the water. The calm rhythm of their movements helped lull Charlotte's over-active imagination, so she stopped and watched them for a while, unaware that they were not the only thing in the garden being watched.

As she crossed the bridge she looked down into the water's depths and marveled at how little time had passed since she witnessed Jendal and Amun as they vanished, fighting under the water. She kicked off her shoes and wiggled her toes in the damp moss that surrounded the lake, reveling in its coolness.

Vax watched her enter the garden. His blood moved a little faster in his veins and the throbbing in his crotch intensified. *Just a little while longer*, he thought as he absently rubbed himself through the fabric of his pants. *I'll show that hybrid just who is worthy of her attention and who is not.* He practically slobbered at the thought.

Charlotte made her way to her quarters and discarded her clothing at the entrance to the wet room. Built to look like a rain forest, it was the Ranic equivalent of the most luxurious spa one could imagine. Open to the sky, it backed up to a hillside. A hot spring fed a stream which entered the room and fell over a cantilevered edge into the smooth river rocks that covered the entire floor, creating a most invigorating shower.

As she stood under the thundering water she could see into a private garden through a wall of windows on the opposite side. Ferns with tropical-looking flowers on the ends of each frond grew inside the room, thriving in the warm, damp environment. A long washbowl was set into a massive piece of granite and a curved chaise covered in lush dark green fabric was tucked into the one private corner that did not get rained on each day. It was luxury in the extreme and her favorite room in the palace.

Charlotte stood for a long time in the steaming water, then wrapped herself in a thick robe and walked out to the bedroom. Her diary sat on the bedside table, willing her to pick it up and write. Instead she dropped it into her pocket along with a pen, intending to curl up by the fire in one of the downstairs rooms and write in it later.

Right now she was hungry, so she rang the bell for Amun's manservant, who had taken the name of Fred, having seen one too many of the illustrious Mr. Astaire's movies that Elyian kept bringing back from Earth.

When Fred still hadn't shown up ten minutes later Charlotte went to investigate. As she walked down the wide curved staircase in the main hall, the distinct impression that something was wrong settled in her mind.

It was too quiet. Normally the house would be bustling with Frey running all over the place going about their daily routines. Now it was deathly calm. Nothing moved anywhere.

She was half way down when she saw the trail. Tiny silver beads rolled down the staircase. They fell, one at a time, into a small bowl under the lip of the last step. She stooped and picked up the bowl, watching with curiosity as they swirled around the bowl and then melted into a single pool of molten silver. Charlotte was nothing if not curious and this had her baffled.

As she straightened, a shadowy smoke drifted lazily out of the wall and swirled around her feet, then moved up between the bowl and her robe. Charlotte cried out and stumbled backward, letting the bowl fly out of her grasp.

Instead of falling it was held unmoving in place as the shadow formed around the rim, holding it steady a few feet off the ground. Fingers of smoke reached out and held her pinned to the floor while more fingers pried her mouth open. The bowl moved toward her and the liquid silver was poured between her lips.

She couldn't move, not one muscle, and the more she tried to fight the smoke the tighter it held her. She tried to force the thick metallic liquid out of her mouth but other fingers of smoke stroked her throat and forced her to swallow.

This is it, she thought as the stuff flowed into her stomach. *This is how I'm going to die.* She felt oddly calm. No panic or fear, just dead calm.

Until he spoke. Then the tendrils of fear spiked up through her gut and slammed into her. Adrenaline coursed through her veins and she shot to her feet.

"No, my dear, this isn't how you'll die." He walked slowly around her, eyeing the tie on her robe.

By the gods, of course! He can read my mind!

Havvol Vax laughed and all the evil he personified coalesced into that single sound. "Of course I can, you stupid girl. You humans continually underestimate me."

Charlotte casually lifted the hem of her robe and crushed the hem in one hand. When it was clear of her feet she moved them.

She made it to the kitchen and fell through the door. Her foot slid out from under her as it hit a slick puddle. She slid through the entrance on her behind and came to a stop when her foot caught the edge of a table. Something was in her eyes, she couldn't see and the burning in her throat and stomach was getting worse.

Charlotte pulled at the soft, wet thing over her eyes and when she managed to open them she wished with all her heart they could have stayed closed forever.

She held in her hand a length of intestines, coiled and slick. It slipped over her fingers and fell to the floor in a pink mess. She heaved and vomited the silver fluid until there was nothing left to vomit.

Then with shaking legs she hauled herself up by grasping the edge of the table. As her head cleared the edge, she came face to face with what was left of Fred. He'd been dismembered and all that was left in one piece was his face. The rest of him was pulverized. Bits of bone and tissue were stuck to the walls, blood and fluids had flooded the floor. Her robe acted like a wick, soaking up the blood until it clung wet and red to her legs.

Vax came in then, having waited a few minutes so she'd have time to really come undone. He peeled her off the floor and scooped her up into his arms. Pulling back his lips to reveal his fangs, he far-stepped them both away without a backward glance.

Chapter 37

in which the deed is done

MORNING BROKE OVER the Shoulen Mountains and the Manos were hungry. A pair of old males stalked their prey. They'd smelled the victims hours ago, and were now close enough to see the smoke from their fire. The Manos slowly circled the camp, making each spiral a little tighter.

Jendal and Elyian, however, had spotted the creatures earlier as they stalked the camp, and now they sat back to back with Agen hiding nearby. As the Manos sprang, the brothers flung their nooses around the creatures' necks.

While the Manos struggled to free themselves, Agen came up from behind and with remarkable speed injected each of them with calming herbs. It took only a short while for the drugs to work, and before long the men were mounted on the animals' backs heading for the hills, where their father's summer home was located.

Amun had already gone. His injury had weakened him, and far-stepping them all from Earth had taken him to the edge of his limits. Unable to take the other three with him, he left the comfort of the fire without them, leaving his two sons and their dear friend behind as he went to face down his own brother. Alone.

Inside the circle of trees, Charlotte was hanging, naked, from an overhanging branch. Vax had taken the tie from her robe and strung her up by her ankles. Then, to add another layer of torment, he locked a spiked chain of Leverium2 around her waist and attached the other end to the ground, tightening it so that the spikes drove into her flesh every time she moved.

Her lovely, thick red hair was sticky and stiff with dried blood and her naked body was bruised and swollen. He'd adjusted the tie carefully so that she hung with her hair just brushing the ground. All through the endless night, ants crawled up her arms and now ran over her face and up her nose as the residue of liquid silver ate away at her insides.

She regained consciousness long enough to recognize the circle of trees that formed Amun's bedroom. *Looks different upside-down,* she thought ruefully, as she fought to quell the terror and replace a little of it with humor, hoping it would help her retain her sanity.

She was relying on her faith in Amun to get her through this ordeal. She knew he was coming for her. Vax had gloated over the fact that he'd tricked them into going to Earth and was now lying in wait for his other intended victim.

Her ability to heal now that she was part Raniculan Vampire allowed her body to mend after each new horror was inflicted upon her. What he'd done to the inside of her body was a whole other matter. The silver was poison, and it was seeping slowly but insidiously throughout her system. Though she'd luckily vomited most of it out, some of the silver was still inside, attaching itself to bone, sinew and muscle, replacing healthy tissue with decay.

When she first swallowed it, the silver had burned her throat. Now that sensation was drowned out by the fire consuming her from her center. It creeped with snail-like slowness, adding silver tendrils down the inside of her body.

If she'd been pure Raniculan she would have died within minutes. As a hybrid who carried the blood not only of Raniculans but of an HH-type human, she was able to withstand and eventually heal from the onslaught to her body.

Vax prowled around the outside of the circle, readying his mind and body for the oncoming fight. He knew Amun; his brother would arrive alone. Vax was sure Amun would have brought his sons back to Ranic, but, not wanting them to get involved in his fight, would have found an excuse to leave them somewhere far away. With the journey to Earth and back, they'd all be weakened and unable to far-step this distance. So Vax figured he had time to play with his new toy a little longer.

He tore the pages out of the diary he'd found in her robe and secured a single, blood-soaked page on each tree on the outside of the circle. He watched with avid interest as his victim hung like an animal waiting to be slaughtered. Charlotte moaned as she saw him approach.

From her upside-down viewpoint he looked distorted, his face a mockery of all she held dear in the normal visage of the Raniculan race. He had the usual tall, broad stature and the clear luminous skin. His hair, the color of a field of wheat, curled down to his shoulders, shining like spun gold. It was his eyes that set him apart. They were dead and cold, with none of the brilliant light that shone in Amun's eyes.

He stopped close to her head and cruelly stomped on her hair, making her wince in pain. The he stooped down and craned his neck sideways to get a closer look at the damage he'd done to her face. She pursed her lips and spat at him. His reaction was instantaneous and violent. Wrenching her hair off the ground, he lifted her head up to an impossible angle and hit her jaw so hard she felt it pop out of its socket. The second punch landed on her temple and blessedly knocked her out.

Vax's distraction with punishing Charlotte gave Amun the couple of seconds he needed. He'd been perched high up in the treetops, watching his monstrous brother terrorize his mate. His vision had gone red with anger and his fangs throbbed with the need to tear Vax's throat out. Silently he dropped from the tree, but instead of slowing his descent he allowed the full force of his weight to land on Vax, forcing him to the ground.

As Vax felt the impact, his prowess at fighting went into overdrive. With a twist he managed to flip Amun over, then slammed his elbow straight down into his esophagus. Amun gagged, then pulled the short, curved blade from his belt. With a sure swipe he drove it deep into Vax's side then pulled it out, bringing a good chunk of his liver with it.

Charlotte regained consciousness a little while later, by which time the forest floor was dark with the combined blood of the men. By now they were in the small river that separated the bed from the trees. Its usually crystalline water was reduced to a murky pink.

They rolled in the shallows, locked together, and to Charlotte it was unclear who was going to come out of the fight alive. The two brothers were so evenly matched. Centuries of hand-to-hand combat training had turned them both into highly skilled killers. They were almost like twins; the same techniques and the same build combined with the equal amounts of hatred festering between them ensured that they cancelled each other out when fighting.

That meant Charlotte needed to help. She wriggled her body, trying again to loosen her bonds. The only result was that the spikes seated themselves further into her body and she groaned in pain. There was no way she was going anywhere.

Suddenly Elyian, Jendal and Agen dropped, silent and deadly, from the treetops. The brothers landed next to Vax and in an instant they had dragged him away from Amun and pinned him down.

While the brothers helped deal with their uncle, Agen cut Charlotte from the tree, carefully released the binding chain, and wrapped her in a covering. She shivered uncontrollably as the shock and pain of her ordeal caught up with her.

Amun lay with his body half in the water, his blood draining into the stream at an alarming rate, but he was still able to raise his head. He watched as Charlotte was cut down, then a hoarse whisper escaped his lips.

"Bring her here."

Agen carried Charlotte to Amun and laid her down. Then he dragged Amun out of the stream and laid him gently down next to her.

Vax screamed in rage, his face mottled and beaten. Elyian and Jendal tightened their grips on his arms and stabbed at him a few times for good measure. They knew better than to kill him. It was Amun who would get to deliver the blow that would finish him off.

Amun and Charlotte turned to face each other as they lay on the blood-soaked ground. Amun couldn't believe what the bastard had done to her. Big hunks of hair had been pulled from her scalp, her lips were puffy and swollen, and one eye was totally shut. A long gash had opened up her cheekbone, although it was starting to knit back together.

The rest of her body was swaddled in the covering but he'd seen her hanging in the tree and knew exactly how the rest of her had been treated.

His anger rose in waves threatening to suck him into oblivion. At last he managed to speak through his own mess of a face.

"Charlotte, my love, I'm here. It'll be all right now."

She surprised him with her rancorous answer. "It will never be all right, Amun, as long as that fiend over there still exists."

Amun tried to lift his lips in a smile, but those muscles had ceased to function. "Don't worry. He's a dead man."

Painfully, slowly, he pulled himself up to a sitting position and picked up his fallen sword. Everyone heard his teeth grate as he braced himself against the wracking pain in his broken body. He flicked his free hand to one side, motioning to Elyian and Jendal to free Vax. They balked a little at the command but then let their hands drop, although they immediately re-armed themselves. With slow, deliberate steps, Amun moved toward Vax.

His voice snarled out of his throat, deep and menacing. "Havvol Vax, you may have been my brother for what seems like a thousand years, but today is the day I will make you finally pay for your sins. No more will Ranic have to suffer your idea of justice, and no more will my mate pay the price for your animosity and jealousy. Twice now you have caused her pain. There will not be a third time."

Vax pulled a dagger from its sheath and stalked toward Amun, low and predatory. They circled each other and for an instant Charlotte thought neither would ever win. But this time Amun moved like lightning. His right arm swung and rocketed back with every muscle in his body fighting to be the strongest it had ever been. The sword flashed as it caught the light, then Vax's body crumpled forward in a bloody heap as his severed head spun in a graceful arc before it hit the nearest tree and fell ignominiously to the forest floor.

Agen officiated at the Ranic high court and watched the couple before him with a smile on his face as they said their vows.

By Ranic royal standards, only a small number of citizens had been invited to the mating ceremony. Elyian, Jendal, Esarelle, and Laila sat front and center, with assorted friends and dignitaries behind. Lining the walls were every other Frey that lived in either Elyian's or Amun's palace.

The room was lit by hundreds of shining orbs that spun webs of silver threads across the room as they wound in and around the pillars. Charlotte had stayed with Elyian at his palace in the weeks preceding the ceremony, as custom demanded, and she ached to be with Amun again. Every window in the court was flung wide open and the light from the moons shone in, bathing the scene in their unearthly blue glow.

As the words were spoken Agen drew a small dagger. Clasping both of their wrists together, he drew the blade swiftly across until their blood mingled, falling into an alabaster bowl.

Amun lifted the milky white edge of the bowl to Charlotte's lips and she drank deeply of the rich liquid. She then held it up for Amun, who repeated her action, drinking until every last drop was gone. As their blood mixed, so did their thoughts. Every memory from the past and feeling they would have in the future was now shared.

Together they lifted the bowl high in the air and smashed it down onto the marble floor, where it dissolved into powder and blew away with the breeze. Amun turned to his mate and the total joy that was written there for the world to see was reflected in the face of the woman who stood at his side. She was his now, and for the rest of their very long lives they would walk the cosmic path together.

Epilogue

SURIANA VAX CROUCHED down, well hidden behind some thick undergrowth on the edge of the woods, watching them. On a lonely stretch of road in the Pacific Northwest, a dozen or so teens played chicken. They were trying to determine who among them could run the fastest, while blindfolded, on the curved stone wall that began a little further back down the roadway.

The edge dropped straight down, a hundred feet or more, to the river below. The first boy, although full of bravado before he began, gave up after just a few feet, his knees visibly knocking as he jumped back down onto the roadway.

The second child was female and she ran fairly fast and sure on the uneven surface. *Probably a gymnast*, thought Suriana.

The third one to try was Jalen, a fourteen-year-old boy, slight of build and with a sweet, innocent face. He lifted his chin, put on the blindfold, and ran.

He ran so fast that the other kids looked on in in amazement as he easily negotiated the imperfections on the brick surface. His feet flew over the stones, and as he reached the end he turned to face the sheer edge that dropped off into the creek. As the peanut gallery looked on, he grinned, and his fangs flashed white and perfect in the moonlight before he took a perfect swan dive off the edge. The other kids all whooped and cheered as they peered over the wall, waiting for him to wave from the bottom.

That's my boy! thought Suriana proudly before she sank way back into the shadows.

In the years since the "Great Debate," right after a single rogue Vampire had murdered the sitting U.S. President, Vampires had been integrated into human society.

An Earth alliance had been formed to debate how to deal with them, and they'd been split fairly evenly over whether to hunt and kill them all or to embrace this new life form. In the end the latter won out and generally it had gone well.

The Raniculan Vampires rarely troubled their human hosts and had taken up positions of influence all over the world. They taught in the school systems and many had gone into the medical field, with a great many becoming outstanding surgeons. They could operate for an entire day and night without stopping for rest. Their hands never shook and the sight of blood seemed to invigorate them no end.

Other than medicine, the field they really excelled in was engineering. They sucked up information on aeronautics and bio-mechanics like they were starving for it.

They were banned from serving in the military or any job where firearms were issued. The humans didn't feel secure enough to hand a gun to a Vampire. As many argued, "Those bloodsuckers have enough ways of killing us all; why help them out even more?"

The world after the Great Debate was a very different place and the Raniculans bided their time, restraining themselves from eating the general population as they played the waiting game. What was another decade or so, when they had already waited three thousand years?

On Ranic, Amun and Charlotte watched with devotion from an upstairs window seat as their daughter Meramun sat quietly in the palace courtyard with an easel propped in front of her and splashes of paint in her hair. Her ancient Egyptian name meant 'Beloved of Amun,' but of course she was beloved of them both.

Meramun was fourteen years old, and thanks to her extraordinary gene pool, her stunning beauty was already apparent. Amun seemed to spend much of his time lately with his hands wrapped around the spindly neck of some adolescent boy or another who had taken it into his head to court his daughter. Sitting as close to Meramun as he could get without incurring either her wrath or that of her father was Connor, the adolescent son of Cam and Irina.

As she concentrated on the art blossoming under her talented hands, Meramun absently brushed her hair back off her face. There, tucked in behind her ear, was a small but unmistakable blue bird, and hanging around her neck was her mother's golden ankh.

Two worlds had taken huge steps to bridge the universe, and the threads of time once floating loose and unfettered now bound them inexorably together.

THE END

Index

ABORINTH: Species from the planet ABOR. Females are humanoid in form but with the addition of a feline tail.

AGEN TRACE: Raniculan. Member of the Interplanetary High Court. Friend to Elyian; father to Violette.

AJIL: Goat-like creature with long, soft wool. Used by the Raniculans for their wool and for food.

AMUN TRAINOR: Youngest of six sons born to Queen Nefertiti on Earth. Elyian's father. Abdicated the throne. Emerald eyes edged in black, dark lashes. Thick, almost black hair with copper highlights. Tall, slender, muscular. Wears an ankh. Hunter and court recorder. Vampire.

ARUN: Frey manservant to Elyian.

CAMERON (CAM) GRANT: Human turned Vampire of Scottish descent. Charlotte's employer on Earth. Botanist and Artist. Blue eyes, red hair.

CHARLOTTE HAYDEN: Born on Earth in 1985 of mixed Ranic and human blood. Tall, slender, green eyes, pale skin and copper/red hair. HH blood type.

CHIMARA: Lover of Agen Trace. Species: Frey. Deceased mother to Violette.

CONNOR: Red-haired son of Cameron Grant (human/hybrid) and Irina (Frey). Pointy ears, elf-like.

CRECK: A small blue creature found on Ranic.

CYRUS: Sire of the six sons.

DANKO: Frey village on the edge of the plain.

ELYIAN TRAINOR: Ruler of the third house of Ranic. Born 1492 Earth time. 6' 5" tall. Broad shoulders, strong, long lithe limbs. Dark hair, forest green eyes edged in gold.

ERIC VANLEN: Gallery director in San Francisco.

ESARELLE: Hybrid human/Raniculan, raised by a Frey. The physician/apothecary's daughter. Works in the palace looking after the children of the Frey that are in service there. Petite.

FAR-STEP: The ability of Raniculans to move instantly from place to place.

FRED: Frey manservant of Amun's (name taken from Fred Astaire movies).

FREY: Humanoid-type species living on Ranic. No fangs. Unable to far-step. High percentage of the population suffers from a birth defect. Generally smaller than the Raniculans. They have a heart and a single lung. Will die from asphyxiation if left in the cold for extended periods.
Arun, Chimara, Danko, Esarelle, Fred, Irina, Laila, Tianala.

GRAIL: Small furry animal that has a deadly bite. Purrs like a cat.

GREYLING: Frey baby who has been damaged at birth and suffers a brain injury causing retardation.

HAVVOL VAX: Head Justice of the Ranic Interplanetary High

Court. Brother to Amun. Vampire.

IRECULIAN: Second planet in the Ranic system. Native species have exceptionally long necks that provide many of them with a superlative singing voice.

IRINA: Frey maidservant at the palace. Mother to Connor. Mate to Cameron.

JALEN VAX: Son to Havvol and Suriana Vax. Born on Earth after his father's death.

JENDAL TRAINOR: Elyian's younger brother.

LAILA: 100-year-old young female Frey born to a farming family and living on plains. Of exceptional intelligence. Beautiful, blond. Trained as an exceptional hunter.

LEVATRON: Mechanical elevator.

LEVERIUM 2: Heavy silver-colored metal found only on Ranic. Has multiple beneficial properties.

LIBRARY OF SOULS: Holds the complete history of all races to be found on Ranic.

MANOS: Beasts of burden and a slave army. Normally vicious but can be calmed and domesticated with certain herbs. Their habitat is the Shoulen Mountains in the north of the planet.

MERAMUN: Daughter of Amun and Charlotte. Raniculan.

QUEEN NEFERTIA: Elyian's mother, who died when he was a child. Mated to Amun.

RANIC: Capital city and planet name.

TRANSPORT: Male Raniculans far-step. Female Raniculans walk. All may use Manos-pulled wagons and river barges.

HOUSING: Everything from small houses to palaces using all types of materials. Towers of metal. Stone and marble used extensively.

TECHNOLOGY: No planes, no fuel-driven vehicles. Mechanical only.

RANICULAN: Humanoid species. Dominant race of Ranic. Physical characteristics: Extreme height, pale skin sensitive to UV, fangs, self-healing bodies, beauty, strong and fast. Agen Trace, Amun Trainor, Elyian Trainor, Havvol Vax, Jendal Trainor, Meramun, Queen Nefertia, Shaela, Suriana Vax, Violette.

SAUL: City on Ranic.

SHAELA: Raniculan. Posted on Earth to help cover up the existence of the Raniculans. Tall, slender, turquoise eyes.

SHOULEN MOUNTAINS: Mountain range closest to the city of Ranic. Habitat of the Manos.

SURIANA VAX: Vax's hybrid wife on Earth. Mother of Jalen.

TERRA PLANETS: The four planets where the Raniculans hunt and send offenders. Three in solar system and the fourth is Earth (the Blue Planet).

THE SIX BROTHERS: Amun (Ranic); Havvol Vax (Earth); Raven (Idris); Ishlen; Ayden; Kahn.

TIANALA: Cook and maid at the palace.

VIOLETTE TRACE: Raniculan daughter of Agen Trace. Her Frey mother died in childbirth.

YALON: Thick brown liquid. Similar to blood in taste and texture. The mainstay of the Raniculan diet.